AZAL

The Retelling of Eve

JOSEPHINE MCCARTHY

Golem Media

Golem Media
1100 County Route 54
Hannacroix, NY 12087
www.apocryphilepress.com

Originally published in 1999 by Mercury Publishing, Lake Toxaway, NC under the name
Josephine Stewart. Golem Media edition 2021. Printed in the United States of America

ISBN 978-1-955821-61-2 | paper
ISBN 978-1-955821-62-9 | ePub

Please join our mailing list at www.apocryphilepress.com/free. We'll keep you up-to-
date on all our new releases, and we'll also send you a FREE BOOK. Visit us today!

ALSO BY JOSEPHINE MCCARTHY

Stories from the Strange Side

The Thirteenth Manifestation

The Last Scabbard

Magical Training of the Initiate

The Exorcist's Handbook

The Work of the Hierophant

Magical Knowledge I: Foundations

Magical Knowledge II: The Initiate

Magical Knowledge III: Contacts of the Adepts

The Book of Gates: A magical Translation

Quareia Apprentice, Quareia Initiate, Quareia Adept

Magic of the North Gate

Magical Healing

Tarot Skills for the 21st Century

CONTENTS

Dedicated to Ma

FOREWORD

Azal was the first book I attempted to write. I started writing in 1997 and the book went into publication in 1999. My first attempt at magical writing was in the form of fiction, as I did not have the confidence at that time to write nonfiction. The story explores ancient themes of humanity using magic to manipulate their environment, the development and polarization of temple power, and the early development of deities. It also explores the idea of reincarnation through ritual patterns; it looks at how souls choose specific times and reasons to incarnate, and how those incarnations can be viewed by future cultures to be deities.

The writing itself is clumsy, awkward and makes me cringe to this day when I revisit the text. But rather than rewrite this story for republication, I felt it was important to allow the reader to see how a writer develops—we all start somewhere. It never fails to astound me that this book made it into print in the first place—not because of the content, which I feel holds many magical concepts and inner histories woven into the purely fictional storylines, but because it was so poorly written and takes a while to get going.

The story reaches back into the very early stages of our current phase of humanity and shows how the influence of ancient lines of humanity colors our future. The tale of the Garden of Eden is explored out of its Judaic context, as a mythic memory of early humanity. It moves forward through time into the early tensions between magical lines of the sun and moon and how those lines of power developed, how their priesthoods grew, and how they became corrupted.

The seed structures of myths are observed throughout the book. The story relates how myths develop and become anchors that we can cling to or learn from, such as the degeneration and destruction of the volcanic fire temple that filters down in history to us as the story of Atlantis, and the birth of the Golden City.

It also highlights the very early step into solar based civilizations and how those in turn grew into warrior/city states. The story reflects the powers that drive those patterns and how those patterns are still evident in our western societies today. The stories of the fire temple and the golden city, while very inspiring to some, also give a nod to the magical line that eventually developed into the magical arm of the British Israelite Movement, a quasi-ritualist mindset that has consistently overlaid and drowned out the quiet natural voices of our land. It highlights how power corrupts, breeds greed, and creates a messianic sense of righteousness.

The first chapter opens with a rather shocking scene of seasonal mating by a line of humanity at its end, and thus corrupt in our eyes in every way. The material for this scene was drawn from anthropological accounts of a native tribe on Papua New Guinea. At the time, I saw this as a total degeneration and something that 'was over there' and not a part of the world I live in. As I have grown older, travelled a lot more and encountered many different cultures, I have come to see that many cultures, our own included, are basically rotting - breaking down and converting to compost, ready for the new growth to appear. It is a natural cycle of civilizations that we have witnessed in history repeatedly.

The final chapter is based in Key West. It grew out of a series of spontaneous visions I had while visiting that island. That experience subsequently started me on a long magical path of discovery into the mysteries of the sea, the weather, and eventually my own birth land.

The book overall speaks of the magical avenues I explored in the early to mid 1990's, of the inner discoveries I made and sometimes could not understand, and the magical contacts I was connecting to and working with at that time. It was an intense decade for me magically, as I bounced from inner temple work to angelic/Judaic lines of magic, through to more ancient contacts rising from the land and the sea. I worked intensively, both exploring and teaching almost to the point of complete exhaustion throughout the 1990's, to the exclusion of all else except my children. They were immensely patient as I went from writing session to teaching session to magical gatherings; because of their patience, I dedicate this book to them—my beautiful, talented, and extraordinary daughters, Cassandra, and Leander.

One final curiosity. In chapter eight, there is a description of a wooden temple built on stilts over springs. It has four huts in the four directions and in the story, it is set on the land that is now part of the Florida Keys. Just after the book came into publication in 1999, the ancient remains of just such a building were found off the coast of Florida by the Keys. One of those hair prickling moments!

Josephine McCarthy
Devon UK, 2012

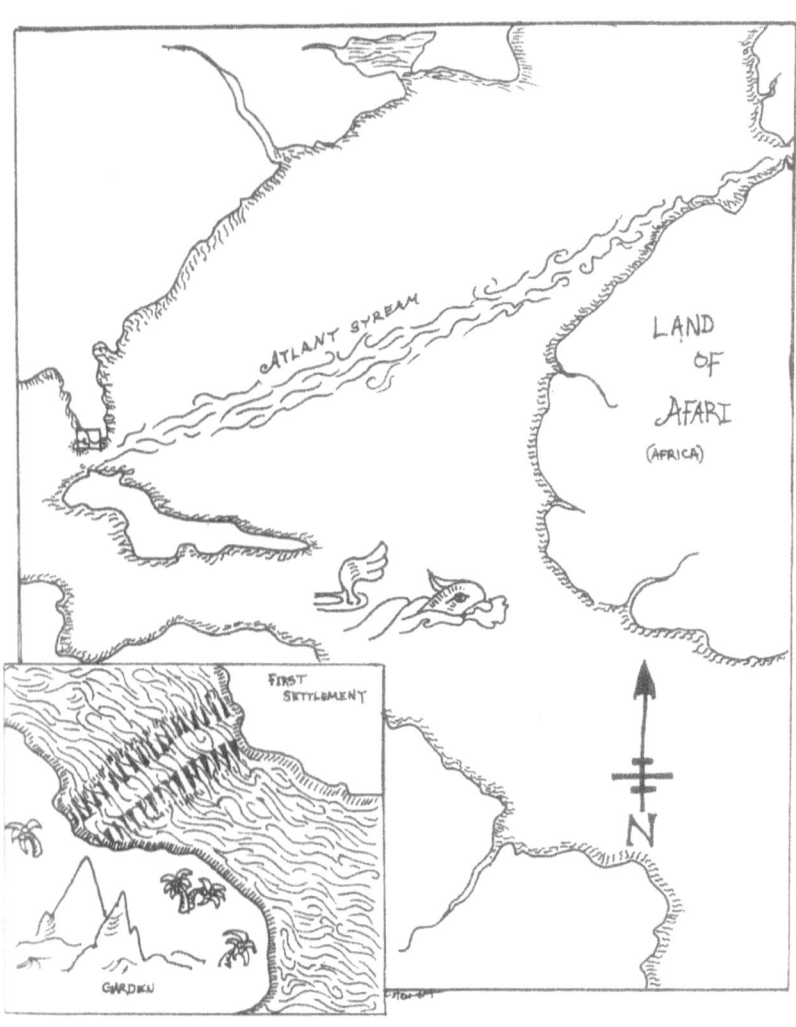

There were those who were born not of blood, nor of the will of the flesh, nor of the will of man, but of God."
—The Gospel of St. John

A zal held her face up to the spring breeze and closed her eyes. She hoped that it would shut out the scene below from her mind, but the voices drifted up to her, defying her to look. Her hands moved quickly to finish tying the prayer banner to the viewing balcony. But the threads became badly tangled, and she realized it was going to take some time to unravel them. She sat back in frustration and looked through the wooden rails at the procession below. Her long red hair fell in waves around her crouching body as she prepared herself for what she was about to see.

The temple sisters shuffled along the great causeway that separated the temple from the outside world, clutching their voluminous blue robes against their old bodies, terrified that someone might contaminate them with a touch. They kept their heads down and their thoughts clear as they prepared for the spring mating ritual of the servers, the planting that would yield more servants. They stepped off the causeway onto a platform decorated with the sacred symbols of the temple and they positioned themselves in the patterns of power. A small dark priest appeared. His skin was thick and wrinkled from years of working in the sun. He held up his arms to the sun and began a rhythmic chant that caused the crowds to sway and hum. Men and women alike, some old and some young, drew closer to the platform. They held their arms up to the sky and swayed like the ocean.

The humming grew louder and louder until the oldest of the sisters stepped forward and pointed at the sun. She then pointed at the great bowl. The fire of the sun flowed through her and ignited the flame in the bowl. The people hummed louder and began to move in unison as though they were one great being. The elder sister closed her eyes and evoked within her a picture of birds, lizards, and the people. She saw them joining in mating and felt the physical thrill of it flowing through her body. She moistened her lips and breathed in heavy grunts.

The people below responded by running their hands over their bodies and then over each other. The men started to remove their clothes, exposing their erections, and holding them in their hands. The sister changed focus and the men seemed to see the women for the first time. They reached out for the women at random and tore at their skirts until the women's genitals were exposed. Grunting and pawing, they bent them over rocks and over the edge of the platform so that they could enter them from behind.

It seemed to get more and more frantic as the seconds passed. The men pushed and gouged into the women. When they had been satisfied, they would move away to allow another next man to take his turn. Saliva, blood, and tears starting to drip from the sides of the women's faces as they staggered in rhythm with each man they encountered.

The priestesses watched in silence as couples copulated in frenzy. Young girls had their hair torn out and throats bitten, and older women staggered and then fell to their knees as they struggled to stem the flow of blood from their damaged wombs.

Azal turned away in disgust. She had never been able to comprehend scenes like this. It was acted out year after year. Her hands habitually went to her hair. She scooped up volumes of dark red hair and pinned it up with a wooden pin. Tightening her hair to her head made her feel more removed from what was happening. She had never thought about why this made her feel better, but the breeze on her neck softened the heavy scowl that had settled on her face. She looked out in the opposite direction to the hills and mountains where the green carpets were starting to fade to yellow from the burning heat of the sun. At least the sisters couldn't reach that. The plants and trees were a class of being that the sisters could not control. Their reproductive system was impervious to emotion. They just doubled themselves from their roots, leaving no process that could be interfered with.

She watched the trees as the breeze caught their branches and imagined she could feel their pleasure, feeling each leaf relax to the cooling wind, but she stopped herself quickly, aware that she had come close to infringing upon a sacred truth. She didn't want to be like them, she didn't want the skill of capturing and training emotion. She wasn't part of them, and she wasn't part of the people. She didn't know what she was a part of. For the first time in her life, she knew she was utterly alone and that she belonged to no one.

The sisters watched motionless as the frenzy burned itself out and the landscape became littered with bodies lying in the sun. Moisture, semen, and blood were smeared across the skin of the women. Those who had died during the ritual were now being removed by the male youths who were too young to have partaken in the breeding. The youngest ones picked through the pockets and hair of the women, groping for anything that might be worth keeping. The older youths climbed on top of the bodies, pretending to penetrate the women, feeling for the women's vulvas, and shoving their hands deep inside them, exploring, testing and finally trying to invoke erections so that they could have their first taste of a woman's body. Most failed miserably, finding it hard to become aroused over a woman. They would kick the bodies in disgust before dragging them by the limbs or hair to the huge pyre that had been prepared for the ceremony.

Those women who survived were led off to the shelter, an area away from the village where they would be watched for any signs of pregnancy. Those who did not bear children would be disposed of. What use is a woman if she cannot bear children? The young boys returned to the male camp, back to the real pleasures of men. Those who had worked hard would be rewarded that night after the cleansing. The boys prepared the water and salt used for scrubbing and cleaning the men from all the impurities they had picked up while in the presence of women. Some men vomited in disgust at the horrors they had been through, but they were soothed and balmed by the gentle touch of young boys. In reward for such devotion, the boys would be allowed to take the men in their mouths, the ultimate pleasure.

Azal walked through the dark corridors of the temple, unable to decide where to go or what to do. Her fingers trailed on the stone walls as she walked, her green eyes flashing as fire torches lit her face. Her walk took her deeper and deeper into the maze that wound itself around and into the stepped pyramid that was at the heart of the temple complex. She didn't notice the drop in temperature nor the silence as she entered the pyramid. She had a feeling of emptiness that seemed to weigh more and more heavily with each step.

If her mother died, she would have no more ties, either within herself or within the temple walls. Then she would belong to no one. She would be nothing. As she walked around and around, the emotional pain tore at her chest and rooted into her very soul, mercilessly destroying her. She did not attempt to block it or interfere with it in any way. This is how it had to be.

The realization that she was truly alone and that the sisterhood was as degenerate in its own way as were the people outside, was finally getting home to her. The feeling was both liberating and terrifying. She alone could carry something new into the future. She had felt this since she was a small child: that there was something in the future that depended on her, but she could not grasp what it was.

She stopped in her thoughts as she realized that she was at the door of the fire sanctuary. She looked around to see if she was alone, and then slipped quietly in. The sanctuary glowed orange from the well of volcanic flame in the center. The room was still and peaceful, its large pillars creating a forest in which she could hide. She loved this room; she loved its sparseness and space. Azal scooped some scented herbs and reverently sprinkled them into the well of fire, allowing her life force to flow into the fire with the herbs. They hissed as they hit the heat, sending clouds of perfume into the room. The smoke wound itself around her hair as she shook it out, allowing the thick red locks to fall to her knees.

Azal walked to the north wall, feeling along the wall with her fingers until she came to a series of grooved patterns. She ran her fingers around the pattern in her own sequence until there was a loud click: she moved back to allow the viewing ledge to open. Doors that reached to the roof started slowly to grind and move, pulling back to expose the temple to the outside world. She waited until the doors had finished retracting and then she stood to take in the scene.

The whole north wall had opened to a beautiful landscape of mountains and sun. Because the sanctuary was near the apex of the pyramid, the view from the ledge was that of a bird in flight. She breathed out as though the breath was her first. She then removed the light blue robe that hung so sorrowfully on her thin tall frame. Azal fingered the linen, remembering the joy of coloring the cloth with herbs and watching the lengths of cloth slowly set their shade in the sun. Azal loved simplicity. She wanted none of the temple. Her dream was to bear children and dye cloth.

She held her arms up to the sun in greeting and worship, trying to tear her very soul from its hold in her body, giving herself totally to the sun. The sun's rays moved across her body, warming her, massaging, and comforting the body that had known so little joy and so much sorrow.

The heat traveled up and across every inch of her body. She turned slowly, exposing every inch to the burning star and, as she turned, the touch of the sun lulled her, drawing her away to another world. She went with that feeling, letting go and reaching out to a world beyond her own, reaching out for something or someone who would ease the pain within her.

Something responded to her inner plea, something reached out and touched her ever so gently, caressing her hair, awakening her soul. Arms that glowed with heat wound around her, stroking and exploring her olive skin; fingers touched her hair, her neck, her face, running across her breasts, down her belly, and in between her thighs. Through the heat of the sun a face bent over to kiss her. His golden hair fell around her face, his eyes of sea glowed with love for her. She cried out in utter joy and suddenly something snapped her back to herself. She stood shaking and crying on the threshold of the world. She looked out to the sun.

"Don't leave me, don't leave me, whoever you are, please stay with me."

☙❧

THE HORN OF CONVENING SOUNDED, resonating around the temple compound, and vibrating through the air wells, turning the temple buildings into one large instrument. The eldest and most senior of the sisters frowned in disapproval.

"We need more time to consider this," she said to the others, casting a long look at the other faces in the room.

They shifted uneasily, not wishing to contradict, and yet, time was running out.

"We have to remove in two moons. We can wait no longer. It will endanger the seeding project." The youngest sister waited for a reaction to her comment and was pleased to see all the sisters nodding their heads. One of the three mountain sisters, a group who wished to keep their distance from the others, turned to comment.

"We can start the process by going first. We do not need to wait for you. The chambers are dug and ready and it will be swift. Our chosen path is much simpler than yours, dear sister. I do not envy you the struggle ahead." The tallest of the three mountain sisters stood up to dismiss the meeting and turned to leave. The others followed, deep in thought.

Azal woke up with a start. The horn. How long had she slept? She had intended to put her head down only for a moment, surrounding herself with the memory of the sun and the joy it brought to her body. She had totally forgotten about the convocation. She was always late, always deep in sleep when she shouldn't be. She scolded herself for the millionth time and threw back the cover on her wooden bed, trying to get her legs to work as she hobbled across the smooth tiled floor. She stepped into the large stone pool at the far end of her chambers.

As she lay back in the hot spring water, she watched the steam rise through the vents, carrying the heat to the central part of the temple, which, without this warm air, would always be cold. A server stepped into the large pool and scattered scented herbs and salt into the water to cover the smell of the sulfur that rose from the hot springs.

Azal's server washed her body down gently, humming tunes that soothed and refreshed.

"Sister," the server whispered, "you have to take better care of yourself. Be ready for unexpected things...."

The server stepped back to watch Azal's reactions to her remark. Azal looked up at the server with a puzzled look. The servers - a race of people always puzzled her, particularly just lately. They all seemed to be watching her and smiling, and yet she had always thought that they had no intelligence, that they were drones. The server nodded at her and smiled again. Azal opened her mouth to ask questions, but the horn sounded again, and she cursed under her breath.

She ran in a very undignified way, with her damp hair slopping around her face, through the various tunnels until she emerged into the main central compound. She stopped short of bursting into the gathering, and instead, darted into the robing room. One of the serving people moved forward to robe her and tidy her up. Azal held out her arms, oblivious of the girl attending her. When the robing was completed, she left the room without so much as a word to the server. The recent experiences she had had with her own server had unsettled her. She needed to be able to understand everything. She needed everything to be simple. Servers don't think, or even speak. They serve.

She looked around the compound. The great fire had been lit in the center and the priests and priestesses were gathered around, waiting for her. There are hardly any left now, she thought as she looked around: the three mountain sisters, herself, two priests and the remaining six sisters. All the others seemed to have slowly melted away over the years. She could not remember anyone ever coming to the temple: only people leaving mysteriously and never returning. She had never been allowed to enter the convocation before and now that she was here, she was beginning to get excited. How could she possibly have forgotten?

For years she had wanted to find out what happened in this strange meeting, what a convocation was, and now that she had been allowed in, she almost lost it by forgetting, turning up late and looking a mess. Then she remembered the sun. How could she forget? She quickly shielded her thoughts, for if the sisters found out about this wonderful pearl in the darkness of her life, they would take it away from her—as they had done with everything else.

The oldest and wisest of the sisters stepped forward to the flame, held her arms up and started to recite in the language of the ancients. This was the only time the sisters used their voices—for invoking. As Azal watched, she felt the pressure in the space begin to rise and she found herself drawn to look in the fire. As the chanting grew louder, she felt something shift within her, at a very deep, almost impersonal level.

Her mind stilled itself and she began to focus only on the flame. She felt herself merging with the fire, stepping into the fire, bathing in its soft flames, becoming renewed and refreshed. She felt the touch of heat on her body and her body responded immediately. She went deeper and deeper into the flame until she found herself in the stars while the sister's chant guided her, lulling her on this wondrous journey. The stars seemed to be attracted to her and the darkness of the void comforted her soul in a way she could not possibly describe.

She felt her flesh fall away, and her bones, and her thoughts of everyday life. Her name fell away until all that was left was the flame within, burning brightly in the void, the divine nothing from which everything comes. She sensed her inner flame move across the surface of the planet, touching the trees, the rocks, the plants, moving, joining, understanding. Her mind melted into the minds of the sea creatures, feeling their feelings, feeling their thoughts and fears. Somewhere in the distance, she heard a change in the chant, which had now become deep and resonant. She drifted in the void, aware only of the chant until her ears became aware of another sound, like the wind playing through the trees. She felt around the space in her mind until she became aware of a pressure building so fast, she thought she would explode. The noise got louder until Azal saw something move in the periphery of her vision.

She turned her consciousness so that she could focus and took a sharp intake of breath as she saw large spinning wheels of fire with many eyes and many wings. Somewhere deep in her mind she remembered hearing about these angels of fire, the beings of creation, but she had never grasped how beautiful and terrifying they were. They seemed to be everywhere at once and as the sister's chant changed yet again, they flew out of the void and into the room, out of the compound and out into the world.

She looked around and was deeply shocked to see that the compound was full of priests and priestesses. While she recognized some from her childhood, others were total strangers. The convening of the priests and priestesses through all times and all the worlds had begun. They processed around the flame, and she felt herself nudged from behind, invited to walk around the flame with them. As she stumbled along, she tried to look around so that she could take in what was happening. She noticed four magnificent gates woven of a beautiful metal, each decorated with strange creatures, one in each direction. She was sure they had not been there before. Each one had a being, half lion, half man, with wings guarding the entrance. She felt drawn to them but dared not step out of the line, and so she looked and looked, trying to imprint on her mind what she was seeing.

As she processed around the flame, a strangely familiar head seemed to be way ahead in front of her. She struggled with her overtaxed mind to remember who it was. The long golden hair and those wide shoulders. The thought suddenly dawned on her struggling mind.

"Oh, great Goddess," she mumbled to herself, trying to speed up so as to reach him.

She tried to pierce her thoughts into his mind, but she couldn't seem to reach him, and with each step forward that she took, he seemed to get further away. He started to turn his head around. Fear gripped her throat. Was it him? Was she hallucinating? What if it was someone else? Would she be able to bear it? As he turned, a tall priest in front of her obscured her view.

"Out of my way!" she pushed sharply into the offending priest's mind.

He turned in alarm and looked at Azal with concern. She looked past him and saw that the golden head had disappeared. She then looked back at the priest, realizing the crime she had committed, and she cried out in anguish and despair. All her power drained from her, all her life, hopes, strength. All her ability to endure her lonely painful life dropped from her shoulders as she was engulfed in darkness.

❧

OUTSIDE THE SERVERS of the people were putting the finishing touches to the burial structures out on the plains. The chambers that had been dug were the depth of four tall men and wide enough for ten men laid side by side. Wooden posts stood at the corners of the pit, and the lattice work was now ready to be placed along the walls. One of the sisters surveyed the work, ensuring everything was right and correct, stopping every so often to drop sweet smelling herbs into the pit. The people eyed her cautiously as they worked. Their lives were driven by the sister's every whim.

A man started coughing while digging in the pit. He paused in his work to try and catch his breath, but the headman shouted for him to continue. He coughed more and more, fighting for his breath until the sister bent over the edge of the pit to see what was happening. She hated getting too close to the people. They smelt terrible and their energy was disgusting. She looked deep into the eyes of the man as he coughed. His eyes pleaded for help. She nodded and looked deeper and deeper into him until he stopped coughing. He stood transfixed by her gaze, held like a frightened animal. Then she pierced his mind with hers, pushing out his consciousness until all that was left was her thoughts. She withdrew her thoughts and the man fell dead.

"Take him away," she thought at the people.

She turned abruptly and left.

As she reached the courtyard of the sisters, the other sisters looked up expectantly. They could feel that something was happening and were curious. The eldest raised an eyebrow.

"The death rate is increasing. One went down at the dig. How many are there in the village and beyond?"

The elder straightened up. "I believe it will take only ten turns of the sun's seasons for the destruction of the servers to be completed. I have heard from others in the far lands that the rate is increasing. Is she ready yet?"

The elder looked inquiringly, waiting for what she wanted to hear. The teacher priestess became uncomfortable and tried to explain.

"Her mixture is difficult. The pattern is unstable but is in no danger. Breeding will balance out the instability through the stimulation of the power center in the throat. Her body will hold the shift well enough, but it needs to happen soon — while she is still young enough to withstand it. All the other samples are ready and held in transportable water. The only hold on Azal now is the mother."

The elder moved towards the door. Her thoughts filtered around the buildings as though looking for something.

"I'll deal with it!" she snapped abruptly and left the room.

The sisters looked at each other in alarm.

"She used her voice," one murmured.

"The time really is coming near. We must all be prepared."

The elder walked down the many tunnels of the temple building and out across the compound until she came to a gate beyond which a steep flight of stairs wound upwards around the outside of the square building on the northern side. Placing her hands on the gate, she felt down into the lock, and with her mind, released the metal joints and the gates swung open. As she climbed the stairs, she wondered what it was like to have a mother, to be a creation with a beginning and an end. To be caught in an endless cycle of life and death. Her mind could not even begin to grasp such a strange and barbaric form of existence.

Azal had grown up around the elder, and the elder had watched the growth of life with amazement and interest. The advent of the removal would mean that the elder would no longer be able to observe the cycle of birth, growth, and death in such detail. It would be a great sacrifice for her. She knew now that the sisters could never return in full physical form because her mind had stretched itself through the flame to see what lay ahead for this planet and the beings that live upon its surface. But we will be there to guide, she thought, we will give birth to, train and supervise the next wave of humanity. She reached the doors of Azal's mother's apartment. She felt herself begin to fade. Not yet, her mind commanded, not yet. Much has yet to be completed. She strengthened her form again by the sheer willpower of her mind, and when she was sure she was complete enough, she entered the room.

Azal's birth mother sat looking out of the window. She had never been allowed to leave her chambers after the birth of the child and for nine long winters she had sat at this window, searching for a glimpse of her. This she had done as a willing sacrifice to enable the soul of Azal to come through her body and grow within her. Now she was weary and ached to see what had become of that bad-tempered obstinate child she had handed to the sisters at the tender age of seven.

The elder looked deeply at her and the woman looked back, trying to sense what was different about the sister. The sister looked deeper and deeper until she broke through to the deepest parts of the poor woman's soul. The woman tried to fight back, suddenly realizing what was happening. She tried to create a barrier, to defend herself, but the harder she fought the weaker her resistance became.

"Azal, Azal, beloved of my breast, be with me, for I will always be with you."

The cry resonated around the empty rooms as she collapsed in the chair. The elder turned and pulled the bell cord that summoned the server.

As she waited, she looked around the simple room adorned with sketches of Azal as a child, and she noticed the drab colors, the thread-bare hangings and the woman's shriveled body. She dusted a small insect off her sleeve and clicked her fingers in annoyance. The server ran in, flustered.

"Your mistress is dying. See to her."

With that, the elder turned and seemed silently to vanish from the room.

Azal stood transfixed, unable to respond, while the server told her of her mother's impending death. Then something deep within her spurred her into action. She grabbed her bag of herbs and ran out of the priestly wing in the east, across the large square courtyard that surrounded the pyramid to the north building, towards her mother's apartment. When she arrived, she found the room filled with the sisters, sitting in silence around the bed. Her mother's body was so shriveled and gray that she didn't recognize her straight away. It had been many years since she had been allowed to see her mother, and now she felt bitter anger and resentment at the intrusion of the sisters.

She unceremoniously pushed the sisters out of the way and pulled back the covers from her mother's tiny body. She stood and looked with profound sorrow at the thin naked frame that had once been her mother. What was left was merely a shadow. She had only clung to life to see her beloved Azal, if only for the last time. Azal worked quickly. She poured oil into her hands and began to massage her mother's frail body from top to toe. She felt her energy flow through her hands into her mother's body. She passed into her the strength that she would need for the death journey. She allowed her spirit to flow over her mother, merging for the last time as mother and child in one supreme act of love and worship.

Her eyes filled with tears of regret and longing for the mother she had never been allowed to grow up with, and when her hands reached her mother's face, she touched her forehead gently in loving worship, whispering visions of trees, the wind, the sun and the moon. All the things she had been denied in her life.

Her mother opened her eyes briefly. She looked at Azal, but her powers of speech had left her. She focused her mind as the sisters did, knowing that Azal would hear her thought.

"My daughter, my rainbow, my life, please carry me to death."

Azal felt her throat tighten to the point where she found it hard to swallow. She stilled herself in preparation for her task and was about to start when the elder cut through her mind.

"No, you must not interfere with the people. They must die alone."

She turned to face the elder. Raw hatred streamed from her eyes and pierced the mind of the elder.

"She was not of the people. She was my mother and, as such, she was my goddess. You will not interfere."

The elder took a step back, not expecting the power behind the fury. This girl's power was unlike anything she had ever encountered before, and she was not sure how to react. Azal's mind was suddenly illuminated with a new understanding. They were not all wise, all knowing and all powerful after all. They also have weaknesses. She smiled widely and triumphantly so that they all could see her, and then she turned to her mother.

Azal started to hum quietly. She stroked her mother's feet and focused her vision inwardly. The hum slowly gathered strength and vibrated around the room, creating a vortex through which Azal could reach into death. As she hummed, she began to see a river and, beyond the river, a large range of mountains. Across the river stretched a wide bridge and Azal saw herself carrying her mother in her arms to the foot of the bridge that was guarded by two angelic beings. She set her mother down at the threshold of the bridge and spoke to her. Her voice was not that of a young girl saying good-bye. It was the voice of a timeless soul reaching through the void in service.

"This is the threshold of the worlds. Beyond lies the divine void and the cycle of rebirth. You must let go of all you have in this life. Let go of me and of your body. Your love for me must flow out to the eternal truth and it must go where it will — just as my love for you goes out in all that I do and all that I say. I will love you forever, but I will not hold you. When I look into the eyes of any life, my love for you will be there. Drink of the river, my mother."

Azal held out a cupped hand of river water and her mother drank of the water. She looked at Azal and then looked through her as though no longer seeing her. She stretched out and touched the bridge, pulling herself to it until one of the guardian beings gently helped her to her feet and walked slowly with her over the bridge. Azal watched until she reached the middle of the bridge and then she retreated from the vision, back to the humming.

She sat for a long time just holding her mother's hand until it became cold. Then Azal was also cold. She was chilled to the bone, exhausted and in pain from the extreme exertion of what she had just done. She looked around her and realized that the sisters had left the room and that she must have sat there the whole night. A cold sheen of sweat covered her body and she felt unable to move, unable to respond to the thoughts that were now trickling into her mind. She knew that if she did not move soon, she would die, but somehow, she just couldn't find the strength. She placed her head on the rough fabric that covered her mother's body and drifted. Just to rest. Just for a short while. How strange. The chill seems to be wearing off, she thought to herself as she drifted into sleep.

She didn't react when she felt strong warm arms pick her up, carry her to her chamber and tenderly wrap her in the softest warmest blanket she had ever felt. She didn't respond when she felt the warm sweet breath on her face, the rough touch of a beard or the brush of soft long hair on her shoulders. She just snuggled deeper and deeper into the comfort, surrendering herself to what she surely thought was death. Warm strong hands slowly and gently removed her robes and began to massage life back into her weary body, gently rubbing and kneading the cold knotted muscles in her shoulders and neck. The face of the man in the sun drifted into her vision. She tried to respond but even as she reached out, she seemed to fall deeper and deeper away in her mind. And then the swaddling. Someone was wrapping her up in warmth and love. Finally, she surrendered her consciousness to the underworld of sleep.

2

The three mountain sisters were hurriedly making final arrangements with the presiding priest for their internment. The sequence of the ritual was repeated over and over, so that he would not forget one solitary detail. He nodded in bewilderment as the sisters took turns driving commands into his brain until finally, when it looked as though he was going to buckle under the weight of so much information, they withdrew, leaving him to rest.

Azal slept deeply and peacefully for the first time in ages. She dreamed of a place surrounded by sea and of a city that shone with the power of the sun. She sank blissfully into the dream, renewing and refreshing her troubled body.

She did not respond at first to the timid voice that whispered in her ear. Somewhere, deep in her dreams, she heard her name being called but could not quite manage to react. Finally, she roused herself as she felt her body being shaken. She opened her eyes to see one of the people bending over her. "The elder sister has requested that you go to her chamber."

The person spoke gently and looked at Azal with tenderness. Azal looked back at her and then around the room.

"How did I get here?"

The server looked surprised.

"But you returned here after the death of your mother. You must have because the sisters left you alone. We all knew what you must have been feeling. Many of my people are dying. There are children every day now on the plains who are left with no mothers."

Azal sat up and looked at the woman intently. Yes, she could feel pain in this woman. But that was impossible. People could only feel strong emotion through the sisters. The server anticipated Azal's line of thought.

"No, great sister, we do have our own emotions, but the sisters have the power to focus and control what we feel when it suits them. Our people are dying, and the sisters are planning something for you. Be careful."

"Why are you telling me this? Why do you care about what happens to me?"

Azal could not understand why anyone would care about her, least of all one of the people.

"Because you are one of us."

The server waited, uncertain of Azal's reaction. She had wanted to tell her for years but had not dared risk the priestess's anger. They were merciless if they were disobeyed.

Azal tried to take in what had been said to her. Her brain could not comprehend the statement, but her body responded with a wave of recognition. Her hands reached out to touch the server. The server became afraid. Azal could kill with her touch if her mind wished it. Her power was something the server had never seen the like of before and it frightened her. Thousands of questions, denials, and accusations flooded into her mind, pushing her already taxed soul close to the edge.

"Listen!" said the server. "I must also leave today, and I will not be coming back. My mother has also just died, and I must go and care for the children."

Azal looked in panic at the server. "You cannot leave now — not after telling me this."

"Beware!" said the server.

"You must also leave. Your mother was a server. She displayed many of the skills and qualities that the sisters had been waiting for many cycles of life. She was trained as a priestess. Yes, we too had priestesses once upon a time. There was a ritual mating of your mother. No one knows with whom or how. One minute she was a priestess. The next minute she was a breeding machine for the sisterhood. You were the product. She was then locked in her apartments and was never released again until you carried her into death yesterday. We all think that you will be the only one of us left to survive and we plead with you to remember us. That is all you need to do. And be warned: something terrible is about to happen to you. Our seer has foretold it. But you will not die, and we will help you as much as we can. Do not mention this to the sisters."

Azal staggered back against the wall. She recalled the frenzied breeding scene in her mind, and she groaned in disgust. How could she be of that blood?

"I know you have always hated us," the server continued.

"You see the disgusting things that happen. But the women are not the same as the men. The men are conditioned from birth by the sisters. What you see is their handiwork."

She was about to continue when the door to the apartment swung open and one of the sisters walked in. The server cloaked herself in an attitude of stupidity, pretending to pick up robes from the floor, and Azal swiftly masked her mind by transforming it into a blank space. The sister stopped abruptly as she entered the room. She felt something strange but couldn't quite grasp it. She probed into the Azal's mind but found nothing, absolutely nothing. Immediately Azal knew that that was a mistake.

"I am exhausted from my mother's passage," she murmured. "I wish to feel and think nothing. Why do you disturb me so when I need rest?"

Azal realized she had spoken out loud.

The sister watched her for a moment and then cursed herself for not anticipating the terrible effect that such dangerous work would have on the young priestess. If she was using her voice, then she must surely be in need of regeneration.

"I'm sorry to summon you but the elder wishes to speak with you."

She turned to the server.

"You did not deliver the message you were sent with. You will feel pain for being so neglectful." Azal threw a glance to the server. She looked into her eyes and tried to absorb the server's pain. But the woman shook her head slightly, indicating to Azal that she should not interfere and so give herself away.

The elder turned to look at Azal as she entered the elder's chamber. She noticed immediately how the girl's energy field wavered and struggled to right itself. She will need work done on her if she is to survive the future, the elder thought. The girl stood expectantly before of the elder, waiting for the discipline and punishment which she knew she was about to receive for her transgressions, both at her mother's bedside and at the convocation.

The elder turned away from her and looked out of the doorway that led onto a viewing ledge. The land was so beautiful here and it always gave her the strength go on in difficult times. Azal looked around the room and was surprised to see that certain ritual objects had been removed. The staff of central balance had been removed and so had the crystal viewing bowl. Azal had never seen these things moved — let alone removed altogether. She felt a danger creeping around her but could not comprehend what the danger might be. She remembered the words of the server and pulled herself in tight so that she would be prepared for anything.

"Child, I want you to prepare for a very important ritual. You will be the main mediator. You will need to strengthen and prepare yourself, for it will be a difficult task."

"What is the task, sister? And why choose me? I am the least experienced here."

The sister ignored the questions and turned around to face Azal.

"You will go tomorrow to the mountain sisters for preparation. That is all. You may leave."

Azal knew better than to push.

Many years earlier, as a child, she had experienced the horrific mental pain that the sisters could induce if you pushed them in any way.

SHE KNOCKED on the door quietly even though she knew that they could feel her approach. A server opened the door, a young girl, who winked at Azal before stepping aside to let her in. Azal was taken aback for a second and then remembered her server's words on the day before she was taken away and never returned.

As she entered the chamber of the mountain sisters, she felt a great sadness descend on her, a sadness that she couldn't explain. She liked the mountain sisters. They were different from the other sisters.

"Greetings, little one."

They raised their heads in unison. Azal thought this was very funny, as she was much taller than any of them. She smiled, and they too shared the joke and smiled. They felt much more relaxed than she had ever remembered them being before, and a sense of playfulness surrounded them. Yet why did she feel this deep sadness around them?

"We have been told that you are to be prepared for the ritual, and before you ask, no, we cannot discuss it with you. Come and lie on this bed, little one. Server! Help her."

Azal climbed awkwardly onto the bed and lay down. It felt good to lie and rest. She had spent so much time running errands lately. Everyone suddenly seemed to be so busy. As she relaxed, she felt one of the sisters come and sit by her head.

The sister gently placed her hands on the young girl's head and, through resting her fingertips on the girl's skull, she was able to feel every part of the young girl's body. As the sister moved her awareness through the girl's organs, she felt areas where the energy was blocked and where certain flows had been interrupted. She moved her fingers very gently over Azal's head and face, twitching and maneuvering the bones and fluids beneath her fingers.

Azal sank into a deep relaxation and noticed random memories from her childhood popping into her mind. She remembered the time she fell from a viewing ledge and banged her head as she landed — luckily — on a balcony garden below. One more span to the right and she would have plunged three hundred feet to her death. Then she remembered the time when she took a wrong turn in the maze and ran headlong into a post. Azal began again to feel the pain that the impact had caused. She was about to say something to the sister about the pain when something popped, and the pain fell away.

She relaxed more deeply and the whispering sisters' voices in her head fell away until she was bathed in a blissful calm. Her mother's face began to form in her mind. Azal saw the youthful look that had formed on her mother's face as she had tenderly carried her to the bridge. Her arms began to hurt, and her head began to throb. She shifted her weight on the table and the sister threw a glance to the others watching nearby.

The sister could feel the terrible impact that the death work had imposed on Azal's body, but there was also something else. Something had impacted on her at a soul level. Although the death of her mother had hurt her deeply, the sister didn't think that that was the cause. The sister struggled to deal with it. Anything like this, any flaw in the child's balance, would kill her in the ritual. Then all the many years of preparation would have been for nothing. She probed and probed until she reached the soul shape itself. Instead of a smooth wavy line, it was distorted in several places, creating inharmonious shapes that affected the way in which the body held the soul. If the sister could restore a harmonious shape to the soul, it would not injure the body as the soul expressed itself in life. If she could not adjust the shape, Azal would be plagued with weakness, illness, and finally death.

After what seemed like a very long time, Azal's inner shape started to release itself and change. The sister breathed a huge sigh of relief. She stroked and caressed the soul until it began to respond and flow. She focused on Azal's inner fire, balancing it, merging it with the central fire of the divine until the power of the divine life flowed over the soul, calming the shape and allowing the whole being of the child to be renewed and refreshed.

They built the fire up in the room and draped Azal with a soft covering. She drifted, listening to the sisters move and think as she slipped into sleep. As she sank into sleep, the face of the sun appeared in her mind. She tried to hold the face, but her body pulled her deeper and deeper into dreamless sleep.

3

Azal had assumed that the pit being dug was for her mother. Her cry had rung through the temple building when she heard that her mother's body had been exposed to the elements on the muck pile. As she sobbed, the server helped her back to her room. She lay on her bed, cursing the sisters and screaming until one of the mountain sisters came to attend her.

The sister sat silently and listened to Azal rant and rave until she finally became quiet.

"Little one, listen to me. What was done there was what your mother requested. Burials are only for special purposes. You know that we burn our dead and that the people expose theirs. Long before she died, your mother requested exposure. Although she was forced to live in the temple with the sisters, she wished, in death, to be identified with the people. We merely carried out her wishes."

Azal sat and thought for a long while. "She was one of the people, wasn't she?" she asked, looking up at the sister.

The sister nodded.

"It was never a secret, child. But she wanted you to feel like a true priestess. She thought that you would be disgusted with her if you found out. And so she never told you."

"What then is the burial pit for?" Azal was becoming more and more confused. "The sisters do not die unless something terrible happens to their bodies. Isn't that right?"

These were questions Azal had never asked before. She had been raised always to accept what she was told and never to question anything or to pry.

"That is correct, Azal. Next week, during the full moon, I and my two sisters will be interred. Our time here is over."

Azal panicked.

"No! You cannot go! You cannot leave! You are the only decent thing here. What will become of me if I am left with the others?"

The sister did not answer but rose to leave. As she got to the door, she turned to Azal. "Just accept what comes, child. We are always with you and will never leave you."

Azal never saw the mountain sisters alive again. And now, as she stood on the ramp, holding the bowl of perfumed incense, she wished that she had gone to their apartments just one last time.

The burial procession slowly wove its way down the ramp. As the bodies of the sisters passed her, she stretched out in her mind to bless and caress them. She could never remember them being overly warm or kind, but they were not frightening like the others. She didn't know why they were different from the other sisters, but they always seemed somehow softer. The furniture for the burial was held high during the procession. The many-colored stones set into the wood flashed in the light and created an aura of stars. The people were held back by servers as the sisters, priests and attendants processed. Azal came up last, bearing the incense burner and clearing away any essence of the ceremony that might be left behind.

As they reached the pit, Azal looked on in fascination as they lowered the sisters one by one into the pit. The burial chamber looked like an underground replica of their apartment. One large bed was covered in rich warm blankets. Its wood was beautifully carved with faces and eyes to watch over them. Accompanying them were baskets and bowls of fruit, vegetables, breads and root broth, stacked neatly in the corner, and pots full of clear water from the spring. As each sister was lowered, she was placed gently on the bed and unshrouded.

Azal gasped. They looked alive! Then she remembered the words of the priest of the mountain. He had told her about certain mixtures of resins and herbs which, if applied to a body, would preserve a body so that it would look as fresh in a thousand years' time as on the day when the soul had left it. He told her of the importance of preserving the body, for if the body remains complete, the soul might stay in this world without passing through death. And that is just how the sisters looked now — fresh and alive.

They were laid side by side on their backs, as though sleeping on the bed. A series of poles and posts were placed around them in the ground. The tops of the posts were flat. Attendants laid beams across the posts and nailed them into position to create a roof over the sisters. Heavy sheets, stiff with mud from the springs, were draped around the sides of the structure to create walls around the bed. Then all fell silent. The sisters in attendance and the priests raised their arms and the people fell silent. When all was quiet, the elder struggled down to her knees. She leaned over the edge of the pit and whispered something quietly to the sleeping sisters. Then she motioned to the attendant servers to begin digging and to fill the chamber with earth. She turned to the priests and priestesses and ordered them to return to the temple.

Azal was loath to leave them here on the plain. Who would attend them? Who would care for them? Who would remember them when the grass had grown over them?

⚜

AZAL LAY STILL while the servers oiled her body in preparation for the ritual. As the time had drawn closer, she had become more and more afraid. Her whole body knew that what was about to happen was very dangerous, and yet she didn't have a clue about what it would be. Her hair was washed, oiled and then braided in tight thin braids until it looked as though her head bore a tangle of snakes instead of hair. She looked in the mirror and giggled at the absurdity of it all. At last she stood while they robed her. Her robes were of a fabric unknown to her.

She was used to cotton of varied weights, but this was some almost ethereal fabric like a web of blue and gold.

The server watched her with interest.

"Great priestess! It is spun from the thread of a small worm and has the touch of heaven."

Azal was shocked. All her food and clothing came from the plants, but this.... It disgusted her, and yet caressed her and fascinated her all at once. She ran her hands down her body, feeling how the fabric traveled across her skin. It felt good.

The server then stood to one side to allow one of the sisters to approach Azal. She hadn't realized that any of them were here. She stood in silence as the sister looked her up and down. When she was satisfied with what she saw, she picked up a palette upon which were spread many different dyes and pigments. First, she drew a small circle in blue on Azal's forehead. Then she traced a thin vertical red line through the circle that stretched from her hairline to the bridge of her nose. On the palms of her hands, she painted a sun of bright yellow, with many intricate flames leaping and weaving around the center. Finally, she outlined two half-moons back-to-back on her feet.

The sister stepped back to survey her work and then, much to Azal's surprise, bent in a deep bow of reverence to the young girl. Although Azal did not know how to respond, she felt a new and profound dignity begin to envelop her.

The sister and the servers withdrew and left Azal to gaze at her reflection in the ornate mirror. As she looked at herself, she began to feel strange. The markings on her face began to look somehow familiar. She looked deeper into the mirror and saw many faces come and go. Yet each face was hers. She saw herself mounted on a strange and ferocious looking being, hacking at someone with a great blade of metal. She saw children, other strange, smaller beings, and then she saw him. She took a quick breath as she looked full into the face of the man in the sun. His clear blue eyes called to her. She turned away, unable to cope with what she was seeing.

Azal wanted to weep. All the pain of the loss of her mother, the loss of the sisters, and her inability to make any further contact with the man in the sun, were becoming too much. Yet she was terrified of crying — at this moment when she should be stilling herself for the ritual. She cursed herself for being so pathetic and sat down opposite the sacred flame that had been lit in her room.

Her eyes were drawn to look into the flame, and she reached deep within herself to find her inner flame. Then she began to see them as one and the same flame, the fire of sacred being. The divinity before the void. It brought her stillness and strength. As the fire expanded in her body, she felt a solid power stirring within her. It flowed through her body, reached her fingertips and toes, and filled her whole being with the light of the void. She rose and turned to the door, knowing that they were coming for her. At last, she was ready.

She processed along the maze of corridors, flanked by four of the sisters. She tried to walk with as much dignity as she could muster, keeping her mind steady so that none would know of the fear that stuck in her throat. Her legs seemed to work independently of her body, carrying her to what felt like her death. Her brain screamed at her to run and not stop until she was on the far side of the mountain.

As they approached the outer doors to the fire temple, Azal became confused. She had assumed that the ritual would have something to do with the convocation. She couldn't remember where she had got such an idea from — but it had dug itself firmly into her conscious mind and now she was really frightened. She had loved to sneak into the fire temple when it was empty and go up to the viewing ledge. But she had always been told that the rituals performed there were dangerous and not for young ones, and so she could only speculate about what could possibly happen in there. She knew that many servers who had attended the priests and priestesses during a fire ritual had died after their experiences in this vast powerhouse.

The priestess in front of Azal knocked on the door with ritual taps. They waited as the huge metal locks were released. As the doors swung silently open, a strong-smelling incense wafted out of the temple room. Through the haze of smoke, she saw that all the priests and priestesses were assembled in a semicircle around the great fire in the center of the circular room.

The huge pillars were painted in gold, and outlines of fish adorned the tiled floor around the flame holder. She was escorted into the room and around the central flame until she stood between the fire and the closed viewing doors. As she looked down, she realized that she was standing on a painting of the sun. The colors of gold, red and yellow were bright and vibrant. How fitting, she thought, to die while standing on the sun.

She looked around the room and felt the space that had been vacated by the sisters of the mountains. The power felt different. The elder approached Azal and put two heavy gold snakes on her forearms. They seemed to lock in place and their green jeweled eyes flashed in the firelight. "Never remove these, for they are your guardians."

Azal felt the gold hot against her skin, as the snakes seemed to melt into her arms and settle themselves.

The elder went back to her position and nodded to the priest. He began to open the viewing doors. As they slowly parted, hot rays from the sun darted between the doors and illuminated the floor of the temple. The sisters began to hum, and the priests began to chant over the humming. Azal stood firmly on her spot, unsure about what to do.

As the chanting rose, so the power rose and the pressure within the temple room became intense. Azal swiveled her eyes to look at the sisters as they hummed. Then she looked again in amazement. They seemed almost transparent. Perhaps it was a trick of the light. The humming changed tone and the elder walked up to her and stared fixedly at her. She flinched instinctively before realizing that the sister was not looking at her. She was looking right through her.

The sister took a deep breath and then spoke aloud.

"Will you be the gateway for the sun in the center of the earth, a bridge to the stars, a pathway to all consciousness, a mediator between all the worlds? Will you, sister of all, daughter of the child of light, mother of the Sun temple, keeper of the snakes of all wisdom, grant this?"

Azal replied, "I will."

She really had no idea what they were talking about.

Although she had spent her life learning specific skills and developing inner abilities, she had never been taught the mysteries. And so the titles, the names and the tasks meant nothing to her. But she was happy to go ahead — and was curious to know what was about to happen. She had also concluded that they were not going to kill her. Her instincts told her that although the ritual was powerful, she would not die.

The elder offered Azal a cup of herbs to drink. Azal took the drink and paused, trying to guess what herbs she was about to drink. The smell was unfamiliar. As she drank it, the liquid seemed to set her throat on fire. She drained the cup and handed it back to the elder.

The drink started to take effect. She began to feel warm and safe. Her mind became unfocused, and her muscles started to relax. She joined in the chant which was low and deep. Her eyes struggled to focus. In the distance she could see the sun, waiting. She felt the warmth of the fire behind her and as the heat began to rise, she felt herself begin to open up deep inside.

The sensation deepened until she had an irresistible urge to pull the fire through her body. Her mind began to focus on the sun, merging with the flame within and the flame behind her. Soon the fire became one. Azal reached her arms out to the sun and let out a terrifying cry that resonated around the room. The fire of the volcano passed through her and out to the sun in a stream of yellow light.'

Azal was bathed in light. She floated in the light and was consumed by it. All she could see, feel and think was this yellow flame. Many voices seemed to be speaking all at once. Many faces passed before her vision, and she felt as though the convocation was been squeezed through her brain. The voices got louder and louder until the noise became unbearable. She cried and fought the sensations that pushed their way through her being as her body screamed for release.

As she felt herself going, she realized that death would be better than pushing through this. She allowed herself to abandon her body, cell by cell. Just as she felt ready to slip into the void, he appeared in front of her. The face of the sun caressed her and pleaded with her to fight and stay alive.

Her body responded and she felt, somewhere deep within her, a will to go on. She tried to focus her mind, repeating to herself over and over:

"It is time to stop. All this must stop."

She repeated and repeated the words until her mind stepped into a void of darkness.

The first thing that Azal felt was the wind on her face. She felt cold, a bitter cold she had never known before, a cold that seemed to eat into her very bones. She tried to move, but every bone in her body felt broken, every shred of her mind felt torn. She opened her eyes slowly and then sat up. She was shocked at what she saw. She was out on the plains in the dark.

The stars were faint, and the moon was hiding Her face for it was Her dark time. Azal shook from the cold and from fear. She looked out over the plains and then looked back towards the temple. But the temple wasn't there. Was it too dark to see? She steadied her battered mind and felt for the temple boundary. But there was nothing. Azal got up and stumbled towards where the ramp should be. Nothing. Only rocks, plants, and the mountains.

Her brain could not cope with this. She panicked, calling out for her mother, and calling for the mountain sisters. The mountain sisters! She started to stumble towards the burial mound. Azal wandered through the darkness, unable to orient herself. Her fear mounted as she began to understand that she might be hopelessly lost. She could no longer see the temple, her only landmark.

She stopped and tried to think clearly. The mound was to the east.

The mountains are to the north. The plains are to the south. She stilled herself, trying to stop her teeth from chattering and her body from shaking. She reached deep within to the flame, and then visualized the flame of the inner convocation. When she held the image clearly in her head, she felt for the direction in front of her. What did it feel like?

As she stretched her consciousness before her, she became aware of heat and fire, and of the fire priests. I am facing south. Azal felt pleased with herself. At last, her training and abilities were coming in useful! She could never understand why they had put so much pressure on her to learn the directions when they were so clearly marked around the temple. But now she was grateful. So if she was facing south, then east was to her left. She turned left and started to walk slowly, shaking and cursing with each step.

As the cold began to eat into her mind, it gave rise to visions of beings who followed her and teased her. She felt the landscape around her in her mind, trying to sense the presence of the burial mound. It had so much power. It should be easy to find. As she walked, she slowly became aware that the ground on which she was walking had become soft and that she was moving up a slight gradient. The mound! She had walked straight to it.

As she got closer to the mound, she saw a faint light. She ran towards it and found a small light burning in a protected lamp. Beside the lamp were clothing, food, and a blanket. She thankfully pulled the blanket around her as she sat down. She realized then that they had known that this would happen to her, and so had left provisions for her to find.

Her anger flared and became so great that it seemed ready to consume anything in its path. How could they do this? How could they vanish and leave her so unprepared — she who had never spent a night alone or away from the temple? Why couldn't they have told her? Where on earth had they gone? How do you lose a huge temple complex? How do you make it simply vanish? She pulled the blanket more closely around her body and her mind became confused and empty of thought. She curled up in a fetal position, hoping for death, and eventually fell into a troubled sleep.

As the sun rose, it warmed her tired body. Slowly Azal began to surface into the conscious world. As she began to awaken, she heard a familiar humming. She opened her eyes and saw her old server cooking over an open fire. The server had allowed her dark hair to fall over her shoulders — something that was strictly forbidden in the temple. Her plump body and rosy cheeks created a picture of motherliness that warmed Azal's bitter heart. She sat up and winced at the pain that coursed through her body. The server came over to her and offered her a cup of herbs to drink. "It will ease your pain," said the server, looking at Azal's questioning face.

"Thank you."

Azal's voice was hoarse and unsteady. She gulped down the herbs, wincing at their bitterness and yet feeling the warmth and healing course through her stomach.

"Are you hungry?" asked the server.

"I have made a broth and collected greens for you to eat. Here, sit."

The server put a bowl of food in front of the girl and watched her eat. Her eyes scanned the burns and bruises on Azal's body, and she cursed the sisters on the morning wind. When Azal had eaten enough to reduce her hunger, she looked at the server.

"How did you know that I would be here, and that I would need you?"

The last twenty-four hours had been too much for Azal to absorb.

"We saw the fire in the sky over the temple. Many of our people had come out to watch. The fire built up and I heard your cries. We thought that you had been burned in the fire. And then the temple just ... vanished. We ran to our mother. She looked into the water and saw that you were still alive and that you had been abandoned. She sent out search parties for you. My little sister found you collapsed on the mound, and she ran back to fetch me."

Azal looked at the server. "I thought that your mother was dead."

"Oh yes, she is. By "mother" I mean our seer. The seers of our people were hunted down by the sisters and murdered. One survived and shrouded herself in motherhood. She told us about you, how you are special, and that you are one of us, and how you will be our future. When you are ready, I will take you to meet her."

She paused and then said, "And my name, by the way, is Ishia."

Azal surveyed her for a minute. She had never thought of the servers as having names.

"Ishia. That is a very beautiful name. How did you get it?"

"When my mother first carried me in her belly, she bent down to the earth in wonder, and as she lay her head on the ground, the great mother whispered the baby's name through the trees and plants that have their roots in her. Then the wind swirled and swirled around her, translating the name for my mother. That is how I was named."

"That is a wonderful story. You are a very lucky woman."

Azal looked at Ishia and wished that she herself had a family and as much love as the server. "No, Azal, I am not lucky. Come to my village and see."

After clearing what was left of the food and packing the supplies in the bag that the sisters had left, they walked towards the village.

"Azal — may I call you that?"

Azal nodded.

"I know I am not supposed to know about the mysteries, but where did the temple go? How did it disappear? My people are terrified. They are hiding in their homes, saying the world has come to an end, and that it was foretold."

"I don't know," answered Azal. "I just don't know. It was as though I had had a bad dream but could not wake up."

Azal fell silent. Her body ached from the impact and the shock.

As they approached the village, they saw women scraping the earth as they looked for herbs. They saw shriveled potbellied children sitting and whimpering. It seemed as though they didn't even have the energy to cry. A heavy smoke hung over the village and a disgusting smell drifted over everything. Azal gagged and put her hand to her mouth. She looked at Ishia with surprise and horror. Was she supposed to live here now? Ishia saw Azal's look and sighed. Azal had been profoundly sheltered. She had lived her whole life in the temple. Now she had to face the realities of what was really happening.

"You must follow me. We will meet the last seer. She will tell you what to do."

As they bent over to enter the hut, Azal was thankful for the aromatic herbs that masked the smell. She tried to focus her eyes through the haze. Suddenly, through the smoke, came the smallest woman she had ever seen. Her skin was black and wrinkled. Her face and body were heavier than those of the people, and her back was more bent. She watched Azal survey her and then grunted and turned around.

"Yes, seed of the future, I am one of the original people from whom the sisters developed. Lie down and let me check you."

Azal panicked and looked at Ishia

"You will be safe. I just want to ensure that they did no permanent damage to you with their savagery."

Azal lay down, carefully trying to avoid the thick dust and the dried herbs lying on the floor. She wondered why the seer had called the sisters savage. The old woman chuckled and, shaking her head, dropped down to the floor next to Azal. She started to sing and clap her hands, swaying to the rhythm that was beginning to fill the hut. She clapped and clapped and sang and seemed to be singing herself into a trance when suddenly she stopped. She sat totally still and was completely silent. Ishia and Azal looked at her expectantly. She remained silent. And then, suddenly, out of her mouth, came smoke.

She bent over and blew the smoke over Azal's body. A strange noise seemed to accompany the motion but neither of the two women could tell where it came from. Then she bent over in a swift motion and, grabbing Azal's head, blew hard into her mouth. Azal coughed and spluttered and tried to fight off the crazy old woman. Terror rooted Ishia to the spot. Never had she seen the seer behave like this before and she backed away to hide in the corners of the hut.

The old seer stood up, pulled Azal to her feet, and looked her up and down.

"Clean! Fresh! Strong! You come here tonight. I will tell stories. Now go."

Ishia's face lit up as she emerged from the corner. Stories! The old seer had not told stories for years. This would excite the villagers. As the two women left the hut, Ishia supported Azal, who was so stunned that she could not speak. Each time she opened her mouth, nothing came out. She could feel that something was happening to her, but she did not know what it was.

As she walked through the foul-smelling village, Azal looked into the faces of the people. All she could see was death, death all around. They were all going to die. How did she know this? She simply knew. She had to get away. Tomorrow or maybe the next day. But soon.

As they entered Ishia's hut, Azal saw the most beautiful child she had ever seen. Although the little girl was in no way physically extraordinary, her inner beauty shone like a star and lit up the whole hut. Azal took a deep breath and sat down.

"Azal, this is my little sister, Orcas. She is eight winters' old. Orcas, this is Azal, the sister I tell you about in the stories."

Azal looked at Ishia and Ishia laughed.

"I tell her of the great temple and the sisters and about you. She loves it! She wants to know every detail."

Orcas, smiling hopefully, crept shyly closer to Azal. She was a small child with big round blue eyes and a dark skin. Her hair was wild and frizzy. It was the color of black that looks almost red. Azal had never seen blue eyes in any of the people before. Azal looked at her friend.

"Her eyes," she said. "I have never seen blue eyes in any of your people before."

"The seer says that her blue eyes come from being conceived in the water."

Azal waited for further explanation.

"My mother refused to go to the seasonal mating. She said that it was cruel and that it spawned the wrong sort of child. And so, when she was in season, she went to the river and prayed to the god of the river and swam about in the water. She says that as she swam, the river made love to her, and she became pregnant. She returned to the river for the birth and Orcas was born in the water. She asked the river for a name for her child and a strange water creature emerged from the deep and made a strange sound like... Orc... Orc.... That is how she was named 'Orcas'."

Azal studied Ishia's face. "Your mother was a very special person," she said.

"Yes," sighed Ishia.

"She was a seer. But she had to hide under the cover of mother-hood because the sisters wanted to kill all seers. They could feel her, but they couldn't find her. They did not know that the seers could have children. It wasn't ever supposed to happen."

Orcas had climbed on Ishia's lap and was now smiling at Azal. Ishia wrapped her arms around Orcas and hugged her as she explained further to Azal.

"She loves stories. Oh, Orcas, I almost forgot to tell you, the old one says that she will tell stories tonight."

Orcas' eyes grew wide in excitement and fear. She loved stories but she was terrified of the old seer. What a dilemma!

As night came on, it grew colder and colder. The villagers built huge fires away from the huts and placed cauldrons of root broth to simmer and bubble on the hot stones. Azal turned to Ishia as they watched the preparations.

"They have enough food. Why then do I see death everywhere? What is happening to your people?"

Ishia sighed. It hadn't occurred to her that Azal might not know. But then, how could she?

"My people — our people — have been dying of some strange wasting disease for a long time now. No one knows what it is or how to cure it. The seer says that our people are coming to an end. It doesn't seem to be a catching disease. It is just something that happens. We have tried every remedy and treatment, but nothing works.

"You must leave here soon! And, if you wish, Orcas and I will come with you."

She didn't look at Azal but kept her eyes fixed on the fire, waiting for a reply.

Azal studied her with her inner vision. She was not diseased. Although Ishia was young and strong, Azal also felt that she should leave. She also felt an intuition that it was important to get Orcas away from the village. And so they would go.

"Yes, I will leave. And I would like you both to come with me and help me. I have never been out of the temple before. I will need your help."

They all settled down around the fires and slurped at the broth while they waited for the old seer to start the story. Orcas' eyes were wide and bright with fear and anticipation. She stared at the old one, fascinated by her wrinkled face and mangled hair. The old woman coughed and spat. She began.

In the beginning, there was only darkness. The darkness was soft and powerful and was all that was needful. The darkness had no time and no thought—only power. Then the power breathed out a huge breath that began to move the darkness. And as the darkness moved, light came behind it. And so there was light and darkness. The light was powerful, hot and bright, and the darkness was powerful, cold and frightening, and they battled for supremacy. As they warred, they became angry,

The power of light said, "If I had a fire I could burn you away" and so the light became fire.

The darkness said, "If I had land, I could bury you" and so the dark became land.

And the land burned with the fire, and the fire was tempered by the dust and soil. Neither could win. So the stars sent a power to mediate. A power of great beauty and strength would surely bring peace! The power fell from the stars to the land and became water. She glistened in the firelight and shone blue on the edge of the land. The land fell in love with her and tried to reach out to her, forgetful of the fire. But the fire became fearful of the water and tried to burn her by blowing burning land up beneath the water in an attempt to harm her. Instead of being afraid of the fire, the water laughed and pulled the burning land up through her belly until it surfaced and became new land.

The fire got very angry and called to the fire within the center of the earth to send a friend. The burning star in the center of the land sent his greatest friend, the wind. The wind blew across the water, making her more and more angry, and then the wind fanned the fire on the land, making it burn and burn. This battle went on and on until they were all exhausted. The water spoke first.

"Can't we all just stay in our own directions and respect each other? I ask this because something special is happening within me." The wind, fire and land gathered around, waiting for her to continue. "I am carrying our child."

The wind, fire and land became confused.

"As we fought and mingled together, we created something new. Out of our anger and despair, new life was created, and now we must all be responsible."

The others agreed. The land went to the north, the fire to the south, the wind to the east and the water to the west. They waited and waited until, after a long wait, beings began to emerge out of the water. The wind and fire looked at the creatures and then at each other. One was a creature of the wind, one was a creature of the fire, one was of the water and one was of the earth. But they would not communicate with each other and they all fled in all directions at once. They were strange-looking creatures, half in this world and half in the other. Some settled and resided deep in the land, and some settled in the inner world. Those who settled in the land were of earth and water and were named "faery" and those who went to the inner world were of fire and wind, and were known as "angels."

The water responded. "Maybe if we come together as friends, the outcome would be better."

So they began their dance. The wind and the sea danced and danced, the fire exploded out from under the sea and created new land, and the land caressed the sea with profound love and respect. Then they waited and waited. Out of the ocean came a creature on two legs. She stretched her arms to the sun in thanks. She touched the earth in love. She caressed the ocean in awe and sang to the wind in companionship.

"Truly, she is good," said the friends. "Now let's make some more."

They made fish and plants and trees and more children. The friends taught their new children everything they knew. But the new children became arrogant and powerful. They used the knowledge given to them from the elements to create their own children. They treated their own created children like slaves and controlled everything they did. The friends were in despair, but what could they do? The children were everywhere and were becoming more and more powerful. They could not destroy them without destroying themselves, for that is the law of balance — you must take responsibility for whatever you create.

But they had to do something. They had to put it right. The water came up with the answer. I will go into the void and look for a solution. She went into the void. The wind didn't blow, the sun wouldn't shine, the earth stood still, all waiting for their beloved ocean to return. After a short while she returned smiling.

"The void gave me seeds of goodness, seeds that are the essence of each of us. The best of me, of the wind, of the fire and of the earth. I will put the seeds from the void into the belly of the slave people, and then we shall see what happens."

Everybody waited in anticipation for the ending. All eyes were on the old woman and her face seemed poised as if to continue — as though she were waiting for someone to whisper the ending. She took a deep breath and poked the fire with her stick.

And so the seeds were planted. The children realized that if they lived with the friends any longer, that they would lose control of their own world and of the slave children they had created. They decided to move into another world, a realm where they could still govern their creations but a place where the elements could not rule them.

In the meantime, the seeds planted by the ocean started to grow. They would be the new beginning, a world of wonder and beauty, of power used wisely and of true fellowship between the beings and the elements. The slaves gave birth to the seeds and the new children shone with the light of goodness, giving hope to all who suffered."

The people murmured and nodded. Yes, to live in such a world would be an honor. The old woman stood up, signaling the end of the story.

Orcas turned to Ishia. "Who are the seed children? Where are they?"

Ishia looked to the old woman. Yes, she wanted to ask the same question but felt that she couldn't. The old woman heard the question and shuffled over to Orcas.

"You will have to wait and see, child. Keep your eyes open, keep your eyes open."

She shuffled off, leaving Orcas totally confused. Should she keep her eyes open? What about going to sleep? That would be hard. Could she blink? Orcas walked around with her eyes opened as wide as she could make them.

The old woman called out to Ishia. "Bring the sister and the child. Come to me."

Ishia looked startled. The old woman never saw people in her hut after dark. No one had ever been in there after dark. Legend had it that spirits visited her in the night, for people had often passed by and heard her talking to someone, and some had even heard replies given in a deep dark voice.

They entered the hut, which was lit by a small oil lamp. The herbs smelt pleasant, and Azal was having trouble staying awake. Her joints still ached. Her skin still burned from her ordeal, and she longed for a clean robe to put on. She had changed into the clothes which had been left for her, but the long robes had soon become soiled in the dirt and mud of the village.

Azal sat on the floor beside Ishia and Orcas and waited for the seer to speak. The old woman looked at Azal.

"What did you think of the story, sister?"

Azal looked at the old woman

"Is the story about the sisters?" she asked.

The old woman nodded.

"So where are the seeds? Are they in the glass vials in the pack they left me?" The old woman's eyes narrowed.

"What vials?"

Azal turned to Orcas. "Orcas, please go and fetch my pack."

Orcas nodded and sped off.

"No, sister. The seeds are not in vials. They are in you and in Orcas. There are two others whom you must find. There is not much time and so you must listen to me and not interrupt."

"The elements put a seed in your mother, and you were the result. The sisters also put a seed in your mother. That seed did not blossom, but it lodged within you. You carry their seed, but they do not know this. They think that you are the result solely of their handiwork — but you are not. You are a creation of the elements and of the powers: both you and Orcas. You and the others will form the foundation for the new world that is being created for you. You are the only hope for this world. The sisters also interfered with the others. But you will not know if they are like you—carriers - or whether the sister's seed took first in them. You will have to use your training and intuition. You have to leave here now, Azal. Take Orcas and Ishia, and go towards the setting sun. Remember: you do not have to be ruled by the sisters. You are strong and powerful—but so are they. You will have to beware of them. They have become degenerate and are setting themselves up as gods."

Azal's mind reeled as she tried to take everything in and not forget a single word. She had one question.

The seer felt it and said, "Ask."

Azal looked up. "What are gods?"

The seer looked deep into her. No, she did not know.

"When you use powers, you use the elements. Is that correct?"

Azal nodded.

"There are many other powers in the world beside the elements and they are all trying to take a form that will allow them to interact with the land, other beings and your people. They take form from your form. If you go deep into the land you will find the power of the land. It will show itself as a woman, a goddess, so that you can commune with her and work with her. She will talk to you. If she remained in her natural form as a power of the land, you would not be able to communicate with her. These are the gods. They are the powers that came out of the great void.

"The sisters have learned how to move from one world to the next. They are in a space that is beyond the elements, but they can still reach you. They will appear to you and will seem all-powerful. They are not. They are false gods, and they are corrupt. If they were permitted, they would eventually wreak havoc in this world. However, there is one group that is not as corrupt as they are. They are now in the center of the earth. But be wary of them, for they are not beyond meddling. They were what you called the mountain sisters."

Azal was getting confused. "So what are real gods?"

The old woman chuckled.

"How did you get so far? You will find out soon enough who and what they are, just as long as you know they are there. They are not all powerful. But they do come in handy."

Orcas returned with Azal's pack. She handed it to Azal. Azal pulled out the vials. The seer snatched one of the vials and held it to her forehead. Using her mind she probed and probed into the vials, penetrating their being. She groaned and cursed.

"They are trying to produce different races of beings. This is the seed information. If it is activated and put into sea, it will reproduce and create. These beings are not of nature. They are not created from the elements. They will therefore be unstable in a world governed by the flow of the elements. Let the elements create their own beings. After all, this world is their creation — not a creation of the sisters."

Having said that, she emptied the vials one by one onto to the dusty floor and spat on them. Then she ground them into the dirt and poured oil over them.

Azal was not sure what to do. Although terrified of not doing the right thing, she also feared the sisters. The seer felt her fear and rounded on Azal.

"You are strong and powerful. Wake up, girl, and fight! You are going to need to learn survival from this point on. It is possible that the others will also have vials. You will have to stop the others from activating them. Do as I have just done here."

The old seer grabbed a handful of her own hair and cut it with a small knife. She then braided it into a length and handed it to Azal

"Keep this with you. Put it in your own hair and I will be with you. It is a link to my power."

Orcas was getting scared and began to whimper. Ishia pulled her close and tried to comfort her.

"Listen to me, all of you." The seer looked at each of them one by one.

"You have to leave tonight. Gather your things and leave before the sun rises. Do not rest until the sun is fully above the horizon. Go in the direction of the setting sun and keep moving. You will know when you have found the new world. It is a land of power and goodness, a place where new things come to pass. Ishia, you are not a seed. But somehow you are immune to the sickness. You must go with them to help and protect. Go, pack your things and prepare."

She grabbed Azal

"Your child. When you bear a child, watch for the seed."

Azal pulled back. Her thoughts went to the mating, and she reeled in horror.

"No! You will not mate like that. The pulling of fire through you has altered you. You are the first. You will bleed."

She pulled up the sleeve of Azal's robe and looked at the snakes.

"You can learn to work with these in a way that the sisters cannot control. Find that way in your inner vision. Your robes will not help you either. Ishia, get her a work cloth and show her how to wind it."

Azal was totally stunned. Gods... bleeding.... What is happening to me? What is this old woman talking about?

"No more time! No more time! You find out!"

The old seer seemed to stumble and weaken. Ishia caught her and held her.

"Go, children, go, before it is too late, and remember, you are the future, you are all we and your ancestors lived for. All that has gone before was there so that you could exist. Do not fail us. But remember us. Your memory keeps us alive."

Ishia darted from box to box, trying to decide what to take. While Orcas slept on a pile of mats in the corner, Azal practiced putting on the work cloth. It was a length of rough cotton that wound around the legs, around the waist and then up over her chest and shoulders to protect her breasts from burning in the sun. She then covered her shoulders with a shawl, picked up her pack, emptied it, and sifted through the contents to see what she would need. She put to one side a small phial of salt, a water flask, dried herbs, tinctures, fire stones, the braid of hair which the seer had given her, a knife and two bone needles. She then began to root around the hut and took a small light cooking pot and three small wooden bowls. What was left she put to one side.

After she had repacked her bag, she sat down and looked at Orcas. The child's eyes had glazed over, and she seemed to be looking far into the distance. Azal recognized the kind of energy that the child was generating. She had the sight! The sight is to see what is unseen both in the future and in the past. Yes, she could well believe that she was born of the elements, for the child had a presence about her that was truly special. Orcas suddenly blinked and turned to look at Azal.

"Yes," said Orcas, "the sun loves you with all his heart— and he will find you."

Azal was rooted to the spot by Orcas' words, and her surprise showed on her face. Before she could speak, Orcas got up and continued to pack as though nothing at all had been said.

Azal saw images of the lover who had visited her from the warmth of the sun, the man who come to her in her dreams. If only he were real. If only she could have a lover in life, someone to walk beside her.

As a priestess she was never permitted to bond with the male servers—not that she would have wanted to anyway, even if the sisters hadn't controlled them so strictly. The few priests that were in the temple had moved into the other world with the sisters, and in any case, they had all been old men.

She did not know what lay beyond the horizon and the thought of finding out both terrified and excited her. Her body ached at the thought of the man of the sun. She realized how much she needed a partner. She needed a man who could match her power and yet allow her to grow.

Azal sighed and brought her thoughts back to the task in hand. She watched Ishia run about like a mad woman, stuffing things into bags and then taking them back out again. Azal laughed and grabbed Ishia's hand.

"You cannot take your whole world with you, Ishia. Just pack what we need to survive."

Ishia stopped, her breath heavy from the exertion.

She nodded.

"Yes, you are right. But it's hard to leave things behind. All my friends and family are dead. Although I'm not close to most of the villagers who are left, I've lived my whole life here. This is the only place I know. All my memories are here. I know I have to let go, but it's hard."

Azal hugged her and touched her forehead. She could feel the pain and sorrow eating away at the poor woman. She drew the pain into herself and held it there, relieving Ishia of the burden. Ishia sighed deeply.

"Gather everything. We must go. There's not much dark left."

She paused for a moment and looked at Azal.

"Whatever you just did there... it felt good. Thank you."

Azal nodded. She fastened her pack on her back. Then she bent over and lifted Orcas into her arms. "Come. Let's begin."

They crept quietly out of the village, walking away from the direction in which the sun would soon be rising. The night was cold, and the wind blew hard. Ishia looked at each of the four directions in turn — as if surveying the whole world in her thoughts. She was leaving the only place she had ever known. Her task was to protect and guide Azal and little Orcas, and it was a task in which she was determined to excel.

"Good. This wind will cover our tracks. I don't know why the seer wanted us to leave at night and in the darkness, but I know she must have had good reasons."

Ishia talked to the wind as much as to her friends, as though to thank the elements.

They walked and walked, taking turns carrying the sleeping child. Eventually the sun began to rise behind them and warm their backs. At first they told each other stories of their childhood, but finally they lapsed into an exhausted silence. Neither had slept and each step they took seemed to get heavier and heavier. Orcas awoke as the sun rose and began to trot happily at the side of the two women, excited at the great adventure. They were going to discover the end of the seer's story and she was going to be the first to see it—before all the other children in the village. She was very proud of herself and couldn't wait to get there.

"Are we there yet? Is it very far? How much longer?"

She chirped and twittered until Ishia finally stopped and sat down. Her round face was flushed and her heartbeat rapidly from the unaccustomed exertion.

"Come here, little one."

Orcas sat down and Azal slumped beside her in a heap.

"The journey is very long. It will take many days and nights. We are going to camp here now and rest. I want you to rest too because we will start again when the sun goes down. Now go and look for plants and shoots to eat. Don't stray too far and get lost."

The child nodded and darted off to look for food. The two women remained slumped on the ground, looking at each other. Ishia spoke first.

"We can camp here. We can hide during the day among those rocks, and we will start again at sundown. Agreed?

Azal nodded.

"Do you know what? Orcas doesn't understand that she is not going back, and I cannot bear to tell her."

Azal nodded again, too tired to talk. The child returned with edible leaves and herbs and two big roots. Ishia pulled out her knife and began chopping the plants. She drew a bundle of tightly wrapped leaves out of her pack. As she opened them, the wonderful smell of wild garlic and broth assaulted their noses. Ishia had drained the broth to make a paste that they could eat. They mixed the plants and the paste together and ate hungrily.

"Next time we stop, we will have the energy to prepare food properly. We should prepare a meal and leave enough to carry with us each time we stop."

Azal agreed. With stomachs full they huddled up together under the shade of the large rocks and fell asleep.

⚘

ONCE SHE WAS certain that Azal, Orcas and Ishia had left the village, the seer poured a selection of dried herbs into the fire and sat waiting. As the night progressed, she felt the cloud of death creep slowly over the plains.

She listened silently to the disturbed sleep of the mothers who drew their children closer as they instinctively felt the danger that approached while not even consciously comprehending it. The children died first, each breathing out a final whisper as their insufficient blood could no longer function in the degenerating matrix of the body.

It took longer for the older ones to die. The withdrawal of the sisters seemed somehow to have accelerated the distortions in the bodies of the servers.

The seer was the last. Because her body was of the same line as the sisters', she had not suffered the genetic damage that the servers had inherited, but she had nevertheless freely taken some of their patterns upon herself to ensure the survival of Ishia and Orcas. She had taken Ishia's death upon herself, knowing that the woman was entwined in the survival of Azal and, therefore, in the future.

Azal was the first to stir. Pain shot through her feet and arms. She groaned at the thought of having to walk through the approaching night. She longed just to lie and watch the sun set. She shook Ishia awake and looked over to Orcas, who was laying on her back and looking at the sky.

"Are you fine, Orcas?"

The child turned her head and looked at Azal. Tears swelled her eyes, and her face was red and taut. "What's making you cry?"

Orcas sniffed and then sobbed.

"I want my mother. Is she in the stars? Can I reach her if we go up a hill? I just want to say good-bye."

Azal squatted down at the side of the weeping child and held her until the sobs became less fierce.

"Listen, child. At dawn, before we sleep, I will take you on a journey so that you can talk to your mother. I promise. Now go down to the water and wash your face. Then fill your water bottle for the day."

The child nodded miserably and wandered off.

Ishia was watching Azal with curiosity. "How will you do that?" she asked.

"Wait and see," answered Azal quietly. "I cannot explain a mystery."

The look in Azal's eyes told her that further discussion was pointless. They packed their few things and waited for Orcas to return, and then set out for another night of walking.

They walked in silence for most of the night, breaking the stillness only to sing occasionally to Orcas. When morning began to break and they were ready to stop, they had already collected whatever edible plants they could find in the dark, and they had a good enough collection of shoots and roots to make a nourishing broth. They found a place in a small cave at the foot of a hill, with a spring running nearby. Ishia washed their metal cooking bowl in the clear water and lit a fire. Then they all helped to prepare the food together. Once the pot was safely set on the hot stones, Orcas sat down expectantly beside Azal.

Azal remembered the promise she had made to Orcas.

"While the food cooks, we will journey."

Orcas groaned. "I can't walk another step today!"

Azal laughed. "Don't worry. We'll make this journey in here," she said, tapping Orcas' head.

"Close your eyes and follow what I say as the pictures rise in your head."

Orcas settled down and closed her eyes. Ishia did the same. Azal took a deep breath and touched her forehead, tracing the sacred sigil of the line and the circle with her finger.

"See yourself falling, falling down through the earth: deep, deep down into the underworld, leaving the surface world behind. As you fall, you feel the earth and rock all around you, supporting you. As you fall, you see a light below and you fall towards that light. You find your-self emerging into a cavern with a river running through it.

"On the river is a boat in which there is a kind old man. He holds a lamp and calls you into his boat. Give him a gift from your heart. As you climb into the boat you feel that you remember this from some-where.... The boat pushes off and you sail down the river at great speed. It flows through many tunnels until you emerge into a land with mountains on one side, desert on the other and a bridge that spans the river. The boat pulls up on the desert side and you see lots of people standing there and waiting. Some are happy and some are sad. These are all the people who have recently died. Call out your mother's name. When you see her, talk to her, and take her to the foot of the bridge. Tell her that she must cross the bridge, but let her understand that once she has crossed the bridge, she cannot return to this life, for she must move on to the next."

Azal fell silent for a while to allow the two to commune with their mother.

"Now it is time to leave. Get back into the boat and we will sail back down the tunnel, back down to the cave. When you reach the cave, step out of the boat and say "thank you" to the boatman. Now you will see steps that you didn't notice before. Ascend the steps until you emerge back in the place where you first started. Now open your eyes."

The three sat in silence for a few minutes. Azal stirred the broth, waiting for the two to re-orientate themselves. Ishia spoke first.

"I saw my mother," said Ishia, "and she said that she was proud of me for coming on this journey. She said that Orcas is special and that I must protect her. She also said that you must wait for your man in the sun. Does that make any sense to you?"

Azal was shocked. She reddened and mumbled. Ishia didn't push what was obviously difficult for Azal, but her curiosity had been aroused. Then Ishia spoke again.

"It meant so much to me to be able to speak to my mother for the last time, Azal. Thank you for giving me that gift."

Ishia held Azal's hand as she spoke. Orcas also nodded, unable to speak.

"Are you back with us, little one?" Azal asked Orcas.

She had wondered if the passing between the worlds would prove too much for the child, but she seemed to have withstood it without any injury. Azal stroked Orcas' hair as the child whimpered to herself. Ishia stirred the bubbling pot, not knowing if she should tell Azal the rest. She had seen the seer. The old woman had said that they were in danger, and that the sisters knew about the smashing of the vials — and that they were very angry. She had said that they must reach the sea and that Azal should trigger the snakes. The sisters wanted to kill both Orcas and Ishia and so isolate Azal, whom they wished to control. The seer had also said that Ishia should tell Azal to use the hair. She wanted Azal to braid the strand into her own hair so that Azal's soul would be bonded to the soul of the seer herself. In that way the seer could protect them.

Ishia waited for Orcas to wander out of hearing range and then told her the remainder of what the seer had said. Azal looked at Ishia with fear.

"I don't know how to trigger the snakes... But the hair... I'll get the hair," said Azal.

She fumbled around in her pack until she found the braid. She handed it to Ishia who deftly wove it into Azal's hair. Then Azal sat back. She didn't feel any different but she knew from experience that powerful things often lay dormant until they were needed.

When Orcas returned, the two women scooped the broth into their bowls, and they all ate hungrily. Then they cleared the remains away and Orcas settled down to sleep. Azal sat alongside Orcas and stroked her hair while humming to her.

"My mother told me that you would always protect me," said Orcas, "and that you would protect my baby when I grew up. My mother hugged and kissed me and told me that I was a big girl now and that I would have a good life in my new home. We're not going back, are we?" she asked, looking up at Azal.

Azal shook her head.

"She then said that your man in the sun would be a father to me and that he would teach me many things. I was also told never to speak to the sisters if I see them. She said that if I don't speak to them, they cannot harm me."

Azal tried not to change her facial expression, tried not to register her thoughts and feelings at the child's vision. She just nodded and said that everything would be fine and that she should now sleep. The child drifted into a deep sleep and Azal crept quietly away.

Azal sat and looked at the snakes. Then she turned inward and, using her inner vision, looked at the snakes and tried to communicate with them. Nothing. She thought hard. Snakes are of fire, and fire is of the future. Prophecy! That's it.

As Azal tried to stretch her thoughts into the future, she felt something stir within her. She probed deeper and deeper until she felt herself caught in a whirlwind. The whirling spun her around at high speed until she could look through the wind. Azal saw herself and her companions climbing into a boat. She had seen pictures on the temple walls of these floating things that carry people across water. As she looked, she felt the seer around her.

"He is good! He is good! But you must remove your fish. They track you by means of the fish. Cut it away." Then the seer was gone.

Azal fell back out of the whirlwind and lay on the ground. As she opened her eyes, she saw Ishia bending over her with a worried look on her face.

"What happened, Azal? I thought that you were going to die. You were just standing there — shaking as though the fire of the sky had hit you."

Ishia sat Azal up and wiped her face with a cloth that she had moistened in the spring waters.

"I was trying to use the snakes. I think that I know how they work now. I tried to look into the future, and I saw a boat on the sea. We were getting into it when the seer's voice came into my head. She said to me: 'The man is good but get rid of the fish.' But I saw no man. I thought all men were dying."

Ishia was excited and wanted to hear the rest.

"The fish! What does that mean, Azal"?

Azal undid her cloth and turned her back to Ishia

"Run your fingers down my spine," she said.

As she ran her fingers down Azal's spine, Ishia stopped. Halfway down Azal's spine, she felt something under the skin. It was shaped like a fish. She had seen the fish shapes in the pictures on the temple walls — and even sometimes painted on the foreheads of the sisters. She cautiously moved it around under her finger.

"What is it?"

"It is the symbol of the sisters, carved in gold. It has been there since I left my mother. They inserted it during the first night I slept in the main temple. They told me that it made me special and that it would help to keep me safe. I had forgotten about it until now. The sisters used to rub oil on my back when I was growing. They said that it was special and that I was lucky to have it. But they never said why they did it and I never asked them."

Azal now turned to face Ishia.

"The seer said that the sisters can track me by means of this fish, and that I had to get rid of it. But how?"

Ishia looked blank. The only way to get it out was to cut it out and Azal would get a sickness if they did it here. They needed salt water from the sea to cleanse the wound.

"We will take it out when we get to the sea. There I'll be able to use salt water. Azal, pass me your pack so that I can see what herbs you have with you."

Azal gave her the pack and her companion sifted through the various pouches of herbs and barks. She separated out four pouches that she could use and gave the pack back to Azal.

"Sleep now," said Ishia.

"We should reach the sea tomorrow. I can already smell the salt in the air."

She turned her head and sniffed the wind. Ishia loved the sea and had visited it twice before on trade journeys undertaken for the village. This would be exciting!

When evening came, they rose, packed their belongings, and set out on another night of walking. Orcas no longer found the journey exciting. She moaned and whimpered throughout the night. Her feet were both sore and bruised. Although both Azal and Ishia had rubbed her feet with a healing salve, they still bled and stung. Her skin was too young and tender for such hardship. They trudged through the night, singing songs to keep the little one amused. As the mists cleared and the sun began to climb, Azal shouted out in amazement. Before her in the distance lay a shimmering carpet of blue edged with white.

"The sea, the sea!" shouted Ishia

She hoisted Orcas onto her shoulders so she could get a better look.

The child looked at the ocean with still, calm eyes. She didn't speak or move. She just stared. "Look Orcas, the ocean! This is what I told you about in the stories."

Orcas remained silent. The two women looked at each other and Ishia shrugged.

"Well, I suppose it's a little overwhelming for a small one."

She put Orcas down and they carried on towards the sea.

"Didn't you like the sea, Orcas?" asked Azal.

Again, she did not respond. They decided not to push her for a reaction, but rather to wait and see what might happen.

5

They arrived at the sea just before midday. They approached the beach at a point some distance away from the village so that they would not be seen. There they built a small fire. Ishia filled the pot with water and threw in a handful of herbs.

"We have to do this straightaway, while there is plenty of light. Are you ready?"

Azal nodded. Although she was exhausted from a whole night's walking, she thought it better to have it done without delay. Azal turned to Orcas, who was staring at the sea.

"Little one, listen. This is important. Ishia must cut my back. I may cry out, but do not fear. She is making me better."

Orcas looked at her and nodded. She was crouching on her haunches, staring wide-eyed at the sea.

Azal lay on her stomach and exposed her back. She chewed on the bark that Ishia had given her, and its potent sap seeped into her body, numbing her thoughts and feelings. Ishia put the knife tip into the fire to cleanse it and then sprinkled water from the pot over Azal's back.

"Ready?" Azal nodded.

She focused her mind on the flame within and gritted her teeth. The first cut made her feel as though her body was being torn apart.

The pain shot up and down her legs and made them twitch and lump. Ishia probed and cut with the knife, trying to be as careful as possible. She carefully mopped up the blood as it flowed from the wound in Azal's back. Azal bit harder and harder into the bark. Her mind was numb from the resin, but the pain still seared through her body. Each cut of the knife merged with the last until her mind swam in a pool of pain. Voices drifted in and out of her brain... the elder, the mountain sisters, her mother and then the seer. Finally, she slipped into the dark void and was surrounded by the comforting darkness, unaware of her own existence.

Once Azal became unconscious, Ishia's job became much easier. Because Azal's muscles were hard and knotted, it had been difficult for Ishia to cut around the sigil. Once she became unconscious, her back muscles relaxed and Ishia found that she could get the knife under the sigil and tease it out. Ishia examined it. It was a simple gold outline in the shape of a fish—the same fish that she had seen in the temple. She looked back at the wound and was about to start sewing the skin closed with a sharp bone needle when Orcas appeared at her side.

"No! Not that way. "

Orcas' voice was powerful and commanding and Ishia looked up in surprise.

"Do not sew. It will damage her further and it will not heal. Put this into the wound and then bind it."

Orcas handed the startled woman a handful of some wet seaweed that she had mashed into a paste. Although Ishia wavered, she knew that something powerful was happening. But if Orcas was wrong, Azal might die because the wound was deep.

"Now, Ishia! Now!" said Orcas urgently. "The wound needs protection."

Ishia took the seaweed paste and packed it in and around the wound and then bandaged it with strips of torn work cloth.

Ishia wiped Azal's face gently and dribbled warm liquid from the herb pot into her mouth. Then she covered her gently with her own cloth to protect her back from the sun. She sat to one side and waited for her to come around.

"Thank you, Orcas. How did you know about the sea plants?"

Orcas looked at her.

"The sea told me", she said simply.

Ishia was about to ask her another question when she remembered what the seer and her mother had said about Orcas being special. She decided to press no further. Then she looked at Orcas and really saw her for the first time. Before now she had always just seen a small child who complained a lot. Now she began to see another side of Orcas, a side that had been there for a long time, but one which she had not recognized before. Now she just seemed like an ordinary child again.

"Could you go and collect some food, Orcas?"

Orcas nodded and sped off and Ishia watched her go. She ran like the wind, her wide eyes darting in all directions as she looked for herbs and plants.

Immediately Azal started to groan. Ishia had poured herbs into a bowl and had put fresh water on to boil for the food. She spooned the herb broth into Azal's lips.

"Drink. It will kill the pain."

Azal drank in gulps and fell once more into a deep sleep. Ishia noticed how Azal's legs twitched in her sleep, and she knew that this was not a good sign. She tried to remember all she had learned from the seer in the temple about healing and herbs. She knew that the back was important and that one had to be very, very careful around the spine.

Ishia looked out to the ocean and felt its strength. She walked to the water's edge, looking back every three steps to check on Azal. As she reached the water's edge, she raised her arms and closed her eyes.

"O great ocean, element of water, I am not a priestess or a seer, but I bow before your great power and strength. Please help my friend to recover. Show me what to do. I know that so much in the future depends on her. Please give her your strength."

And a server of the children cried out to the beloved ocean, reaching out in wonder and worship, calling on the power of the friends to help in the healing of the special one. The ocean looked kindly on the server. She called out to her companions, the earth, the fire, and the air. "One of the servers has turned to us in despair. One of the servers sees my beauty and beholds my power. I will help her even as she helps the special one." And so the ocean reached into her depth and brought out her healing power and allowed it to flow into the server. All the love of the ocean flowed into the woman. All the power of the ocean touched her feet and the breath of the ocean flowed across the surface of the water to whisper wisdom into the ear of the woman. "Behold my power, woman. I will be with you, for it has been foretold that whosoever acknowledges my power and stands in awe at my feet shall be protected and guided by me."

Ishia was rooted to the spot. She felt the energy flow into her from the water as it swirled around her feet. She felt the ocean reach out to touch her. As the water lapped around her, she felt her body become more and more energized. She felt someone approach. Orcas appeared next to her. She didn't speak but gazed out to the sea and smiled.

"She likes you. She will help you."

Ishia turned to Orcas. "Who likes me?"

The child turned to face Ishia. "The ocean," she said.

They returned to Azal, who was slowly regaining consciousness. Ishia bent over her, lifted the bandage, and examined the wound. It had stopped bleeding and was already starting to dry. Orcas also inspected the wound. She removed the seaweed and washed the wound. Then she turned to Ishia.

"Place your hands on the wound and the wound will be healed."

Ishia looked at the child sadly. "I cannot heal. I do not know how. Only the seers know such skills."

Orcas began to get annoyed.

"I know that you can because the ocean has told me. Just do it!"

The woman looked at the child, who by now was almost crying with frustration. Orcas was getting strange fancies, probably from not having children to play with. Maybe she should just humor the child, it could do no harm.

She sat down at the side of her friend, who was moaning with pain. She placed her hands over the wound and then let them rest gently on either side of the cut. At first she felt nothing. Then she felt a pulsing in her hands that grew stronger and stronger. Her hands began to burn and ache, and the power continued to get stronger and stronger. Azal whimpered and then slipped into a deep sleep as Ishia's hands pulsed and throbbed. After what seemed like an eternity, the pressure eased and eventually Ishia withdrew her hands. She slumped back, exhausted but exhilarated at what had happened.

In the meantime, Orcas had been preparing the broth. She filled Ishia's bowl and laid it before her. Hardly able to move, Ishia managed to get some broth inside her before falling asleep.

※

ISHIA WOKE WITH A START. A shadow had passed over her face and had roused her from a deep sleep. The sun was nearly setting. She sat up and cried out in horror at the sight of the man who stood over her. He was tall and lean. His arms were burnt from the sun and his face and hair were covered in a cloth mask. He held out his arms in a gesture of peace.

Orcas appeared from behind him.

Ishia panicked. "Orcas! Child!" she screamed. "Come here! Come away! Come here!"

Then she looked around to where Azal lay near the packs. The man followed Ishia's gaze and saw the slightly sheltered spot where they had placed Azal out of the sun. He stepped to her side and dropped on his knees.

"What happened? Let me look at the wound."

Ishia tried to stop him.

"She does not need your help. The wound is healing."

Azal was finally coming out of the heavy sleep caused by the herbs. The man's voice seemed familiar to her. It tugged at her, waking her, pulling her back to life. Her head ached and her back felt as though it was on fire. She tried to speak, but her throat seemed closed up. All she could manage was a hoarse whisper. The man bent over to hear what she was saying. He gently stroked her hair and murmured to her.

Ishia stood firmly at the side of the man and tried to pull him away.

"Thank you for your concern, but I really don't think that you can help us."

Orcas sat on a rock, her eyes wide and staring, taking in the whole scene without comment.

"Your little one over there told me that you need a boat to cross the sea. I have a boat, but no one has ever crossed that sea before. We sail up and down the coast, trading, but with the sickness there is little point in trading with the dead."

Ishia backed away from him and he laughed.

"Don't worry! I'm not infected with it. It doesn't seem to touch me. What about all of you?"

He gestured to the three of them with a dramatic sweep of his arm and laughed again. Then his voice grew serious.

"I have had many dreams about crossing the sea. I was thinking of trying it anyway. I would be honored to take you all. But you'd have to learn how to work the ship. No crew would ever come with us on such a journey."

Ishia didn't know what to say. Yes, this is what they had journeyed for—but could they trust him? She wished that Azal was well. She would have been able to make the right decision.

The man's voice drifted in and out of Azal's dazed consciousness. I know that voice... I know that voice.... But from where? He bent over Azal again and his eyes grew serious. She opened her eyes and was startled by the mask. She tried to move but as soon as she got to her knees, the burning in her back seared through her. She cried out and fell back onto her stomach.

"You have to get her into shelter. She will die of cold out here tonight. I have a shelter just down the beach, near the ship. Stay tonight and decide by sunrise tomorrow if you wish to sail with me or if you want to sail with one of the cutthroats."

Orcas marched up to him.

"We will stay with you." She spoke with absolute conviction.

"Can you carry the sister?" Orcas asked him. "Just be careful of her back."

He bent over and ruffled Orcas' hair.

"Of course I will be gentle, little one."

He turned to Ishia. "Are you coming? Or do you have other people to carve up?"

His voice had an edge to it and Ishia became defensive. She wanted to explain to him what had happened but decided against it. She nodded and picked up the packs. As he bent to lift Azal, Ishia put her arm out to stop him.

"She has a large wound in the middle of her back, just on her spine. Something that was killing her has been removed. You will have to be very careful not to press on that wound."

The man nodded.

Gently he bent to lift Azal. He stood up straight and held Azal in his arms. As he stood up with Azal, Ishia's eyes seemed to become unfocussed. As she struggled to refocus her eyes, she saw Azal standing by the water's edge and cradling a small child in her arms. The child was a boy with golden hair. In the vision, Azal was laughing. Behind her, very faintly visible, she could see an almost transparent image of a man with long hair.

Ishia blinked and the vision was gone. She looked down and found that Orcas was holding her hand. Orcas looked up and smiled.

"All will be well, Ishia. Just don't worry."

The child's eyes looked into the woman's eyes, and Ishia felt the great strength and wisdom that lay behind those eyes. She nodded.

The man's shelter was only a short walk away. It was obscured from view by trees and high shrubs. As they bent to enter the small doorway, they were greeted by the heady aroma of resins and herbs. Inside, the shelter was both warm and comfortable, and the man lowered Azal gently down onto a pile of soft cushions. Azal lay on her side, drowsily watching the scene before her. But she grabbed his hand as he moved away.

"Why do you wear that mask? It's very frightening."

"The burning of my face is more frightening to the people around here. They do not understand it and they attack me. Are you in pain?"

His question was obviously meant to change the subject. She sensed his intention and probed no further.

"Yes, I am. The herbs dull my senses but do not kill the pain."

He ran his hand over her head to check for fever, and then looked into her eyes.

"I have something that will help you. It will make you sleep again. Your body needs sleep. When you awake, you will feel much better, and your wound will almost be healed."

He went into the corner of the hut and searched through many bottles and pouches. Ishia and Orcas watched him in fascination. He could feel them watching him. He turned to them and said:

"Rest and sleep tonight. Tomorrow at dawn I shall leave. You may come with me if you wish. I am the only one who can take you over the sea. Take those blankets and cover yourselves. Sleep. I shall watch over your friend."

Ishia's mind told her never to trust anyone who was not of her tribe, but her instincts told her that this was a good man—and a healer. She lay down and was soon fast asleep.

Now I can work in peace, he thought to himself. He bent over Azal and put his hand on her head. He surveyed her body and stopped when he saw the fresh blood stains on the cloth covering her thighs. He was about unwind the cloth to look for the wound when something stopped him. He remembered the prophecy that a new race of women would appear who would not breed seasonally but who would be bleed and be always fertile. They would have the ability to choose when to create life.

He held his hand over her thighs and used his inner vision to check for wounds—just in case this was indeed a wound. There was no wound. Instead, he felt a swirling vortex of power. Azal opened her eyes and looked at him. She could see that his eyes were closed. His eyes and mouth were all she could see of his face. They seemed familiar to her - as did his voice. She knew all of the men who had ever been to the temple, and she knew that this man was not one of them.

He checked her energy levels by placing his hand softly on her head. Her levels of energy were strong, and something was already working in her. Good, he thought. That will make it easier. Maybe her companion was not so useless after all. He prepared a tincture from a bottle, mixed it with water, and then shook it very hard in short successive shakes. Then he leant over and whispered to her.

"Take a sip. Good. Now another. Good. Turn over so that I can apply some to your back."

Azal turned and the pain was etched on her face. He also felt her pain and it surprised him. He had recognized her as soon as he had seen her. This was the priestess whom he had seen in his dreams. But he hadn't realized till now how strong the bond had become. Gently he dabbed some of the tincture onto the wound. It was already starting to heal. The tincture will complete the healing, he thought to himself.

"How do your legs feel?"

"Fine," she replied drowsily.

"You have the blood of fertility. I will go and find a clean work cloth and some grasses for you." She looked at him in confusion. She doesn't know, he thought. He tried to think quickly.

"Do you know what the blood of fertility is?"

She shook her head.

"Have you ever bled between your thighs before?" She shook her head again.

He sat back on his heels to think. He thought again of the prophecy and tried to remember the details. If she was the one in the prophecy, the first woman to bleed, which she obviously was, then maybe the pain caused by the cutting that her friend had done on her back had triggered the fertility bleeding. He tried to explain the prophecy, but the pain caused her to drift in and out of consciousness, and she was unable to hear him.

Azal strained as he held another dose of the tincture to her lips.

She sipped it slowly and was comforted by his care. His touch was giving life to her body and it was responding well. Already the pain was seeping away.

"Sleep, special one. I am here now, and I shall care for you."

When she woke in the morning, she found him sitting and looking at her. Azal sat up carefully and looked around. The other two were curled up together and were still fast asleep. She realized that the pain had gone, and that only a slight stiffness remained in her back. Cautiously she stretched and then she looked back at him.

"Where did you come from? Why did you help us? What is your name?"

He laughed quietly at this sudden flurry of questions.

"My name is Belinos. But you may call me Belin." He told her of his chance meeting with Orcas and of how Orcas asked him to take them over the horizon and to heal her sister friend, Azal. "And so here I am."

She felt immediately that he was not telling her everything, and he felt her apprehension.

"You will be safe with me. I will get you there. To that purpose I pledge the very honor of my soul."

Azal gasped. He had pronounced the pledge of the priesthood.

"Are you a priest?"

He looked away, as if in pain.

"I was," he said simply.

His manner did not allow for any further probing. She could feel that something hurtful had happened to him—maybe the very same thing that had happened to her. At least a priest is a known quantity, she thought.

She knew what she was dealing with. She knew that if he said that they were safe, then they were safe indeed.

By now Orcas and Ishia had been aroused by the sound of their voices. Ishia was amazed to see Azal looking so bright and cheerful. They ate quickly and then began packing for the trip. Azal sat watching Belin as he worked with Ishia. His body movements seemed vaguely familiar to her. She probed her memory, wondering where she had seen him before, but she remembered nothing. He had already gathered enough provisions for the trip and had filled water barrels for the journey. These he stored securely on the ship.

In the full light of day the ship was magnificent. It was moored out beyond the waves in a sheltering cove and had a mast that seemed to reach to the very stars. The ship had a figurehead, a beautiful carved goddess of the sea, half fish, half human, with four faces: one face for each direction. Azal had only seen such ships before on wall paintings, and she had had no idea how big they might be.

They loaded their packs and belongings into the small rowing boat that would take them out to the ship. Orcas laughed and giggled as she dipped her hands into the sea. She leaned over the side and whispered to the water.

"The sea is excited! The sea is excited!" she yelled.

Her face shone and her eyes glowed with a freshness that the two women had not seen before. Azal and Ishia smiled at each other.

Once they had embarked, Orcas ran up and down the ship,

checking each corner and each closet. Azal went to the face of the Goddess of the waters that looked over the deck of the ship. She lowered her eyes in reverence. This is what a god is, she thought to herself. She could feel the power flowing from the image—which acted as a window for the flow of the divine power. The divine power allowed itself to be filtered through an image and be modified in such a way that humans could receive and understand it. In her head she spoke to the Goddess.

"O Goddess, please grant us your protection on this journey and help me to learn the ways of this world—a world I know nothing about." She was about to turn and leave when a voice spoke in her head.

"And what will you give me in return, daughter? Open your hands. Whatever you see there is mine. You must give it to me by throwing it into the sea."

Azal, using her inner vision, opened her hand. In it lay the golden fish that had been taken from her back. She reached into her hip pouch and pulled out the fish. She held it up to the sun to view it properly. She hadn't had the strength to look at it before now. Then she went to the rail of the ship and threw it into the sea. As it hit the water, a large fish leapt up and caught the golden shape, swallowing it whole.

"Daughter, I will always be with you—wherever you may be and whoever you may be. You are my beloved."

Orcas appeared at her arm.

"Isn't she beautiful?" said Azal. Orcas nodded.

"But the ocean is even more beautiful," said Orcas in a serious voice.

"They are very different kinds of beauty. But they are both beautiful," said Azal, trying to explain to the child.

"No, they are the same," said Orcas.

"The ocean is herself. And this carving is how the people like to think she looks. They feel that they cannot talk to the sea. But they can talk to a face. It's just that people are so limited."

Azal was astounded by the wisdom that came out of the child's mouth. Of course! She is right. Azal had to admit that she found it easier to talk to the face than to the open sea. She was humbled in her assumption that she knew better simply because she was older. Orcas possessed a wisdom that was older than the stars.

Azal set off to explore the ship. There were three cabins in the main body of the ship and a hold for provisions. On the deck itself was a large shelter. She marveled at the amount of food and water that the man had brought on board.

"You could keep a whole temple for a year with this lot," she shouted down to him as he stacked provisions in the hold. She smiled at him. '

"We will need them, believe me. The journey is long and danger-ous. And who knows what it will be like on the other side?"

He tried to obliterate any trace of fear in his voice. He had never sailed out into the ocean like this before, and he had never worked with the inner contacts of navigation. Although he had trained for many years as a priest and although part of that training had been in inner navigation, he had never had to use such skills in a practical way. Until now.

Later that day, they set sail towards the west, towards the land of eternal power and youth. Since Belin was a small boy, he had been told of a fabled land of new beginnings, a land where things were pure, fresh, and powerful. A land that did not allow corruption—for the land itself would swallow up and destroy any who tried to misuse it. For Azal and Ishia, this was a land of new beginnings, a land the sickness had not reached, where they could settle and give birth to the new world that had been foretold by the sisters.

Belin looked out across the vast expanse of the ocean. She was the most beautiful being he had ever seen. He momentarily bowed his head in reverence to her and then closed his eyes as he began to use the techniques of the inner navigation. He moved his consciousness inwards, towards the flame of his inner fire, where the stillness of the void resides. Then, using his inner sight, he looked out over the ocean and called for the navigator in the language of the sea. He called and called until he became aware of a presence beside him. An old, old man with long white hair and a beard stood beside him on the deck as he steered.

"My son of the sun, there are many pathways in our sacred ocean. Some are slower than others and some are faster and more dangerous. You must take the fastest - even though it has its dangers. There will be a great storm in three weeks' time—and you must be out of the water by then. Steer south until you feel me stop you. Then lower your sail and you will not move for one night. You will drift into the right position. Then, when the sun touches the horizon with his fingers, hoist your sail and you will travel at speeds you had not thought possible. After five days, lower your sail once more. The current will take you to the shore within twelve days."

Belin repeated the instructions over and over to himself so that he would not forget them. He lowered the sails and told the women that they were going to drift for the night. Ishia and Azal lay on a pile of sacks and looked up at the stars.

"Azal, I was very scared of you for a long time," said Ishia, "and then I thought that you might think that I was a savage. But now I feel as though you are a sister to me and to Orcas. I so longed to speak more to you in the temple, but I was afraid of the sisters."

Azal lay silent for a while, and then she took a deep breath.

"I too feel that you are my kin. I was also afraid of you—afraid of what I was and afraid of the future. I'm still afraid of the future, but I know now that we will be protected."

They both lay there in the silence of the night, watching the stars process through the directions.

Belin also watched the stars and the two women. He ached to take Azal into his arms, just as he had done in his dreams, and yet he had begun to question himself. Was he just imposing his dream on the nearest priestess? His thoughts wandered to Orcas. She had also decided to sleep under the stars and had curled herself up in a little nest of straw and sacks. Deep in sleep, she sucked her thumb. Her face radiated power and light as she slept. Belin wondered what the future held in store for them - for this would be a most fateful journey for each of them.

As the boat drifted through the night, Belin struggled to stay awake. He was watching for the sunrise. As soon as the first light crept over the horizon, he hoisted the sail with a loud shout that roused the others. The ship seemed to rock and dip until suddenly it lurched forward as if carried by some great hand. As the ship increased speed, the three travelers looked at each other in amazement and wonder.

Orcas skipped over to them.

"So. You have found the Atlant Channel. Good for you! Did the old man tell you? Did he ask about me? What did he say?"

Orcas was jumping up and down with excitement.

Ishia turned to Orcas and grasped her by the shoulders.

"What are you talking about, Orcas'? What old man? What's the 'Atlant channel'?"

Belin stepped in. "Let me answer everyone's questions at once. The old man is the inner navigator, the boatman of life, death and the ocean. No, he did not mention you and I don't know what the Atlant Channel is, but this is where the navigator told me to go. Tell me, little one, how do you know all this?"

He softened his voice and, as a friendly gesture, went down on one knee in front of the child in a comic gesture of reverence. Even so, he felt a deep reverence arise in his soul for the wise and powerful soul being nurtured in this small child's body.

"The navigator is my grandfather," said Orcas simply. "He taught me everything I know about the sea. The Atlant Channel is a stream of water that travels fast. It is powered by jets of boiling water and steam from underground waterspouts." When Orcas realized that the two women had no idea what she was talking about, she tried to simplify it.

"Azal, you know of the sun within the earth?" Azal nodded.

"Well, heat from that inner sun pushes the water. When the heat collides with the cold water, it pushes it ever faster. The hot water makes a pathway of swiftly flowing water in the ocean. If you allow it to catch you, you can also move at great speed. This pathway also carries the information and knowledge of the sun within the earth to the land of eternal youth. That is why we are going there—because all the knowledge of the sun is there, and all knowledge of life is held within the water, and that water feeds the land so that the land is wise and powerful."

Orcas finished and waited expectantly for praise. She had now returned to being a small child in search of adult approval. The other three stood around in awe of the child. Ishia did not know what to say. She had never seen this side of Orcas until recently. But then, when she thought about it, she had never had much to do with Orcas until her mother died. Ishia had been at the temple most of the time, and Orcas had been with the village children. Now she realized just how very special Orcas was, and how it was her duty to protect her.

In fact, she now felt like the one who had been left out. She knew that Azal was important for the new world. She now knew that Orcas was also important, and it was beginning simultaneously to dawn on her that Belin was more than just a sailor. He was a priest of the sun and was like Azal. So where did she fit in? She remembered what the seer had said. She, Ishia, would have to protect them. Well, she thought, that is exactly what I shall do.

Later that evening, Orcas and Ishia played a shell game. This left Azal and Belin alone for the first time since her injury. He felt awkward and she had so many questions that she wanted to ask him. But they just seemed to mumble polite words to each other. Finally, when Azal spoke, she echoed what Ishia had been thinking.

"You're far more than a sailor, aren't you? You are far more than a simple priest? Correct?"

He nodded.

"So where do I feel I know you from?"

She looked inquiringly into his eyes, searching for the question that had hounded her for days now.

"I cannot tell you about myself until you tell me about yourself. Then I may be able to piece this all together."

He waited for her to speak.

"Mine is a short story," said Azal.

"I was taken from my mother at a young age and raised by the sisters. Ishia was my server. On a day not long past I took part in a ritual of fire, and during the ritual the temple vanished. Everything I knew disappeared. Ishia found me on the plains and took me to her village. The old seer there said that I should go west over the water and take Orcas and Ishia with me. That's it."

Azal peered at Belin's mask. He was deep in thought. He was thinking about the fire ritual that she had mentioned. He knew what had happened. They had used the power of bridging to move into the inner realms and then they had left Azal there to fend for herself. Now he was convinced that Azal was one of the seeds—as was Orcas.

Despite this conviction, he still could not feel whether Azal was a seed of the elements or whether she was a false seed planted by the priesthood. As soon as he had seen Orcas, he had known that she was a child of the element of water. But Azal was somehow more complex. He could feel that many things were happening, but he couldn't understand all that he felt.

While he pondered these questions, Azal used her inner vision to survey him. This was her first opportunity to look at him in this way. Using her inner sight, she looked at him in depth. She saw his power, which burned bright and balanced, and his heart, which was good, and his emotions. She blushed when she saw the love for her that she found deep within him.

She saw that he had no scars on his face. An image of his face swam before her inner vision, and she finally recognized him as the man in her vision of the sun.

Without thinking, she grabbed the mask and tore it from his face. His face radiated the light of the sun and his eyes glowed soft and warm. He had tried to stop her, but she had been too quick for him. Then she just sat there, basking in his light, while her own face glowed with love.

Now at last she recognized him. His heart leapt as he held out his hand to her and stroked her face. "I have traveled many days and nights searching for you. I have searched the stars for you. I searched the oceans, the mountains, the caves. I even searched among the inner convocation of priests and priestesses. I thought that I would never find you. I thought that I would grow old and die without you."

Azal gasped at the mention of the convocation. So it was indeed him that she had seen during the convocation ritual.

6

A zal opened her eyes slowly. Strange clicking noises and the sound of splashing had awakened her from her deep, troubled sleep, and she found that she had been weeping. Throughout the night she had strange dreams which she knew contained both warnings and prophecies. In her dream the mountain sisters appeared to her. They were in a cave deep near the center of the earth and they stood around a well in the floor as if transfixed. Azal could hear the chanting of the sisters. They told her to look down the well and, as she did, she fell in. She fell and fell until she had fallen through the body of the earth, emerging out into the stars. She looked down at the planet. It was so beautiful and calm, and it glowed with the light of the void. As she looked closer, she saw the land mass moving and changing, breaking up into smaller masses with the sea all around them. Azal watched the weather change to a cold forbidding sheet of ice that covered most of the land.

Two small areas of land were populated, but the rest of the planet's surface was devoid of life. Only the sea held an abundance of beings. She began to weep for the barrenness of the land when a comforting presence enfolded her. It whispered to her:

Do not despair. Before the coming of the sisters the void sent out those who guard and protect, those who teach and guide, those who create and assist birth and those who destroy in judgment. These angels chose only to watch until now, but my song has traveled over the face of the deep, calling them to help. Their work will reach through time and space, and they have pledged to walk with the children of the elements.

You, child of the four friends, will be the bridge of life and death, of new and old. They will guard you and the land where you will work, which will be known as Paradise."

The being moved a hand over her face and she saw before her a world that she could never have imagined, populated with many kinds of beings, and with plants of such beauty that she held her breath lest the vision fade. She wept with sadness and joy at what was going to come, and hoped that she was strong enough to undertake the task of bridging - whatever that might be.

Azal heard the noise of splashing accompanied by wild whoops and giggles. She scrambled to the side of the ship where she saw Belin sitting on a wooden post that jutted out above sea, and Orcas swimming with some of the strangest beings she had ever seen. They were large fish who leapt into the air when they surfaced so that they could breathe. Azal had always been told that creatures of the sea could not breathe air. They had faces that smiled and many spines down their backs. Orcas swam and giggled among them. She darted in and out of the water as if playing a game with them. They made clicking sounds that Orcas answered by making clicking sounds of her own. She seemed to be able to communicate with them easily. Azal was entranced and yet fearful. She called out to Orcas to be careful—which, of course, Orcas ignored.

Ishia came onto the deck to see what all the noise was about and stopped dead when she saw Orcas swimming with the sea beings. Fear rose in her throat, and she ran forward to shout at Orcas when Azal stopped her.

"She is of the ocean. She is a child of water. The ocean will not harm her."

Ishia also knew deep down that Orcas would not be harmed. But she feared losing the child who needed and depended on her. This was a new Orcas—someone both knowledgeable and strong. Ishia had also felt unwanted since she had found Azal and Belin curled up together, like two cats asleep under the stars. She had seen his face at last, as he lay sleeping beside Azal. She had grown used to the mask, and the sight of his face quite shocked her. It was not badly scarred as she had imagined. It was round and radiant like the sun. His skin had an unearthly glow, like the glow of a fire lighting the dark night sky, and his hair and beard were the color of gold.

She had gazed at them, sensing the bonds and the love that passed between them even in sleep. Ishia had known the moment he first arrived on the beach that he and Azal had some link through time or through the worlds. She had tried to discourage him and keep him at a distance—to protect Azal. But now it seemed as though they had at last found each other and Ishia knew that nothing would change that.

Nobody now seemed to need her or want her. She gazed at Orcas as she splashed with her sea friends and she realized that she did not even really know this child, that Orcas was a total mystery to her. This hurt her deeply. Azal felt her friend's hurt and put her arm around her. As she whispered into her ear and stroked her hair, she tried to impress through her hands how much she had come to care for and depend on her friend.

Ishia broke away, not wishing sympathy to be heaped upon her already growing pile of resentments.

The passing days and nights brought nothing to ease Ishia's growing feelings of isolation and resentment. She did her appointed tasks, was friendly and kind to everyone, but as her pain grew, her appetite for life lessened. Orcas felt her pain and tried to spend as much time with Ishia as possible. But it seemed to do no good. Eventually Azal realized that nothing they could do would help. She knew then that she would have to use her inner vision to search for a solution.

She went to the back of the ship and found a quiet place. There she sat down. By using her inner vision, she journeyed to Ishia's side and took a long look at the state of her body and soul. Azal was shocked to see a heavy weight suspended over Ishia, a weight of grief, pain, and suffering. It was a level of suffering that was not intended for one human being and Ishia's soul was struggling under the burden. Azal could not understand what could cause such terrible suffering. It was not the situation on the ship: that was far too trivial to cause grief of this magnitude.

She reached out and took the burden onto her own shoulders for a while in an attempt to understand where it came from. As the weight descended onto her shoulders, she felt the overwhelming feeling of loss and pain that is caused by sickness. She used the power of the serpents to transform the feeling into a vision so that she could see the full story.

Azal was struck with horror as the vision unfolded before her. She saw people in one country after another dying in agony from a terrible sickness. She saw children convulsed by pain and mothers weeping in horror as their children died around them. She saw scene upon scene of rotting bodies. She saw the sick and dying.

So! This is what the seer warned about, she thought. This is the clearing of the earth that will remove the entire serving race of people. They are all dying. And the more that die, the fewer are the people left to carry the suffering of these who are in the agonies of near death. Ishia is probably the only fully healthy one left—and so she carries the full weight of all this suffering. But what of herself and Orcas? Do they not also partly have the blood of the server race in their veins?

The answer came from deep within her. Only those of full blood share the burden. Azal and Orcas were of a mixed blood, the blood of the old and the new, both bridges. She realized that was what the vision meant when she had been called a bridge. She knew the moment that she saw Belin's face that he was not of the race of servers. His features were too fine, and he had a glow in his face that was something she had never seen before—although in her training she had heard mention of it.

She knew at that moment that she had to protect Ishia from this burden before it destroyed her. It had already occurred to her that Ishia was being allowed to escape her fate as a server and that being the only survivor of a race held terrible responsibilities. However, this burden was too much for one soul to carry. She sat awhile, thinking how she could help her friend in her struggle.

An idea dawned on her. She went deeper into a space of inner still-ness and then, seeing the flame within, she followed it into the void. She reached out in her mind with a request to approach the convoca-tion. Her inner flame grew bigger and bigger until it became a wall of fire before her. She stepped through the fire and emerged into the convocation of priests and priestesses. She carried in her arms the burden of suffering that Ishia had so valiantly held, and she called out to the assembled masses.

"Friends. I come with a terrible burden, a burden that no being should have to carry alone. The being that carries this burden is the last of her race and I am a bridge between the old and the new. Please help us in our task of birthing a new wave of life on our planet by carrying a small fragment of the pain of the old. As we carry a small part, so the suffering lessens until it finally dissipates. We all take part in the birth of the new world that is to come. In return we shall grow and multiply and be ready to carry your burdens should that time come."

The priests and priestesses of the convocation came forward one by one. Each took a small piece of the suffering and carried it away. Her heart was filled with love and respect for their selflessness. She thanked each of them in turn. When it was done, she took her own piece of that huge burden. She placed it near to her heart where she would transform it into love and so make it fruitful.

She emerged from her vision feeling utterly drained and exhausted. She managed to find her way to the deck shelter and found some food which Ishia had put out for her. Azal ate hungrily, oblivious of her surroundings. Belin came to her side almost immediately.

"Azal, What have you done? Your life force seems so weak and frag-ile. Let me help you. Eat and then rest."

Azal looked around.

"Where is Ishia?" she asked.

Belin looked curiously at her.

"She has gone below deck. She was struck by a great tiredness and so she went to sleep."

Now Azal felt that she wanted to do the same.

She told him what she had done, and he nodded slowly. He had felt that some great power was moving, but he had not realized that it was happening on the ship. He put his hands on her and allowed his life force to flow into her, energizing and feeding her. Then she lay down to sleep and recuperate. As she slept, he watched over her, protecting her from any intrusions. Her body energies had drained down to the barest minimum, and he wanted to be sure that nothing would take advantage of that.

When Azal woke up, Belin was still sitting and guarding her. His face still glowed with love and power. She reached up to touch his face and the touch of her hand aroused his body in the way that he had been fighting to suppress. He had tried to keep his dreams to himself, and not once had he tried to touch or caress her lest he offend her. When they had lain together under the stars the night before, he had urgently desired to take her into his arms and make love to her. But he had fought the feeling, knowing that it was she who must initiate such an act of power.

But now she had reached out to him. Ishia was still asleep and Orcas, who was exhausted, had gone below deck. Azal stroked his face and ran her hands down his bare chest, nuzzling into the thick hair that covered his body. He slowly removed the robe that she was wearing, and then softly ran his hands over every inch of her body, pausing to kiss the scar on her back. His hardness pressed against her, waking energies and powers within her that she did not even know existed. She had never had a man's body so close to her. No man had ever penetrated her. Her body knew only of the visions of this man from the sun. And now he was here, kissing every part of her body, awakening her and worshipping her. With her fingers entwined in his hair she pulled him onto her, searching for his strength, until they were joined as one being.

The pleasure that she felt was something that she had never known. Her inner vision was triggered, and the serpents' eyes began to glow. She saw herself and Belin in the plains alongside the river. As they made love, the river swelled and spilled out over the plains, renewing the parched earth, and bringing new life to the land. And then she saw a whirlwind that reached up through their bodies into the stars, a whirlwind that reached right into the inner realms, welcoming a soul into their world.

Her body's urgency grew and grew until she growled and pulled at him in passion until their inner selves exploded into ecstasy. They became as one being, merged through the power of creation. Her whole body rocked with pleasure. Her wound pulsated with pain, and she held onto him in exquisite union, not wanting to let go. He laughed with joy and pleasure, trying to untangle her fingers from his hair as he moved to lie alongside her.

Down below, Orcas smiled and sang to herself as she drifted in and out of the visions and dreams of the life that lay before her.

The time had come to lower the sails and the two women and Belin struggled to get the large expanses of fabric under control. As the sails were being lowered, Orcas bent over the side of the ship and listened to the noises of the sea. She seemed to be holding a kind of conversation by exchanging clicking noises with invisible friends. Finally, she climbed back onto the deck and watched the sails being stowed. When the sails were secured, Azal and Ishia sat down on deck and Orcas approached Belin, who was tying some knots near the stern.

"There's a nasty storm blowing up, Belin. What are you going to do?"

Belin stared at the child for a moment.

"The navigator said that a storm was coming in three weeks' time. That will give us enough time to reach land before it overtakes us. We will be all right."

He smiled at Orcas, trying to reassure her.

"No," said Orcas. "You do not understand. The sea has just told me that there's a storm just over the horizon and that it'll be here in an hour's time. The sisters have sent the storm. They're angry and they want to destroy us."

Belin became alarmed. Why was the sisterhood pursuing them? He now knew that Azal was what they had been hoping and waiting for—for their seeding project. But he also knew that the other two were of no real value to them. Why then kill Azal after all the work that they had done?

He posed this question in his mind—more to the wind than to Orcas, and he certainly expected no reply.

"Because she is of the elements and not the sisters," Orcas answered quickly. "When Ishia removed that fish from her back, she would have died if she had been of the seed of the sisters. The fish was what they used to control the seeds; it also acted as a lifeline from the sisters. When they realized it had been removed and she had survived, they knew that their seed had not taken and that something had gone terribly wrong. And now, she carries the child of the future: the child of the sun, the start of a new race. Your child."

Belin groaned at Orcas' words. He had known that they would have a child, but he didn't realize that Azal would conceive so soon—and in the midst of such danger.

He tried to focus his thoughts for action. A storm was coming. They had to be ready for it. He called the two women and told them a storm was coming. But he made no mention of the sisters nor of what Orcas had told him. They started to prepare for the oncoming chaos, fastening everything down and making space below.

※

THE ELDER SISTER laughed as she stirred her hand around and around the water pot, creating a whirlpool. She looked deep into the water and saw the boat sailing into the storm. Then she drew a deep breath and blew across the water's surface. The boat tossed and pitched under her breath. She held her cloak over the water pot and the sky grew dark. She stirred and blew until the storm became a gale and then she sat back to watch. The other sisters also gathered around to watch.

"Why does she not die? How does she survive?" one sister asked the elder.

"She has with her," the elder sister answered, "the son of the sun: the divine power of fire made man, a god given to the world by the element of fire. He is helping to give birth to a new race—a race that will counter ours. It must not be allowed. Although he is strong, his power is diminished by manifesting through human life. He is putting all his power into bridging with the navigator. I cannot stop it. His diminished power is still greater than mine."

⚜

THE SISTERS WATCHED the ship and the people on board as they struggled to control the vessel. They watched as the women tied themselves together in the hold, and they smiled as they saw Belin, weakened by the bridging, fall into the sea. The sea enveloped and caressed this child of the sun, taking his body deep into the belly of the ocean. His body came to rest on a ledge far below the water's surface, and his soul was released back to the sun. The water glowed with his light and became calm, allowing the storm to pass even though the sisters continued to blow.

The elder became angry. She had wanted them all to die. Most importantly, she had wanted Azal dead. The powers that were now invoked in all directions were too strong for her to control coherently. She would deal with Azal later; first she needed to refine her skills in this new realm. The change to the inner worlds was not as smooth and simple as she had imagined it would be. Many of her powers worked differently in this new realm and she had not yet managed to adjust. But I will, she thought. I will.

⚜

THE THREE FEMALES clung to each other, moaning and retching. As the sea calmed, they untangled themselves from the ropes that bound them together in the hold. Orcas wept and Azal seemed stunned. Ishia finally managed to steady herself. The storm had passed, and the ship now rocked gently. Ishia grabbed a bucket and filled it with sea water so that they could wash themselves down. All three of them were covered in vomit and were shaking from head to foot.

The storm had seemed to go on forever, but Azal calculated that it had probably only lasted an hour. She poured water over herself and climbed up to the deck. She looked around at the devastation. Part of the shelter had gone. Much of the deck was littered with broken wood and seaweed, and the sails had vanished.

She looked around for Belin, but she couldn't see him. Frantically she searched every corner for him in case he had been knocked unconscious, but she couldn't find him. She ran around the deck again, calling for him. Orcas stood and watched her silently. When Azal realized that Belin had been swept overboard, she threw her head back and wailed both inwardly and outwardly. The wail rang through all the worlds as she fell to her knees in despair.

Immediately Ishia was at her side, holding her, restraining her as she tried to climb over the side of the ship to join him. Orcas ran forward. "No, Azal, daughter of the four friends! You must not die. You carry him within you."

Orcas pulled at Azal's sodden robe. But Azal couldn't hear or see. All she wanted now was to die. Orcas pulled her to the floor and knelt at her side, holding her face until she was forced to look into Orcas' eyes.

"Azal! Look at me! His child is now in your womb. He died to save your child for the future. Your child is the future. Belin fought with the sisters, and he won. Your child will live, and he will be beside you."

She grabbed hold of Azal's hands so that Azal could see what she saw.

Azal looked into the vision, and she saw herself holding a small child with golden hair. Behind her stood Belin. The sight of him tore at her afresh, the pain becoming almost too much to bear. Ishia reappeared with a vial of herb tincture.

"Here, this is his medicine. He was teaching me about it. This will help you until you are able to face the pain."

She held the vial up to Azal's lips and Azal drank the bitter draught. She sank back, waiting for the tincture to work, waiting for it to block out the pain in her chest, the heartbreak, the despair, and the emptiness that swirled in her mind.

Ishia watched over Azal as she whimpered in her sleep. She looked around at the devastation on the deck and realized that a portion of their food and water supply had been washed away. She groaned, knowing that Belin's death was not the only disaster. They were now with insufficient food and water and none of them knew how to sail a ship.

Orcas was once again leaning over the side and talking to the sea. Ishia watched Orcas as she conversed with the water, and she tried to make some sense in her own head about what might lie before them. She was deep in thought when Orcas sat down beside her. Orcas whispered so as not to disturb Azal.

"The navigator has told me that we are off course. I think I know of a way to get the ship back on course. Please don't be frightened by what you see. I will do nothing that will threaten us in any way."

Ishia just nodded. She was beyond even trying to pretend that she was in control of the situation. She looked around herself and then at Azal. What pain and suffering would she have to endure when she awakened?

Orcas stood at the front of the ship, next to the image of Goddess. She bowed her head in reverence and then started to make very high-pitched noises, the like of which Ishia had never heard before. She continued the noises for a long time and then suddenly stopped and smiled.

Ishia stood up to look over the horizon as she felt the water around the ship start to become turbulent. She became frightened and peered over the side of the ship. She saw what seemed to be moving islands coming alongside the ship. She cried out in horror as she realized that the islands were in fact sea creatures of a size that she could not comprehend. They moved slowly and gracefully in pairs, coming up to blow air before sinking slowly under the water again.

Orcas laughed and clapped her hands, making more high-pitched calls to her friends and leaning over to see them better. She called back to Ishia and told her to go to Azal and hold tightly onto her.

"These friends are going to move our ship back on course, back into the Atlant Channel. Hold on and enjoy the ride!"

Ishia braced herself and leant protectively over Azal's unconscious body.

The ship started to creak and groan as the sea creatures pushed and maneuvered it, slowly nudging it back on course. The creatures called to each other and to Orcas as they swam with the ship wedged carefully between them. Eventually Ishia felt the ship lurch forward into the stream of fast-moving water. Orcas danced about on the deck, squealing, and whistling to the creatures.

Then she suddenly fell silent and turned inward. She moved herself deeper and deeper into herself until she found that place within her from where her roots had come—the ocean. She thanked the creatures and the ocean for their help and pledged herself to their service if they should ever need it.

The ocean responded, echoing the call of fellowship and love around the depths of the sea, and declared that her child was the greatest gift that she could have given to her friend, the land. The creatures that swam within her responded to the pledge and echoed her name throughout the oceans of the world.

Azal swam in a dark pool of fear, pain, and loneliness. The tincture was beginning to wear off and the pain in her heart was returning. She found herself wandering in inner vision in the desert of death, looking for her mate, calling his name, but no one responded.

She searched fruitlessly and stopped only when a being placed its hands on her shoulders and turned her around. She looked back at the being, which appeared to her as a transparent form of brilliant light. As she looked through the being, she saw Belin.

Her heart jumped as she tried to reach out to him, but something stopped her. She watched him as he washed himself and then robed in the bright white robes of the Sun priesthood. He stood in the court-yard of a temple that seemed to glow as powerfully as he did. In the center of the courtyard a flame burned brightly. He looked into the flame and saw Azal looking back at him. He smiled and lifted his hand in the sign of sacred union, telling her that they could always meet—for he was not yet returning into the cycle of life and death. He had decided to remain in the inner temple of the sun so that he could be with her throughout the whole course of her present life.

As the vision faded, she cried out for him to come back. She awoke with a cry that brought Ishia running to her side. She sobbed while Ishia held on to her, soothing her, comforting her and yet allowing the pain within her to spill out and disperse. Azal looked around, disorien-tated, until Ishia asked her to lie back down and rest for a while until she felt ready to walk about. She lay and watched Ishia as she counted the water barrels and tried to salvage the food supply. She thought about her vision of Belin and how he had reached out to her. It gave her comfort to know that she could reach him in spirit. And yet her body ached for him to be there, with her, in this life. She continued to watch Ishia with half-glazed eyes until she slowly realized what Ishia was doing.

The food supplies! Until now she had not been able to think clearly. She had not realized that they were still in danger. Azal forced herself to get up and join in the salvage work. She drowned her sadness in the sea of physical hard work, hauling food sacks and stacking water barrels. Some of the water had been contaminated by the sea water and so was useless. They now had enough for a few days only—and food for even less.

The sun came out and scorched them mercilessly as they worked. Azal almost enjoyed the burning sensation, for the fire of the sun on her exposed back was a touch from the son of the sun. She worked naked because her cloth had been torn and soiled beyond use. Slowly, her body darkened under the hot skies. Orcas perched on the deck. She kept glancing between the women laboring on the deck and the sea. She talked to the image of the Sea Goddess and told her about the wonderful and magnificent temple that would be built in her honor—a beauty, however, that could never surpass the outstanding beauty of the ocean herself. No being could ever recreate that.

As the days and nights passed, the three rationed the water and food to an absolute minimum while simply allowing the ship to travel wherever it wished in the Atlant Channel. Azal immersed herself in a haze of obscure dreamlike thought that obliterated all feeling and memory.

Ishia tried to keep herself busy by cleaning the ship, organizing what was left of their belongings and supplies, and by tending to Azal, who seemed to drift further and further away from her.

On one of these dreamlike days, Orcas suddenly darted to Ishia's side.

"The sea tells me. . . "

Orcas stopped to pant and catch her breath.

"The sea tells me that we only have one more day left until we reach land."

She stopped to smile, and her smile widened irresistibly until she erupted into jumps and whoops.

Being on the sea had been both wonderful and terrifying for the child. Ishia finally allowed herself to relax and let go. She wept and wept from the pent-up stresses that had accumulated within her and from her fear that Azal might not survive another day in the scorching heat—locked as she was in her silent world.

As they sighted land, Orcas dived overboard and swam ashore. She waded out of the sea and onto the sandy beach. Beyond the sandy beach lay a line of trees and thick ground cover. As she approached the shrubs, something moved quickly. Orcas, startled, cried out in fright as many strange small birds rose into the air and flew away. They flew up and off across the water towards the boat, complaining loudly at Orcas' intrusion.

Ishia stood on the deck of the ship and watched the exotic-colored birds rise into the sky, and her eyes were wide with awe. She had only seen creatures like that on paintings on the temple walls. Now, in real life, she saw how beautiful they were.

Orcas, in the meantime, was using her inner sense of touch to reach out and feel for the presence of water in the land. She felt a small stream nearby and pushed through the undergrowth to reach it. She emerged into a small clearing through which a stream ran, and she drank long and deeply from its cool, clear water. She then sat back to survey the land around her. Orcas was amazed at what she saw.

On many of the trees grew beautiful collections of multicolored petals around which tiny insects ceaselessly buzzed and fluttered. Her whole being responded to the beauty of what she saw, and she began to cry. The Goddess of the ocean felt Orcas' emotions and she responded to them.

What you see, child, is a gift. A gift from the Mother Earth below your feet, a gift from the wind that blows through your hair and a gift from my depths. Guard this gift wisely for the new people who will come—for their survival depends on these gifts. These are flowers. They are the start of the new creation, a wave of creation that has grown from seed, as is the child within Azal. The flowers are the physical expression of the emotions of the people, and while flowers continue to exist, no being can ever control the emotions of the people. This, Orcas, is your duty. You must never leave this land. You must stay and guard the plants, the trees, the flowers, and the creatures of the air.

Ishia grew more and more concerned when Orcas did not return to the ship. She tried to wake Azal from her deep sleep. She was terrified that if she left Azal to search for Orcas, Azal might die in her absence.

Azal finally awoke and nodded when Ishia told her what had happened. Although she found it difficult to speak, she understood that Ishia was going to look for Orcas and that she would return soon.

She sank back into the makeshift bed and fell into a deep and troubled sleep. She began to dream of the place where their boat had just run aground—the place where they would live. She dreamed of a forest with strange creatures, and a landscape with hot springs and swamp. She looked around and saw many children playing in and around the trees, and creatures playing with the children. She saw angels of the inner realms watching and guarding the children, and other, beautiful nature beings peeking out from behind the bushes. She looked further on to where a village was being built. She watched as many men and women struggled with wood and water to build shelters and a sanctuary. One of the guardian angels approached her in the dream and spoke to her.

"Behold, child of the four friends, this is your destiny. You must build and raise the inner temple—a place of worship and honor. We will work with you and we will be your materials, your building blocks. First you must meet your mistress, the great Goddess. We are honored that the Gods have chosen to touch this world and become a part of it. They became angry with the corruption of the sisters, and they stepped out of the void to rebalance what had been done. I, Uriel, will be with you as you work. Come, follow me."

The angel led her down through the forest of the new land until they came to a hot spring. The angel motioned for her to step forward and touch the water. She bent down and ran her hand through the water, which was wonderfully warm. A pair of feet appeared near her hand. Quickly she withdrew her hand from the water. As she stood up, she looked at the face of a woman who seemed both timelessly old and young. Her beauty and ugliness were beyond compare, and the power of the void streamed from her eyes. Her hair was black, and fire flicked in and out of her locks. Blood ran from between her thighs and tears dripped from the edge of her face. A profound love and fear rose within Azal. She reached out to touch the Goddess who caught her arm and held it in a tight grip.

"Azal, named altar of the light of the void, beloved of the four friends, do you vow to me? If so, what do you vow?"

Before she could think, words spilled from Azal's taut mouth.

"I vow to honor and love you, to serve you and to be your priestess. I give you my life. I give you my soul. I am bound to you throughout time and space and when time and space have no purpose, I will reside within you, close to your heart."

The Goddess reached between her thighs and dipped her finger in her blood. She placed her finger between Azal's thighs, marking her with blood. She then reached to Azal's forehead and scratched into her skin a sigil of two crescent moons back-to-back. Then she drew a line down the middle on her forehead, mingling the blood of the Goddess with that of Azal.

"So be it."

The Goddess vanished and Azal turned to the angel, who had also vanished. She looked around her at the landscape, and she knew what she had to do.

Ishia shook her body in excitement. "Come on! Wake up! Guess what we have found? Come on! Wake up!"

Azal opened her eyes and brushed her hair away from her face. Ishia drew back in shock.

"Azal! Your face! What has happened?"

Azal put her hand to her face as though asking a question. Then she remembered her dream and put her hand to her forehead. A shape had been outlined in her flesh and Azal fingered the dried blood.

"Don't worry, friend. It is a gift."

She didn't expand any further and that left Ishia even more concerned and curious.

"What is it you have to show me?"

Azal's curiosity had finally been aroused.

Ishia grabbed Azal and virtually dragged her up on deck.

"Follow me, Azal. I've much to show you that will make you happy."

The two dropped overboard and swam to the shore. Ishia kept close to Azal, watching her for any weakness. When they had reached shore, they rested for a while. Then Ishia took them both deep into the forest until they reached a clearing.

Azal took a sharp breath. Before them lay the hot springs of her vision. She bent down to touch the water and, with great reverence, she bowed her head to the waters. She then stood and raised her arms until they were stretched out wide.

"O great Goddess, the void made manifest. I will make this place sacred to you and I will tend this place and bear my children here. My children will serve you and my children's children and all who go beyond me shall call your name sacred."

She felt something rustle around her and used her inner vision to see what it was. Her heart lurched as she saw Belin, smiling and laughing. He bowed to her and spoke.

"This truly is a sacred place. It is the first place where the Goddess chose to step from the void and bring forth her army of angels and creatures. You are truly honored, and I will share that honor with you. I will always be with you!"

Before she could speak to him, he had vanished. Her mind was torn by conflicting thoughts and emotions. She wanted to stay with Belin. She wanted to know about the angels: who they were, what they did, where they came from. She also wanted to know about the other beings that appeared only to the inner vision—the beings of the forest. She sat down to try and take everything in, and Ishia sat beside her.

Ishia had watched Azal while she touched the water and invoked something. After that she had appeared to be somewhere else as she stood in the shallows of the water, staring out at the forest. Orcas appeared at Ishia's side and suggested that they get what was left of their belongings before the ship drifted out to sea with the changing tide. She also warned them that another storm was coming. She assured everyone that the storm was natural and that it would not harm them. But they had to be quick.

The sisters, angry at their failure to destroy Azal, now turned their attention to the other seeds that they had planted around the world. They watched as these seed bearers traveled, drawn by an inner urge, towards the land where Azal and the others were.

"The creation will still go ahead," thought the elder, "and our race will be triumphant. The creatures that we create will serve and feed our race and our race will dominate and rule over the many different creatures."

Azal and her offspring would slowly be destroyed and overtaken. Of that, they were sure.

It had taken a few days to build a shelter that was stable and functional. They had daubed mud from the hot springs over the wood and branches and this had made durable walls for the home that would insulate them against the heat. Azal had learned a considerable amount about building, food and survival in a very short time, and her hands were finally beginning to harden with the work that Ishia forced her to do every day. ·

At the end of each day of building, Azal would go, in the evening before darkness, to the springs to build the inner temple with her mind.

She worked in the convocation and collected energy from the four directions, an energy mediated by the priests and priestesses. She condensed this energy into a tightly wound ball. She passed from the convocation back to the outside world, to the swamp, and unraveled the threads of power. She began to weave them into a shelter, day by day, teasing the lines of power around the directions until a structure had been built. Then she created doorways in each direction so that the Gods and Goddesses had defined spaces through which they could manifest. Then she sat and meditated as to how it would look when it was built. That vision was imprinted over the structure to give it shape. It was finally finished. Soon the outer structure would be built.

Azal went out every morning to examine her new world. She watched the flowers bloom and fade. She noted the different plants and trees and listened to the creatures of the air as they talked to each other and flitted in and out of the treetops. She also sat and inwardly felt the child she now knew she was carrying. She had known before, but now she could feel the child grow within her. What had confused her, however, was that when she talked to the child, two voices, rather than one, answered her back. She hoped that the child she carried would fuse itself into one coherent being before she gave birth. A child with two voices would be a bad omen.

She lay and thought of Belin and how he had come to her in the spring. She had not seen or felt him since. Nor had she felt the Goddess. She reached up and touched her forehead and traced her fingers along the scars. They had healed but not gone away. Although they had remained red, there was no pain or infection in them. She realized that she had made a serious commitment in her vow to the Goddess whom she had met, and yet she still didn't fully understand the implications of that commitment. She lay in the sun as she turned her thoughts over and over, enjoying the warmth as it touched her dark skin and rejoicing in the beauty of the land that was now their new home.

Her thoughts drifted to Orcas. She pondered the problem of whether she should teach Orcas the Mysteries. Orcas was certainly able and strong enough to learn them. Perhaps she would talk to Ishia about this matter.

Her thoughts were disturbed by screams from Ishia. She ran back to the hut to find her friend pointing out to sea and shaking with fear.

"I dreamed about this! I knew it would happen! We will all die!"

Azal looked out to sea and saw a ship on the horizon. She was convinced that all the people had died and that all the sisterhood had gone over to the inner world. She had really thought that they were all alone on the whole earth. But then she remembered something that was said a long time ago in the village by the seer—something about her not being the only seed bearer. If that were true, then whoever was on that ship was a product of a sisterhood. Would they be hostile? Would they know that Azal had broken away and was no longer a puppet of the sisters?

She told Ishia what she was thinking, and she calmly explained all the consequences and possibilities. Ishia in turn went to find Orcas so that they could warn her. They had about one day before the ship would arrive.

The two women prepared food and set out water for the oncoming visitors. They realized that they might be close to death—as they themselves had been when they first arrived. Orcas kept going down to the water's edge to listen to what the sea had to say. When she returned she passed on the information to the women as they built a fire. They pondered what she said in silence. Azal spoke.

"Four people. If they choose to be hostile, we cannot defend ourselves against them."

She was about to sink into despair when Ishia had an idea.

"Let's start with them as we wish always to be."

Azal looked at her with a blank expression, not understanding what Ishia meant.

"When I first went to the temple to work," said Ishia, "I was terrified of the sisters because of the way they behaved and carried themselves. When I worked for you, I was in awe of you because of the way you carried yourself. Now you must do the same. When these people come ashore, they are going to meet the most powerful priestess on the land, and they will feel fear and respect. Do you understand, Azal?"

Azal's face lit up as she understood what Ishia was saying. Although the events of the past few months had shaken her badly, she had in fact learned how to function and respond like a normal person and not just a priestess. But she could slip back into the priestess role if she had to, although it was not a prospect that she relished.

She had enjoyed being as equals with Ishia, and having her as a friend and companion, not just a server. This equality had opened a whole new world for her, and she didn't want to return to the old life. Ishia deduced her train of thought from the changing expressions on her face.

"Don't worry, Azal. It won't be the same. You're in a different life now. It will be a new experience. I am no longer your server. I'm also now your friend—and I always will be. To them I will not be your server, but a village seer. I have lived around a seer for long enough to become one."

She smiled in a wicked, conspiring way.

Azal also smiled broadly and nodded.

"I have a little story to tell Orcas," said Ishia. "I'll be back in a minute."

Ishia sped off to find the child while Azal sat on the beach and fed the fire that they had lit and looked out to sea.

They kept a vigil by the sea throughout the night and took turns keeping the fire burning. Azal wanted whoever was out there to know that they were there and that they were expected. She wanted no surprises and no secret landings. She could not jeopardize the lives of the others. She slept fitfully through the night, and just before dawn she awoke with a start. Something had changed. Her inner sense of danger told her that the people were preparing to come to land. She built up the fire and put away her sleeping mat. She crept into the undergrowth and waited.

Sure enough, after she had been in a cramped position for an hour, a small boat came ashore carrying two people: a man and a woman. Azal scrutinized them carefully. Orcas had said that there were four people. Two therefore must have stayed behind. She could not hear another boat and this bay was the only safe place for a landing in the dark.

She watched as the two climbed quietly out of the boat and walked toward the fire. They slowed down as they realized that there were two people asleep around the fire. Azal crept around behind cover until she was directly behind the two people. She sneaked up behind the woman and put her knife across the woman's throat. The woman whimpered and Azal hissed in her ear, commanding her to kneel on the floor. The man spun around and faced Azal. His face was scarred and covered with matted hair, and his eyes were full of pain and fear.

Ishia and Orcas awoke immediately and Ishia sprung to her feet, taking in the situation with one look. Azal asked the man his name. As he stepped forward, she pressed the knife harder against the woman's head. He stepped back and held his hands up in the sign of harmlessness.

"My name is Taran, and the woman is Bregh."

Azal motioned for them to sit by the fire and eat. She watched them as they ate. She waited for them to finish eating before she asked them what they were doing in this place.

Taran spoke first.

"We have traveled for many turns of the moon over land and sea. Our people are all dead and our priests vanished—leaving the temple empty. They left us maps and food. We were guided here by the maps and the ocean. We met others along the way with similar stories. We mean you no harm. I can see that you are a priestess. I vow to you on the honor of my soul that we intend no harm."

Even though this was a vow of the priesthood, something didn't feel right to Azal. She looked at him deeply and saw nothing within him that was bad or dishonest. Yet something still bothered her. She turned to the woman, Bregh, and looked at her. She was still obviously afraid, snatching at her food while watching the blade of Azal's knife. Azal looked at the woman with her inner vision and saw a woman who was quiet and honest. She was not of the priestesshood and yet she was not totally of the people. She had no outstanding strength or power and would pose no inner threat. Azal motioned for her to sit back.

"Tell me about yourself," said Azal. She waited as the woman looked from Azal to Taran. Taran then stepped forward and placed a hand on her head.

"She cannot speak. She has many disabilities. She was bred by the priesthood, but something went wrong and she was born like this."

Azal nodded. "And so? Who else is on your ship? Where are the other two?"

Azal could see that Taran was astounded. How did she know about the others?

He looked at Azal more closely, and for the first time he saw the sigil on her forehead partially covered with hair and the snakes on her arms. He groaned inwardly. He had spent months trying to escape from the clutches of the priesthood as they followed his progress in the inner world. But now, it seemed, they had walked into another version of the same thing. He saw Azal waiting for his answer about the other two on board.

"There are indeed two others—a man who is injured and a male child. We left them where they were safe while we came to find out what was here and who had made the fire. We had been told that we were the last people alive on earth."

Ishia, who had stood in the shadows with Orcas, stepped forward.

"I feel you are sent here to work with us," said Ishia. "You and your friends will be welcome. But should you threaten any of us in any way at all, you will be killed. We will share our food and shelter with you, and you will answer to Azal."

Azal looked at the man and felt his inner weariness and distress. She reached out and placed her hand on his shoulder.

"You are welcome here, and it will not be as you think."

She smiled reassuringly at him and Taran looked back.

When she touched him, a surge of power flowed into him from her and regenerated him. He recognized the level of her power, but also the greatness of her compassion. Her touch had reached down to the depths of his soul, and it had left him naked before her. He knew then that they would be safe.

Taran and Bregh ate, drank, and talked, and waited for the sunrise so that they could fetch their friends.

7

Azal groaned as she tried to rise from her knees. Her body, bloated by pregnancy, weighed her down to the extent that it had become difficult for her to move at all. She finally stood and looked out at the construction that was being built over the hot spring. The work was progressing efficiently and quickly with the help of the new people who had arrived by sea. Already the shell of a primitive temple building was in place.

They had constructed five basic platforms—one in each direction and one in the center. On each of these platforms, wattle and daub huts would be laid and pathways on stilts would lead from building to building, linking them all together. They were laid in a circle around the spring and the center hut would have a well in the floor to allow the steam to rise.

She staggered back to her hut to rest. She had been feeling strange for the past two days and decided that she needed more sleep. Ishia and Bregh watched her as they smoothed the wood they were preparing for building. Ishia was growing more and more alarmed at the course of Azal's pregnancy. It had gone on far too long already and she was too big. Was she going to give birth to a fully grown man? Ishia knew that a pregnancy should only last six cycles of the moon, but

Azal was now into her eighth month. Impossible. And the size of her... It was unhealthy. How would she be able to deliver at that size? Ishia had never seen a pregnancy like this before.

She had been confident at the beginning that she could deliver the child and that all would be well. But this was something beyond her knowledge and capabilities. She grew more and more afraid for Azal and for the child. She could not bear the thought of losing Azal, and yet she could not see how Azal could survive such a birth. She had been present at the birth of many children, and there were always certain signs that birth was imminent. Six moon turns after the breeding festival, the women would lie down, and the baby would slide out. It was always so simple. But Ishia knew that this would be different.

As she carried on working and thinking about these problems, Orcas skipped up to her. She had learned how to flip her body head-over-heels and was proudly performing around the front of the huts, squealing and laughing each time she landed on her bottom.

Her playmate came racing around the corner with his head down. Then suddenly he lifted his head up and leapt in the air. As he did so, he twisted his body around in a full circle before landing again on his feet. Then they both stood together and waited for the women to approve. The two women roared with laughter and the two children fought with each other as to who was the best. Ishia waved her hand at the boy.

"Fynn! Go and find some roots for our food tonight. And take Orcas with you."

Orcas had stopped laughing and had become silent. She stood totally still for a moment and then looked at Ishia.

"The babies are coming! I must go and get some herbs!"

Before anyone could say a word, she darted off and Fynn turned and ran after her. Ishia shouted after Orcas, "Are you sure it's now? Are you sure?"

Orcas didn't reply. She just vanished into the forest with Fynn hard on her heels. Ishia and Bregh went straight to the hut where Azal was sleeping. Ishia crept quietly inside and knelt beside the sleeping woman. Ishia saw that her sleeping mat was soaked through.

Then, as she placed her hand lightly on Azal's abdomen, she felt it tighten. She nodded to Bregh, who went to fetch water and the tinctures. She shook Azal lightly. Azal moaned and then opened her eyes. Azal's eyes were full of pain. This shocked Ishia. She helped her out of her work cloth. When the water arrived, Ishia bathed her from head to toe.

Azal's mind was caught in the whirlwind of intense pain. She and the pain had become one. Through the pain, she could hear someone in the distance calling her name. She tried to reach out, but her body did not respond. It was trapped in its own rhythms of contortion and agony—leaving her only regular but brief moments of peace before the next onslaught of pain returned.

Through a haze of agony, she could see people moving about. She saw a beautiful being of light stroke its arms through her body as if realigning her. The being then went to her head and she could feel its touch reaching deep inside her. The being maneuvered and shifted her muscles and bones, assisting her body in its struggle to survive. She vaguely remembered this feeling before somewhere in her past, somewhere with the mountain sisters. She called out to the sisters in despair, hoping that they would come and take her away from this torment. Azal's contractions continued relentlessly throughout the day without relief, until she was utterly exhausted.

Ishia massaged her contorted body and prayed. She had no idea what was happening. She had never seen a birth like this before. Azal started to arch her body, twisting from side to side. Then she turned onto her knees and cried out. Ishia was around her side just in time to see the baby's head appear.

"I can see it! I can see it! The baby is here, Azal! Just push! Carefully!"

Ishia was both excited and relieved to finally see a child emerging from such a frightening situation.

Azal felt as though she had been split in two. She cried out and cursed, thrashing her head and moaning as she pushed. The sound was deep and resonant, coming from the very center of her being. She became aware of small creatures moving around her, whispering in her ear.

"He's coming! He's coming! Push, sweet maiden. We are here to protect him. He will be our king! Push, sweet child of the friends."

She tried to look through the pain to see who was speaking. All that she could see were wisps of fire.

"Who are you? What are..."

Her words were cut short by her body demanding that she push. She bore down hard and felt the bulk between her thighs slither out, reducing both the pressure and the pain. She breathed out long and hard and collapsed back in a stupor.

"We are the Salamanders of the fire, the original creations of this world, along with the creatures of the earth, the water and the wind. You, friend, are a part of all of us. When you bred with the son of the sun, you gave us a king whom we will serve and work with. It is he who shall in turn protect us from the children of the sisters. We reside in the south, in the heat and in the fire. Should you need us, call into the fire, sweet maiden. Call into the fire and we will be there!"

Azal drifted in and out of the conversation until she heard a child's cry. This brought her back so that she could focus on Ishia's voice.

She felt the cord being cut, and then felt the being of light who had been at her head reach over and cut an inner cord. As soon as that was done, Azal felt something deep within sever, separating her from her child.

She opened her eyes and saw the baby as it was brought to her. He was a beautiful boy with a tuft of golden hair and eyes of the purest blue.

Although Azal was exhausted, she put the child to her breast. As he fed, she felt all her learning, all her experiences, pains, sorrows, rituals, and joys pass through the milk into her child. She gazed at her new child in wonderment and worship. His little face glowed in the same way that Belin's face had glowed. She sobbed out loud for Belin, her loneliness magnified by holding the child he would never see.

She also felt a new wave of pain. She cried out in surprise as the pain cut through her, hardening her abdomen, and forcing her to hand over the baby. Ishia and Bregh looked at each other in panic. They had no idea about what might be happening. Azal tried to get up and found herself squatting in the corner. She moaned and wept from the pain as she felt another bulk lowering into her birth canal. She pushed and cried until another head appeared. Then she lay down in the corner to allow the child to slip out. She growled and whimpered until the head revolved and the baby slid effortlessly out. Azal collapsed into the corner, leaving the astounded Ishia to pick up the baby. She cleared the child's nostrils and tied a string around the cord. Again, the being of light bent over Azal and cut the inner cord, separating the child from its mother. The remainder of the birth products slid out, and Ishia placed them with the first issue. She would cook them for Azal to give her strength.

The second child looked very different from the first. This second child was a girl with dark hair who laid in Ishia's arms calmly. Ishia checked her from head to toe and found that she had an extra finger on her left hand. She turned the child over and gasped when she saw the birthmark on her back. Just where Azal had had her sigil removed, there was the outline of a fish in the form of a red birthmark. She bathed the child and presented her to her mother. Azal put the child to her breast, but this time she felt nothing flow into her.

Ishia was speechless. She had never seen two babies born at once from one mother. This was truly a day of great omen. After the two women had bathed Azal, they gave her a clean cloth and then laid the babies alongside her. They padded them around with straw for warmth and then threw covers over them all so that they could sleep and regenerate. Ishia told Bregh to stay and sit in the corner to guard them. Bregh nodded and squatted in the corner.

As Ishia emerged from the hut, Orcas came racing around the corner.

"They're here, aren't they? What do they look like? Are they beautiful? Can they talk yet? Can I play with them? Is Azal happy?"

Orcas hopped from one foot to another foot in her excitement— demanding answers to her questions. Ishia looked long and hard at Orcas.

"How did you know that there was more than one child?"

Orcas stopped and looked at Ishia in confusion.

"Because they talked to me, of course. One is the son of Belin, and one is the daughter of the sisters. The daughter of the sisters is great fun. We will play together. But the boy is serious—not like Belin.... I miss Belin. He was funny. May I see them now?"

Orcas stood waiting.

"No, not yet. Let Azal sleep. Her body has been under terrible strain. I've never seen a birth like that before. I didn't think she would survive."

Orcas looked at Ishia and saw the worry on her face. She stretched her hand to reassure her friend.

"I knew she would be all right. Don't worry, Ishia, she is strong and will recover well. The difficult birth was because she is a child of the elements. They must suffer terrible things to bring life into this world. It is a warning to us that we should not copy the sisters. The sisters, through their experiments, brought life, the servers, into this world without proper consideration, and they thereby caused all sorts of problems. And so the elements were ashamed of the sisters, of their own creation. Thus, when they gave of themselves to give life, to redress the imbalance, they made a great sacrifice. The outcome of that sacrifice is that Azal, Taran, Fynn, Belin and I all have sacrifice and suffering entwined in our very structure. We must suffer greatly to bring forth life. I will die bringing in life, but that is fine. That is how it must be. When that happens, I shall return home to my mother the ocean."

Ishia wanted to protest to this strange wise child but thought the better of it. She understood what Orcas had said and just nodded. She knew that Orcas was of no ordinary life, and that Orcas struggled with having to perform her destiny while still in a child's body.

"Your words are a great gift of wisdom, Orcas, and I thank the ocean for allowing me to be part of your life and hear your wisdom."

She changed her expression when she saw Orcas becoming uncomfortable. She then realized that Orcas was also enjoying being a child and didn't want profound or worshipful speeches.

"Go and fetch some food for preparation! And be quick!"

She spoke with mock severity. Orcas grinned and ran off.

Taran and his companion, Vran, were still out at the springs, working on the building. She would send Orcas later with the news, for now Azal needed to rest. She went back to the hut to sleep alongside

Azal and the babies. As she approached the hut, she saw a strange light spilling out of the doorway. Her first instinct was that it was fire. She cursed herself for leaving Bregh in charge. Although the girl was dimwitted, she had not supposed that she could be so careless.

As she entered the hut, she drew her breath in sharply. Bregh was asleep in the corner and at the foot of the bed stood Belin, his body clothed in a soft golden light. He was gazing at his beloved and at the children, and Ishia noticed that the male child was glowing in the same way as Belin did. He raised his hand in blessing over the sleepers on the bed and then vanished. Ishia was left standing alone in the darkness of the hut, her body frozen in fear and wonder.

Azal awoke and nuzzled her babies as they sought her breast. Ishia was still staring in amazement.

"Azal," she called softly. "I will cook you some food to increase your strength and your milk. I will also cook your birth matter for you to eat."

Azal propped herself up on her elbow, and her swollen breasts fell free as they filled with milk.

"No, I will not ever eat blood. I am sworn from birth, and it will be like that until I die. No child of the elements may eat blood. If they do, they sever their links with the four friends. I know which herbs I must eat. Send Orcas to me in the morning. She will find them for me."

She fell back, and her face showed the full extent of the suffering she had gone through. Ishia straightened the covers and straw. She gazed at the wondrous scene of the babies who were curled together— as they had been even in the womb. Azal was curled protectively around them, and her body heat kept them warm. Ishia's heart lurched at the scene. She backed quietly out of the hut and watched as the moon rose through the path of stars. She lay down on the threshold of the hut to rest lightly. She dare not fall asleep. She wanted to be able to hear and respond if she were needed.

Orcas prepared food for everyone. When she saw that Ishia had fallen asleep, she crept around her and tiptoed into the hut, carrying a bowl of broth for Azal. She had been out in the woods collecting whatever herbs the rising moon told her that Azal needed. She cooked them lightly and now spooned the broth carefully between Azal's exhausted lips.

Orcas whispered to the babies and kissed them both before wiping Azal's face and allowing her to lie back down and sleep. Azal caught Orcas' arm and smiled to her.

"Thank you, friend and sister. May you always watch over my children. In return I shall always watch over yours."

Orcas nodded in assent. Then she quietly crept out of the hut and stepped lightly over Ishia so as not to disturb her.

ON THE THIRD morning after the birth, just before sunrise, everyone gathered outside Azal's hut for the naming ceremony. Azal emerged with the two babies in her arms and smiled at everyone. She looked old and tired.

Although her hair was drained of color and her tall frame stooped, her eyes shone in happiness. She nodded to Orcas, who came forward, took the babies into her arms and sat down. Then Azal prepared the space.

She processed in a circle around the directions and then stood in the center of the circle that she had made. She felt the inner fire rise and saw the flame of the convocation before her. She gradually became aware of the priests and priestesses emerging out of the four directions to be with her and she opened her arms to welcome them.

She then went to each direction in turn and called on the four friends. In the south the fire Salamanders appeared once again. Behind them stood Belin. The priest held his arm up in greeting to Azal. She smiled but did not allow herself to be distracted. Then she moved on to the west and, in her inner vision, saw the ocean and the beings of the ocean. From among them emerged a tall, heavily built woman dressed in long robes. She wore a band of silver around her head, and she saluted Azal with a curt nod of the head.

Azal saluted them by bowing deep and thoughtfully. She continued to the north and again passed into the direction in her inner vision, where she saw the Dark Mother in the form of rock, with her beings of the earth, the hidden ones of the forest and plants. Azal also thought she saw a faint outline of the three mountain sisters standing behind the rock. She strained to see, but the vision faded as she stepped back. She finally approached the east. As she looked with her inner vision, she saw the beings of the wind and behind them, a whirlwind. She acknowledged the beings and then returned to the center. She motioned for Orcas to bring the children to her. She took the boy from Orcas and Orcas went to stand in the west with the other child.

Azal carried the little boy into the east. As she looked up, she saw the sun just peeping over the horizon. She held the child high in the air and declared:

"Behold my son, child of the sun, king of fire, child of the elements, keystone of the new world, keeper of the knowledge of the sun, and builder of the Golden City. Beings of the four directions, tell me his eternal name. Tell me the key to his soul. Tell me the sound of his summoning."

The wind started to blow and the ocean started to swell. The gathered company became afraid—all except Orcas, who smiled. The wind whipped around Azal and the baby and whispered the sound of her baby's fate. The name resonated through the wind and her mind caught the sound and translated it to words.

Parsa.

"So be it!" cried Azal. "My child is named Parsa, king of fire."

The baby cried and the wind calmed. She handed the baby to Orcas and took her daughter.

Azal walked around the directions, searching for the directional connection to her child. She could not find one. Instinctively, she was pulled to the threshold of the ocean. She stepped out of the circle and walked to the water's edge. The company followed. She sprinkled water over the child, who calmly lay in her mother's arm, gazing up at her. She closed her eyes and reached out to the ocean in her inner vision. She then became aware of a swell in the water, and of something coming out from the ocean. She saw a female figure coming out of the water. She heard the others gasp behind her and she opened her eyes.

Out of the water walked a tall, beautiful woman with skin of shining black, hair of flames and blood dripping from between her legs. Azal recognized the Goddess who had marked her and she fell to her knees in fear. The others backed away, all except Orcas, who ran forward to greet the Goddess of the warm ocean. Behind the Goddess a trail of flames flickered on the waves, marking her passage.

The Goddess commanded Azal to arise and hold out the child. Azal did so and looked upon the Goddess in awe.

"Your child is of the seed planted by the sisters. It was their desire to make a new race and a new world to serve them. It was their desire to make themselves as Gods and Goddesses. That should not be so. Your child will have the mark of a true Goddess. I am She of the ocean and the hot lands. Where the ocean makes love to the land, that is where you will find me. I am She who governs blood and sea, fire within ocean, disease, and death. I reach out my touch to this child and bless her with my blood.

"Although her line will be powerful, it will also be troubled as the influence of the sisters emerges.

"In order to counter this, I give her three gifts: the gift of sight, the gift of knowledge and the gift of bond between her line and myself. Her name will talk of this bond. Her name will be Isca, which means 'of the Goddess.'"

The Goddess reached out and smeared blood across the face of the child before turning and walking back into the sea, leaving, a trail of fire behind her.

Azal turned to face the assembled company who, apart from Orcas, were cowering on their knees. She went back to the circle and turned to each direction. She thanked the beings for the naming of her children and closed the contact down. She suddenly felt very weary and began to stoop. Orcas moved forward and took the silent child from her, while Vran picked her up in his arms and carried her back to her hut. Orcas and Ishia put the babies in the little nest of straw on the bed and Vran placed Azal very gently onto the bed.

He looked at her as she lay exhausted, his eyes full of worship. From the moment he had seen her, he had desired her. He wanted to be partnered with her but had kept his distance while she was with child. Now that that was out of the way, he could start wooing her. His bright ginger hair fell over Azal's face. She opened her eyes slightly and saw the golden glow of the light coming from behind Vran's hair. Her mind became confused through her exhaustion.

"Belin, my love, come lie with me."

Vran stepped back in disgust. How could she want a dead man when he was here in the flesh? She was stupid and ungrateful. But she would come around to his way of thinking—of that, he was sure. He left abruptly, and Orcas stared at him as he walked off. Her eyes did not leave him until he was out of sight. Fynn, who was at her side, also felt the threat and gazed at Orcas without fully understanding what he felt.

Orcas found Ishia sitting next to the hot springs. She told Ishia what had happened in Azal's hut, how Vran was a possible threat to Azal, and the feelings of lust and hate that had come from the man as he was rejected. Ishia sighed. She had been hoping that a feeling of community would appear now that they were all building the temple together, but it had not happened. They would have to do something soon to bond the people, even mating, if they were to survive and grow. "Orcas, please tell Taran that I wish to speak with him."

Orcas looked around the construction site to see if he was there. She spotted him high up a tree fixing rope to a branch. She ran into the woods. When she got to the tree, she climbed it quickly and expertly. Taran nearly fell out of the tree in shock when he reached absently for a rope and Orcas held it out for him.

"Ishia needs to speak with you. She is sorry to take you away from your work, but I think it is important."

Her piercing eyes had always fascinated him. He nodded as she looked deep into him. He felt something pass into him from the child, something strange and yet safe. He did not fight it, but let it flow through him. His life as a priest had trained him in the use of power, but the power that resided in this child was like no other. Taran trusted her and so submitted to whatever was needed of him.

She turned and vanished out of the tree like a raindrop. He tried to watch her descend but she was too quick. He gathered his ropes up and secured them, and then prepared himself for this meeting. He had tried hard to avoid really becoming a part of this little group. He spoke as little as possible and knew that Vran was doing the same. As he approached Ishia, she looked at him very carefully. She had not really bothered to take much notice of him until now. She had felt the distance between the newcomers and themselves, and yet she had had no wish until then to change things. But now Azal was under threat, and that must change. This threat had made her realize that they had to bond if they were to survive. It was only Orcas and Fynn who seemed to have a balanced friendship.

Ishia motioned for him to sit down, and then told him of what had passed between Vran and Azal. He listened intently and nodded. Vran was an unknown entity to him. He had found him wandering on the route he was taking, dying of thirst, and mumbling about a cursed priesthood that had left him behind. It was the same story as his and then, it seemed, Azal's. Fynn was the only one who had no knowledge of a priesthood. His family had all died. Everyone in his village had died. But he, for some reason, had survived, and he had attached himself to the two men when their paths crossed.

"He cannot even hope to mate with Azal," said Ishia. "She will have no other after Belin. He must be paired with Bregh, for I will certainly not pair with him."

Taran wanted to protest, for he felt that Bregh was too vulnerable for such a union, and he had kept the poor woman away from Vran.

"But don't you see?" continued Ishia.

"He is perfect for her. He wants a woman to care for him and lie with him, and she needs someone to protect and provide for her. And we need children for the future."

Taran thought for a while. He realized they could hardly be choosy about partners and that they must provide children for the future. He had avoided such thoughts in the past, but now it was time to face them.

He looked at Ishia and saw her strength and clarity. She was not obviously beautiful, but her strength gave her face character and that, in turn, made her beautiful.

"And who will pair with you?"

His voice was slow and deliberate. He had long admired her ability to hold everyone together —despite the lack of any common understanding among them, and he enjoyed her company. He had not yet thought about pairing for children. He first desired to flush his hatred for the priesthood out of his system before he moved on to a new life.

He sat with one eyebrow raised, waiting for her answer. Her face flushed red with embarrassment. He spoke again, hoping to lessen her embarrassment.

"There is only you and I left."

As he reached out to touch her face, Fynn came crashing out of the overhead tree. Orcas tried to suppress her laughter, but made loud snorting noises, her body shaking so hard that she also nearly fell from the tree. Ishia got up and fled in embarrassment and anger. Fynn stood before Taran as Taran shouted at him. The boy tried very hard not to smile but eventually his mouth got the upper hand. Fynn slapped his hand over his mouth and fled screeching into the woods. Taran looked to the sky in a gesture of hopelessness and then sat down and laughed.

When he finally returned to the huts at the end of the day, Ishia was quietly stirring broth and adding herbs. Azal was propped by the fire, holding her sleeping babies, and Orcas was playing with her feet. Fynn was gazing into space with his mouth open and the other two were nowhere to be seen.

Taran approached Ishia carefully. He could see that she had been crying. Clearly, she had been distressed by what had happened. He thought that it might be so. After she had run off, he had stopped his work in the springs. He had sat there and communed with the Goddess. He had realized that he was at a turning point in his life, and he had to make decisions, not only for himself but also for the future of others.

The Goddess listened to his fears and worries and in return she showed him a brief glimpse of the future. It was a vision of him as an old, old man surrounded by great grandchildren. In the vision he saw himself telling them the story of how he had spoken to his wife under a tree that rained children. The Goddess then directed him to a spot in the woods where she said he would find a gift for Ishia—something that would make amends. He searched and searched until he saw something glinting in the afternoon sun. He picked it up and turned it over and over. It was a white crystal; veins the color of the sun were running through it.

Now, next to the fire, he gently spoke Ishia's name. She turned to look at him, half afraid of her own reaction, and half afraid of ridicule. He squatted down beside her and apologized for having embarrassed her.

"I would still like to be your partner if you will allow that. Here, hold out your hands."

She shot a look at Azal, and she nodded back at her. She held out her hand and he carefully placed the stone in her palm. Ishia opened her hand and gasped as the stone glittered in the light of the fire. He told her about the Goddess and what he had seen.

He told her honestly about his feelings prior to their conversation: how he had not initially wanted to get involved with the women in any way. Ishia accepted his gift and agreed to be his partner.

Azal sat herself up and spoke to Taran.

"I know the feeling and fear you have about this place becoming an echo of the old. But that is not what we want. We want to start something new here, a place free of the corruption of the sisters. It is important that you two bond with each other, for we desperately need children for the future. My children will also need companions for their adult life."

She smiled and Taran nodded.

Orcas broke into the conversation.

"Where are Vran and Bregh?"

She looked around. They had not been seen all day. The others shrugged and Azal was relieved that Vran wasn't there. She now felt very uncomfortable to be near him after what had happened. Orcas went to look in his hut. Then she looked in Bregh's hut.

"The huts are empty," said Orcas as she returned to the fire.

They all nodded absently.

"No. You don't understand. They are all empty. There is nothing in them at all. Everything has been taken."

Three days went by and the missing two were still not found. Everyone had searched and called and they eventually found certain items that had been taken from the other huts, things necessary for survival in the wild. During the gathering around the evening fire to discuss the matter, Orcas stood before Ishia.

"I know of a way to find them but I'm not old enough to do it. It is not of my element, and I do not yet have the strength. But Taran does, and he is of the air. He is a child of the wind."

Taran raised his head in surprise.

"What are you saying? I am not of Air. I was born in the temple, like Azal."

Orcas raised her hand to him.

"Yes, you were born in the temple, but the friends placed a seed in your mother—a seed of the air. You are the result."

For a moment Taran pondered this mystery. Then he asked:

"What is it that I can do that you cannot?"

"Fly," replied Orcas.

He looked at her as if she were mad.

"No, you do not understand. You can fly in your inner vision and search from the air. Try it."

Taran shook his head in confusion.

"But I don't know how."

Orcas gestured to him. "Come here and sit next to me. I will try to help you."

The others settled down to be quiet and Orcas placed a hand on his shoulder.

"Now close your eyes."

Taran closed his eyes and felt the hot little hand on his shoulder. He turned inward to his inner vision. And in his inner vision, he stood up out of his body and walked around the camp. He felt Orcas alongside him and heard her whisper into his ear.

"Just fly, Taran! Just fly! Open your heart and your soul and reach out for the stars."

He did as she instructed and found himself lifting off the ground like a bird. Taran flew over the camp and found himself looking down on the assembly below. He circled and then flew off over the forest, screeching and looking this way and that. He flew deeper and deeper over the forest until he could see smoke in the distance. Just before the hills he could see a clearing. He flew towards it and looked down to see what was there. He saw a fire and saw Vran and Bregh sitting together next to it. He sang to her while he combed and oiled her hair, and she laughed and smiled.

Vran heard the bird screech above and looked up.

"Look, Bregh! The king of the skies. Hail, king of the skies!"

Bregh giggled again.

He went back to combing her hair. The others drifted into his mind, but he tried to push them back out. They would start their own village without people who can read your mind and women who give birth to too many children at once. It was obscene. Bregh was different. She worshipped him and cared for him, and he would give her many babies—one at a time. They had no need of strange goddesses that walk out of water. He had finished with that the day he had left the temple. Now he would lead a good and honest life with his woman and children.

Taran took in the scene below and immediately understood what was happening. He returned to the camp and settled back into himself. He told the others of what he had seen and sensed. Ishia was relieved that they were safe, and Azal was relieved they had gone.

That night Azal had a terrible dream. She dreamed of the vials and of strange creatures emerging out of the sea and land. They warred and killed each other, feeding off each other's flesh. She saw them grow and change as the shape of the land grew and changed, and wherever they went, a dark cloud followed them. The dark cloud would rain its droplets down on the creatures and some would die from its touch. She saw horrible men with faces that showed their ignorance and degeneracy. She watched hands reach out from the clouds and refashion the faces until they no longer reflected what was in their souls. They looked like children of the elements, but they were not. They were empty shells filled with...

Azal cried out in the dream. They were filled with souls created by the sisters! The empty people had control of all the creatures and the land, and they worshipped the sisters as their gods.

She woke up, sobbing aloud, and Taran, thinking she was in danger, rushed into her hut. He found her sobbing and the babies crying. He knelt beside her as Ishia rushed in to see what was wrong. He gently stroked her hair and whispered to her like a child. Once the sobbing had subsided, she told Taran and Ishia of the dream. Ishia did not understand it, but Taran put his head in his hands and groaned. Azal and Ishia looked at each other.

"Do you know what it means?" asked Azal.

Taran nodded. He sat back on his heels and told her about a collection of vials he had carried. He had been instructed by the priesteshood to empty them over the land and sea at the end of his journey. When he saw land, he had emptied his vials over the sea. He emptied two over the land. Vran had done the same. He too had carried vials. Azal waited for him to finish and then told him of the vials she had carried and how the seer had destroyed them.

Taran turned the dream over and over in his mind. The women told him of the story of creation that the seer had told in the village, and how a lot of the story made sense. He nodded sadly as he realized he had really been a pawn of the sisters when he believed he was finally escaping from them— free at last from their degenerate minds.

He tried to piece together as much of the picture as he could, to make sense of the wider story. Azal fed and snuggled the babies until they fell asleep, while Taran thought and Ishia sat trying to work out what was going on. When it was all quiet, Taran spoke.

"I think I've got a picture of what is happening, has happened and will happen. The sisters created a race, right?"

The two women nodded.

"And they also prepared a new race of many different creatures. They would war with each other and eat one another. Because the new race of servers would be as ugly as their souls are untrue, the sisters would adjust them to look like us. The creatures and the people would change and develop over time as the land changes. They would breed and die, breed and die. They would govern all lands and give power to the sisters for generation after generation until they, the sisters, would be as Gods. If this is the new world of which we have been told, I want no part of it. I will walk into the sea now."

He got up to go but spun around as he heard Orcas' voice. No one had heard her come in nor seen her squatting in the corner as she listened.

"Taran! Although what you have said is true, there is still something missing in your story. I am of the ocean. The ocean gives and withdraws life, and she governs time by the turning of her waters. In her there is no time. When I swim within her, I see. I see what you have spoken of and what you, Azal, dreamt about, but I also saw other things. I saw the children of the elements grow and multiply. I saw the ocean also give birth to creatures who would redress the balance. I saw the children of the elements carrying the flame for the true Gods and Goddesses and for the elements. I saw them carrying a thread through time so that when the abominations of the sisters fade and die, the children of the elements will rebuild and be fruitful on the land. They will only eat plants. They will sing to the flowers. They will rejoice in the wind, the sun, the earth below their feet and the sea as she lies before them. They will act as a bridge through time. They will carry the inner flame or the void through life and death until the creations of the sisters have finally wiped themselves out.

"Then the children of the elements can live out the pattern of existence until the universe is once again in balance. Then they will return to the four directions. But remember: the future in time has many paths that it can take. Your actions determine which path will open and which path will close. How you and your descendants live determines the future of us all."

Orcas fell silent.

"Orcas, how can you know all of time and yet still bear to live?"

Taran's voice was tender and carried with it his understanding of the suffering she must endure to stay in this life with them.

"I am a part of the ocean. And the ocean is simply here for you to sail on. I hold out my hands to you for only a short time. When what the sisters were planning became known, the elements responded in many ways. I was one. I will seed a future line but will not take this form again. I may take other forms to reach out and support other beings. But I am tired. I must leave." She got up abruptly and left the assembled company.

"She is progressing too fast. She has grown from child to elder in a few turns of the moon. She will soon die."

Ishia's voice broke as she tried to stop herself from weeping.

"No, she will not die yet. She still has a child to bear."

Azal repeated the prophecy in a whisper as she tried to comfort Ishia.

While Taran walked back with Ishia to her hut, he tried to think of ways to comfort her. But he was at a loss for words and so remained silent. When they got to the door, she turned to face him. "It is not always good to know the future. We have heard too much from Orcas and the seer. We should just live our lives and allow the elements, the sisters, and the Goddesses to do their work. Our lives are quite hard enough as we try to survive here."

"Taran."

He looked up at her and saw how her face had relaxed.

"Taran," she whispered, "give me a child."

⚜

THE SISTERS SURVEYED their handiwork over the surface of the planet.

In two areas, the seeds had taken and new worlds would grow from them. But all was not well in their domain. In the inner realms the sisters could see the future as well as the past, and not all of the sisters liked what they saw. The mountain sisters within the earth refused to cooperate with those in the inner world, and this severed a long tradition of cooperation between the sisterhoods.

Since the other sisters would not support them, they were now trapped for all time in the center of the earth. So long as the land existed, they would be there. And so they conversed with the Ocean, who took pity on them and helped them build a well of stars that went from the center of the earth down to the surface and then out into the stars—so that they could at least see out of their dark world. In return, they agreed to help the new friends of the Ocean fall from the stars through their well and into the world. The ocean was happy with this arrangement and together they formed a bond.

The sisters in the inner realms tried to maintain their power over the first creations of the elements: the beings of fire, ocean, land, and wind. But they did not succeed. The angels and the faeries came together within the void to decide what should be done. The angels decided that they would work with the sisters in false service so that they could undo some of the damage that the sisters had caused through their greed and arrogance. As long as the sisters interfered with life, the angels would work to modify the damage, and this would give hope to the future and guard the world against destructive power. The faeries, however, refused even to contemplate communication with the sisters. They spat in the face of these abominations and swore to uphold the purity of the elements. They committed themselves to guiding and protecting only the creations of the elements.

And so, the angels stayed in the inner realms with the sisters, watching and waiting for the times of great importance upon the earth, where they would have to pass into the outer world to redress imbalance or herald the threshold of a new time. The faeries chose to fall into the underworld, where they would reside in the body of the mother and be of service to the forests and the waters, the children of the elements and the creatures. They traveled across the face of the ocean to prepare a garden to rival all others: a place where all the creatures of the elements could reside together in harmony. On a day in the future, they would call upon the children of the friends to come and join them in the garden called Paradise. But, in the meantime, they had to wait.

8

Azal sat on the platform that was suspended over the hot springs and breathed in the steam. Her mind slowly became calm and balanced, free from all worry and pain. She readied herself for the task which she knew she must face. She called on the inner company of priests and priestesses, the angelic beings of the void, the faery beings of the elements, the creatures of the sea, and finally the dark Goddess of the ocean and fire to be with Orcas during her ordeal. She then rose and walked slowly to the hut which was now set aside exclusively for giving birth. As she walked, she looked around her. Much had been achieved in the five short years during which they had been here. The temple over the springs was now complete. The four huts in the directions and the center sanctuary hut with the steam well stood proudly in the morning mist. The wood carvings which were dotted around the building made it look like some strange creature rising out of the steam.

She looked at the small village which they had built. The three children of Ishia and Taran toddled in and out of the huts in play while Ishia struggled to keep Orcas alive long enough to deliver Fynn's child. It saddened Azal to know that Orcas would never grow old enough to see her child dancing around the huts or see the temple grow and flourish.

Everyone knew that Orcas was about to die. She had told everyone as soon as she became pregnant. Now everyone had gathered to say goodbye to their beloved child of the sea.

As she entered the hut Azal saw Orcas arching her body against the waves of pain that assaulted her. Ishia was wiping Orcas' face and giving her bitter herbs to fend off the pain. Ishia's own baby slumbered in a basket in the corner while she worked. Azal bit her lip and moved forward to be alongside this precious young woman. Fynn sat at Orcas' head. Tears streamed down his face, which was haggard with pain and distress.

"I don't want to lose her, Azal, I love her so much. Please, is there anything. . .?"

Azal shook her head. Such was the destiny of this woman, a destiny so profound that nothing could interfere with it. Orcas started to moan and squat. Ishia readied herself for the baby and Fynn stroked her hair with the lightest of touches, whispering of his love for her. She moaned deeply as the head of the child presented and panted as she allowed the child to rotate before slipping out. As the child left her body, Orcas fell back in exhaustion, her eyes fixed on Fynn in love and pain.

Azal worked with the inner beings to sever the inner ties with the mother and to support Orcas' soul while she readied herself for death. The child, a baby girl, was placed at Orcas' breast. She propped herself up and looked deeply into the child's face as she fed her. The child suckled healthily, and Orcas whispered into her ear.

"Remember me, child of the ocean. Remember who you are. And when you are in distress, call across the sea and the ocean will be there for you. Goodbye, my little one, my love, child of my dreams and sister of the moon. I will always love you, whatever you are and wherever you may be. Carry my line, protector of the creatures and the sea."

Then Orcas grimaced as pain enveloped her.

The placenta had not come out and her body contracted in vain to expel that which no longer belonged there. She began to bleed heavily and Fynn began to cry as he held the baby. Ishia tried to help Orcas, but she had by now journeyed too far towards the threshold of death. She would now be in Azal's hands. Azal guided her soul over the threshold and as she stepped into the void with Orcas, the Dark Goddess was waiting to absorb the child of the ocean into herself. Azal greeted the Goddess and stepped back to allow Orcas to move forward. Orcas stood before the Goddess in worship. The Goddess started to whip her hair over her head until the hair shot out, wrapped itself around Orcas and pulled her into the Goddess. Thus was Orcas absorbed into the Divine Feminine, leaving Azal standing in awe and wonder before the Goddess.

⚬

"AZAL, *child of the friends, you will be the teacher and guide of the child. You will name the child Afari, and she will mate with your son. She will become mother to my chosen people, the people of the hot lands. Guard her well, Azal and hide her from the sisters.*"

Azal was about to ask the Goddess how she should hide her when the Goddess vanished, and she found herself out in the void.

She awoke to find Fynn wiping her face with a damp cloth. She sat up in surprise.

"Why am I on the floor?"

She looked around in confusion. Ishia was washing Orcas' body while Taran resumed his walking up and down the hut and humming to the baby.

"You cried out and fell to the floor. You frightened us."

Fynn spoke softly to Azal as he wiped her face.

"What happened? Is she all right? Can I reach her?"

Fynn's pain grew stronger and stronger as he pushed against what was going to be the answer. Azal reached out to stroke his face. So young to suffer such pain. So young to be left behind.

"Yes, she is well. She has gone to the Goddess and will not return. But you will not be able to reach her. "

Taran nodded in agreement. He had long since understood that Orcas' soul was of the quality that does not need a cycle of birth and death. She had been here to serve and teach and now she had returned to where she truly belonged.

Azal hesitated to tell them the rest of the story. Taran picked up the thought and asked her inwardly if she should keep such vital information back from the only family that Orcas had known. Azal looked across at Taran. Yes, she nodded to him, your priestly powers work well, and you are right. I should not withhold this information. She looked at the others and took a deep breath.

"There is something else. The Goddess named the child. She is to be called Afari, and she must be betrothed to Parsa, my son. Together they will be the parents of the line that the Goddess calls her chosen people."

They had all quarreled about how to deal with Orcas' body. Fynn wanted her body given back to the sea. Taran wanted the body to be cremated for cleansing purposes, but Azal had a strong intuition that she should be buried near the entrance post to the temple. She won the argument by the sheer force of her will and the small party of people and children gathered around to say a final farewell to the shell that had carried their beloved friend in life. The burial pit had been dug near the entrance to the temple compound. The trees that acted as gateposts had intricately carved heads attached to them, and these heads stared down on the activity below. Through the posts, the mist and steam swirled around the temple stilts—creating the illusion of a large spider rising out of the steam from the hot springs.

In the pit, Ishia laid a bed of her finest weaving and surrounded it with Orcas' favorite possessions. As they laid the body on the bed, Azal jumped down into the pit with Orcas and braided Orcas' hair into the roots of the trees that acted as the temple gateposts. Ishia called to Azal and threw down something she wanted to give to Orcas. Azal caught the object and when she looked at what she had caught, she saw the crystal with threads of gold running through it that Taran had given to Ishia. She smiled as she placed the beautiful gift of the earth into Orcas' hands and closed her fingers around it. She kissed the young girl's head and withdrew as Fynn motioned that he too wanted to go down to say his last good-bye.

He jumped down into the pit and squatted beside Orcas' body. He began to sing a song of the ocean, a song about how the ocean gave birth to life. He then sang of his love for her, and the vibration of his voice and his love traveled through the worlds, reaching out to the stars and down into the depths of the ocean. Somewhere, deep in the depths of the sea, a young woman smiled as she drifted with the tide. Fynn climbed out, sobbing for his love, and as he was handed the child, he held her up to his face and breathed in the scent of babies. The child lay quietly, unruffled by the grief that surrounded her. Fynn's tears dripped onto Afari's face. The child licked the saltwater, the tears of the ocean, and she smiled.

Azal raised her arms in invocation, calling on the four elements to acknowledge the passing of their child and friend. She then went down to the ocean's edge and gave thanks to the ocean for allowing such a gift as Orcas to have been in their lives and for the richness she had given them.

Ishia carried the baby of Orcas beside her own baby of three months. They would feed together and sleep together as twins. Ishia's baby would comfort Orcas' child for the loss that the baby must feel at a very deep level. After many months of being curled in the loving warmth of Orcas' womb, listening every day to her mother's voice and slumbering to her mother's heartbeat, the baby must surely feel the loss. The naked children darted about, the younger ones falling over as they tried to keep up with Parsa and Isca. The assembled adults, having completed the final ritual of Orcas' passing, sat down in the hot sun to watch the children frolic and play.

Only Fynn could not bear to look life in the face after such a loss. He walked through the temple posts and through the forest of stilts that held up the circular buildings of the temple. He walked to the center where the hot springs bubbled out of the earth and the steam hid him from prying eyes. He sat down and wept until no more sound or movement could flow from him. Then he became still and allowed the power of the springs to flow over him. His vision blurred and he fought to focus his eyes. Then, through the steam, he saw a beach that was not anywhere he knew.

He saw a woman. The woman was not Orcas but looked like Orcas —with her black skin and warlike hair. She was talking to a group of assembled people and spoke with authority. He realized that he was seeing into the future and that this girl was his descendant, a child from the line of Afari. It came as cold comfort to him that something of Orcas survived into the future. He wanted her here, today, now. He rose and left, passing through the gateposts to pause at Orcas' burial place at the edge of the entrance. He didn't feel the light touch on his shoulder, nor did he see his impish lover perched on a rock that lay near the left post, at the head of her burial plot. She watched him walk back to the village and saw how he avoided the gathering that was happening and the children playing. She whispered a poem of love to him that he never heard and blew the touch of her body upon the wind that swirled around him. But he never felt it.

Ishia watched in amusement as Isca tried to teach Tarish, Taran's younger son, how to stand on his head. Each time he tried and fell over, Isca would dissolve into giggles. The female child of Ishia and Taran, Seti, who by now was only two turns of the seasons old, decided that she would be able to perform this trick. She toddled in front of Tarish and put her head to the floor. There you see... simple! She stood up again, waiting for her adoring audience to love her. Everyone screamed with laughter at the little imp. Abrim, Taran's eldest son of four seasonal turns, stood aloof from such a childish display.

Isca had snuggled up alongside Ishia to watch the babies feed and to drink in the glorious smell of mother's milk. It held wonderful memories that she was not quite ready to let go of. She placed her hand on Ishia's breast and put her thumb in her mouth. Her spare finger, which was attached at the thumb, went up her nose.

"Take your thumb out of your nose, daughter," Azal called out absently. She had got the comment down to an automatic reflex every time she saw her daughter with her finger stuck up her nose.

She was thinking about how Orcas would be rolling around on the floor with the little ones, giggling louder than all the others put together, if she had been there. Parsa could feel his mother thinking sad thoughts and he sidled up to comfort her. Lately he had had many dreams about a large creature with four legs, a bushy mane of hair surrounding its face, and a mouth full of ferocious teeth. The creature had told Parsa that he guarded Parsa's mother, Azal. But Parsa himself was strong and fierce. He didn't need strange creatures taking over his job.

Azal was Parsa's whole world, and he worshipped her. He was the oldest of all the children and was also the man of the house. Azal was his to guard. At the tender age of five turns, Parsa felt that all this standing-on-one's-head nonsense was quite beneath him. Running around was fine, but he drew the line at headstands.

He stroked his mother's long hair and touched her breast in worship. She smiled down at him and saw Belin looking back at her through his child. Her heart contracted in pain.

"It's all right, mother. I know you miss Orcas but that's how it has to be. I will take your pain away. " She smiled at her valiant son and ruffled his hair.

"I was thinking how much you look like your father and how much I miss him. I grieved for Orcas for a long time before she died. We were ready to part, and I have let her go within me. But your father was taken from me suddenly. I couldn't even say good-bye. That is what hurt me so much."

That night Azal dreamed of Belin. She found herself walking along the banks of a river that flowed through a desert. In the distance she could see a bridge with many people lined up to cross. Some were refusing to step onto the bridge. She watched them from a distance and jumped when she felt a hand on her shoulder. She turned around to find Belin behind her, his face blazing with light and his eyes shining with love for her. He traced his finger over her face and down her neck, pausing to kiss her shoulder. She dared not move lest he disappear. And so she stood very still, the tears dripping from her chin. Her tears woke her up. As she opened her eyes, she saw the ceiling of the hut and cried out in pain.

She was still crying when Taran came to the door of the hut to see if she was in danger. He could see the faint outline of her body as it shook from the sobbing. He crept into the hut and knelt beside her. He stroked her hair and whispered to her as she sobbed, feeling the pain and the loss flow through the woman. He nodded to himself when he realized that she wept for her lost mate, Belin, and not Orcas. He kissed her lightly on the forehead and crept quietly out into the night.

᠅

AZAL WAS WALKING BACK DOWN to the temple for what seemed like the fiftieth time when she stopped at Orcas' grave. Although Orcas had died only five months before, it seemed like only yesterday. Something made her look at the grave. Plants had grown over the grave within weeks, but now something else seemed to be coming out of the plants. She looked more closely and realized that it was a part of the plant. It was a cluster of tiny bright blue flowers that had formed into what looked like a little face. As she bent down, she smelt a faint and wonderful smell. She sat back in amazement. These were the special flowers that grew by the sacred spring. But they grew in no other place. What were they doing here? She was about to reach out and touch them when a voice within her stopped her. She tried to reach out to it a second time and the face of the Goddess appeared in her mind.

You may eat of the herb and the root, the leaf, and the fruit, but do not touch the flowers, for they are the emotions of the world. These gifts are the beginning of the new world. They seed just as you, Azal, seed. They seed like the animals which I will send as seed, and they will outshine the abominations planted by the sisters. I have scattered the seeds of the flowers to the four winds, and they will take root in every corner of the earth. Protect them, Azal, child of the four friends, protect and live alongside them, for together you will live in Paradise. And when you die, be buried in the rich soil; I will then preserve your body so that you will walk the garden I make in your honor, and you will teach and guide in the temple.

✨ 9 ✨

Many, many years later...

The child giggled and squealed as she watched birds performing in the trees. The birds, which had a large wing-span, curved beaks and sharp claws, swooped and dived among the trees, putting on a fine performance for the children. The little tree dwellers, the creatures of fur who stole the village food, chattered in anger at the birds as they disturbed their afternoon slumber. The child threw a piece of bread in appreciation to the birds and clapped her hands. She realized that she had already been too long in the forest, for the sun would soon be making love to the ocean and then it would be dark.

She got up and ran as fast as she could through the forest and out into the clearing. She arrived back at her village just in time to gather with the others to watch the sunset. All the villagers, the priests and priestesses and the children, sat to watch as the sun kissed the ocean and then slowly vanished as the night stretched her wings to cover the world in darkness. The child looked up at the trees and smiled as she saw how all the birds also sat silently in the trees to watch the sunset. The old priest got up and held his hands out to the sky.

"O great Belin, Lord of the sun, God of fire, you who bring warmth to our land, we thank you for our day of warmth. O wondrous Azal, Goddess of the four directions, we praise you as you lie in wait for the sun to join you in the darkness. We plead with you to release him at the end of the night so that he may light the world once again."

All the villagers mumbled in agreement, for should the great Goddess Azal decide to keep her lover with her, then the world would surely die from darkness and from cold.

And now it was story time. The child clapped her hands with glee, for there would be a special story tonight. And tonight was the night when she would finally be named. She had waited all her short life for this day, the day when she would be old enough to be called by her own name—instead of just being "child" to everybody. Tonight, she would hear the story of her line and her name, and she would finally know who she was.

All the children in the village were raised by all the women. Most children did not even know who their real mother was. But I do, thought the child as she twisted her tight black curly hair. Not many look as I do. Not many have a skin as beautiful as mine that shines like a dark sun. Not many have my white teeth that glint like the foam of the ocean in the sunlight. She dashed off to the storytelling that was scheduled to take place next to the sacred spring tonight.

Because a naming ceremony is the most important of all ceremonies, it must be held by the temple. She ran toward the fires. As she arrived at the threshold of the temple entrance, she paused to touch the tall stone that stood erect there. It was a sacred stone to mark the resting place of her first ancestor—or so she liked to think.

Everyone else, including the priests, had scolded her for her grand claims.

"It's just a stone to mark the threshold of the temple grounds."

This pompous priest told her this every time he had seen her touch the stone in reverence. But she knew the truth. Ever since she could remember, she had paused there to greet the beautiful woman who sat on the rock looking out over the ocean. One day she had plucked up the courage to ask her who she was.

"I am your mother," the woman had answered.

The child had been confused by this answer and the beautiful woman had laughed and shook her head.

"No, child, not in that way. I was the first mother of your line. I am your first ancestor, the child of the ocean."

Now, as she was going to her storytelling and naming, she invited the lady to join her.

"Alas child, I cannot do that. I cannot leave this rock. Only part of me is here—that part that can speak to you. The other parts of me are within the belly of the Goddess. And so I must stay here."

The child didn't understand what this meant, but she shrugged. She had to go and so she waved a good-bye to the lady on the rock and skipped into the storytelling circle. Everyone started whooping and clapping. She blushed deeply and took her place at the foot of the storyteller.

The old teller waited until all were silent and then he cleared his throat.

"And so it began. God the father and God the mother decided to have children and so they had many. Soon they had so many children that the noise became unbearable. Then God the mother said, 'Let us make a place where our children can grow without disturbing our sleep.'

"God the father nodded in agreement. They made a land and put water on it. Then they filled it with plants and creatures. Then they put the best of their children in this garden and asked them to tend it. There was Azal, Goddess of the four directions; Belin, the God of the sun; Ishia, Goddess of birth and death; Vran, God of journeys; Bregh, Goddess of metals; Fynn, God of stones, and Orcas, Goddess of the ocean. Then came the children of the Gods and Goddesses. They were: Parsa, God of the sacred fire; Isca, Goddess of children; Abrim, God of sacrifice, and Eve, Goddess of the trees. Finally came Afari, Goddess of the creatures and flowers. And all the children lived together in the garden where they played and sang. The Gods were happy. All this continued until one day, when the God of mystery—he who is many and yet one, he who is a sisterhood and yet a God, the ultimate mystery—became jealous and angry.

"He commanded Vran and Bregh to leave for the hills to start a new tribe whom he would protect. He sent large storms to drown the other children, but the Goddess Orcas calmed the storms with her words. He brought the sun so close to the earth that it burnt and scorched the land, but the God Belin smiled and removed the sun back to its proper place. Then he sent too many children so that the women would die, but the Goddess Ishia gave birth to all of them herself and bore the pain so that the children might live. And so finally he sent monsters and demons, creatures so large that the earth shook as their feet touched the ground. People fled in fear until little Afari whispered to the creatures and they agreed to stay away from the garden.

"Thus they all lived in harmony, until one day they realized that this land was not big enough for all of their children. They then decided to go back to the world of the Gods and leave the garden for their children. And the children grew and prospered. They built a temple in honor of the Gods and Goddesses, and in return, the Gods and Goddesses made a pact that they would always be accessible through the temple to teach and guide their children.

Now in those days women were made pregnant by the river. On each full of the moon, any woman who wanted a child would bathe under the waterfall. Then the water would give her a child in her belly.

"One day Afari decided that she wanted a child. She went down to the waterfall and sat beneath the falling water. She called out to the river to make love to her and give her a child. The river did as she asked. She gave birth to a child whose line gave birth to a long line of women and they in turn gave birth to this child's mother. This child's mother went to the same river and stood beneath the waterfall and called out: 'Give me a child of the water. Give me the fruit of your lips. Give me a woman who will carry my thoughts into the future so that I will live forever.' The river smiled and gave her a child. And today that child is here to be named."

The old man stood up and held his arms to the sky.

"I call upon the winds and ocean, the moon and the flames of the fire, and I call upon the earth below my feet to choose a name for this child."

HE FELL SILENT. This was the oldest ritual that anyone knew. He listened with his inner hearing for the name.

Azal smiled as she watched the fire and listened to the stories. She smiled at the innocence of the people gathered and took joy from the faces in the crowd that showed her mark and that of her beloved Belin, *for whosoever of your kin survives shall be marked with an inner mark on their foreheads, which may be seen by those who have the gift of vision.*

She looked at the child who was to be named and saw Orcas' mark on her head. She saw the suppressed giggles of Afari and the beauty of Fynn. She thought how the new child was truly the bearer of the best gifts that she could have been given. *She also has a beauty and strength that surpasses all others and so her name should reflect this.* She went up to the old priest and looked at him. She shook her head in despair at his ignorance. He couldn't see her. The child had more natural sight than this trained priest had. Azal had been aware that the child could see her and was watching her. She put her lips next to the priest's ear and spoke.

"This child is beloved of the Goddess. Treat her well and raise her by the springs. She has an inner beauty that surpasses all others, and her name will reflect her beauty. She shall be known as Nubia—which means 'She who dazzles with her beauty.'"

The priest was startled by the clarity of the message. In many of the ceremonies, he had heard nothing, but tonight the contact was very clear. Nubia. What an unusual name. He approached the child who was looking past him, and he put his hand on her head.

"In the name of the great Goddess I name thee Nubia—which means 'She who dazzles with her beauty.'" `

Then he stood back and looked at her. He certainly thought the name rather strange, as this child was as ugly as could be. Her skin was too dark, and her hair was like a wild forest. The girl smiled past him and then remembered to look at the ignorant priest.

She then turned to the assembled company, who signified by their clapping and cheering that they accepted this girl into the company of adults. The old priest stepped forward and raised his hands for silence.

"Now we must find her a husband, for her blood arrived at the last quarter of the moon."

The girl recoiled inwardly but fought not to show it. Azal, who was observing the proceedings, became angry. These people are in the presence of a child who is the only one at present capable of learning the mysteries and they want to give her in marriage. All of my blood and the blood of my companions has slept for so many generations, and now they want to bury this one. No, I will not allow it.

She raised her arms in power and called to the Goddess of the springs. She called from deep within her, sending a vibration out through the void and deep into herself. The Goddess heard the call of her devoted servant and appeared before Azal. Azal bowed deeply and told the Goddess of her dilemma. Azal had been charged on her death to remain as an inner contact for the new people rather than go back into the life cycle. She had agreed to serve a length of earth time, but her work had been barren since the last priestess with power had died. Now there was no one who had any real ability except this child. And because she could not reach the priest, she was afraid of what might happen to the child.

The Goddess agreed to help. She turned to face the assembled company, who were oblivious to her presence—all except the child Nubia, who gazed at the scene in fear and wonder.

Azal stood behind the Goddess. When she was ordered to do so, she walked through and into the Goddess and used the power of the Goddess to project the human shape she had had before she died. Immediately she became visible to the crowd, all of whom cowered on their knees in fear, all except Nubia, who bowed deeply in love and respect. The priest started chanting and singing to herald the arrival of the great Goddess Azal. He coughed and spluttered as he chanted, fighting at times for his breath. She turned with weary despair to look at this ill and empty man.

"Be silent, priest! Stop that wailing! It assaults my ears and the ears of the Gods. Hear me well, people of the garden. This child who stands before you is my very own child, Nubia. She, Nubia, a child of the Gods, shall be your priestess. Train her in everything you know and give her free access to the sanctuary, for she shall serve me all the days of her life."

Azal looked over the crowd. She used the vision of the Goddess whom she had entered to see why the couples had yielded such ineffective, useless priests and priestesses, who had no inner sight and were unable to access the inner worlds. She looked into the face of each one of them and saw their intricate patterns of blood lines and dormant skills.

Then she realized. Of course! They had been paired off with the wrong partners and so the information that was stored inside them had not been triggered. She looked again at the various people and smiled.

"Bring all the people who are not paired but are of an age to bear children here to me."

She looked over the handful of young adults who had not yet been paired. She saw the mark of her own blood and that of Belin, Taran, Orcas and Vran on the heads of some of the people before her. Some had diluted their bloodlines so much that the marks were fading, and they would soon be useless. She picked out three couples—rejecting those with faded marks and those with Vran's blood. Vran had tainted his gifts by developing a tribe in the forest that lived off blood and death. They used metal taken from the earth to kill and had joined their power with that of the sisters.

The three couples stood before her.

"You shall be paired together, and your children will be called sacred. They will be priests and priestess of the future. Guard them well and give your children to Nubia to train when they reach the age of twelve winters."

She stepped back from the Goddess and reeled with the strain of such a blending. She vanished into the void to regenerate and left the Goddess to guard the assembled people. None of them could see the true Goddess, for to see her, one must have eyes within, and to see her is to destroy within you that which no longer belongs there. The people could not do this, for they clung to that which they did not need, and they feared everything they did not know.

It was not so with Nubia, who was of the line of Afari and the child of Orcas. Nubia looked at her and held back nothing. She gazed on the face of the great Goddess with profound love and the Goddess smiled back. The people could see that Nubia was communing with someone, but they could not see who. The Goddess asked Nubia to follow her, and she did so. They walked into the forest and past the springs, walking in the light of the Goddess, and emerged into a small clearing, where the Goddess stopped.

Should you need me, little one, this will be our special place. Dig with your hands, Nubia, child of the ocean. Dig! Nubia began to dig with her hands but found nothing. She dug down until she was up to her knees in dirt, but still there was nothing. She stood up in confusion and she looked at the Goddess smiling at her. She looked back to the hole she had dug, and it was starting to fill with muddy water.

Tell no one of this spring for it is truly my blood and should only be used wisely This shall be your secret and you will guard it with your life. One day you will gather some of this water and take it to a new world to sprinkle over the land. Tend this water as you would tend your child.

Nubia looked back down at the water which had filled the hole and was now spilling out over the land. She looked up again and the Goddess had gone, leaving her alone in the dark forest. She became afraid that she might fall in the dark and so she curled up in the clearing and went to sleep.

That night she drifted into the realm of frightening dreams. She saw a group of Goddesses who were evil and who were trying to destroy the garden. They laughed at everything she tried to do to defend her people. They had a garden too, one that was full of creatures that ate each other and people who ate the creatures and drank blood. They wanted Nubia's garden to fail and theirs to flourish. They tried to reach out to touch and destroy the people within the garden, but they couldn't quite reach far enough. She was about to call upon the help of the Goddess Azal when she saw yet another garden far off across the land and sea, in the direction of sunset, to the point where the west and the east meet and hold hands. This garden was worse than the first one in the dream. It was bigger and had more people. The people practiced terrible magic on each other and ate each other. They looked strange and ugly. Nubia was so terrified that she felt unable to breath. She woke up suddenly and realized that it was only a dream. But deep down inside her, something told her that what she had seen was true.

It was dawn. She got up and was amazed to see how the spring had grown up overnight. It's water flowed red and she remembered the words of the Goddess, "This is truly my blood." She vowed that she would tend the water that flowed off into the forest. She bathed her face in the water and then drank some. She sat and felt its power awaken her body. After reciting a prayer over the water, she set off to find her way back home.

Everything seemed so bright and colorful as she walked through the forest. Now she could see things that she hadn't noticed before and she could see the life force flowing in and around the plants, the trees and birds. Their colors danced in her vision, and she could feel their thoughts as she passed by them. But the flowers were special. Now she understood why one must never pick a flower. The color and energy that flowed from the flowers reached out and touched everything around them. She could feel the flowers touch her, caressing her, making her feel happy and calm. They were truly special. The flowers in turn could feel her respect and awe and so they opened especially for her. As she walked past, they opened their inner selves to her and beings of immense beauty rose out of the flowers to greet and bless her. Their bodies were patterns of joy and hope, love and happiness, heartbreak, and pain. They smiled at some deep sleeping part of her soul, energizing, and strengthening her.

The whole village had turned out to escort her to her new home within the temple compound. She felt embarrassed and really just wanted to get on with it but the villagers insisted that the transfer be done with as much ceremony as possible. Horns were sounded, children danced and sang, and the old priest waited for her at the threshold of the temple. He tried to speak, but every time he opened his mouth, the fresh, biting air made him cough. He held out her robe of priestesshood to her with one hand, and, with the other, he held out the pouch of herbs that only a priest or priestess may carry. The girls who were escorting her to the temple stopped at the gate posts. The crowd drew back and waited while the priest droned on and on in a language that no one could understand, pausing only occasionally to cough.

He sprinkled Nubia with water and motioned for her to take off her body cloth. Nothing of the old life could be carried over into the new. She dropped the cloth and her dark skin glistened in the sunlight. She reached her arms to the sky in worship and then bent to touch the ground on the threshold of the temple. The priest came forward, spat out the blood that had risen in his throat and robed her in her blue robe. Then he handed her the pouch. The crowds clapped while Nubia, desperate to get away from the ceremony, walked through the gate area as quickly as she dared.

When she was finally alone, she decided to explore the temple. It was occupied only by the old priest and his helper. In the old days there would have been five priests or priestesses, but it had been hard recently to find people who were willing to make a commitment of their whole life to such a vocation. She really couldn't understand why that should be so. Surely working with the powers and communing with the Goddess is the most exciting thing a person can do.

She wandered up and down the walkways that linked the small circular temple buildings. It had been torn down and rebuilt many times in the past and it now looked as if it should be torn down again. The wood was rotten from years of steam rising from the spring, and the whole building smelt of old men.

She found her way to the central hall that was suspended over the hot springs. A well cut in the center of the room allowed the steam to rise into the hall—giving it an eerie and mysterious atmosphere. In each direction was a simple wooden altar and on each altar was nothing but one wax candle. She processed around the room and lit each candle.

Each direction glowed in the steam. Then she went to each direction and put her hands on the altar and shut her eyes. She felt herself instinctively reach out beyond the threshold of her world and into that of another.

As she reached out in the south, she felt a contact reaching out to her. She focused her mind until she heard the voice of Azal.

"Relax! Don't concentrate! Let me flow into your mind."

She relaxed. Immediately she felt a light touch on her hand. She opened her eyes and looked up to see a handsome young man with a face that glowed like the sun. He smiled at her, and she shook with fear. His eyes laughed in a kindly way at her fear, and he reached out to touch her again.

"I am Parsa, lover of Afari. I am your father. Hail to you, child of Orcas, child of my love!"

He looked deeply into her eyes and his face grew serious.

"There is a terrible danger ahead. The tribe of Vran has been driven by the sisters to attack your village and kill you. You are a threat to them and the sisters. Gather the couples who were matched by the Goddess and bring them to this room. Tell no one else of what you have heard. Go quickly, Nubia, child of Orcas."

Nubia panicked. What of all the other villagers? What of all the children? She ran out of the room, leaving the candles burning. She raced out of the compound gates and down to the village. The sea glinted in the light of the full moon, but its beauty only compounded the fear and sadness that Nubia felt. In the face of danger, such beauty passed her by.

They had never in the history of the settlement's existence been attacked. Since they had always lived in peace, no one really knew what danger might be. They had all heard tales of how violent the tribe of Vran was, and they had accommodated many refugees from the tribe who had been cast out to die. But they had blended in well over the years and generations, marrying and giving birth to children that had the blood of both tribes. Nubia had often wondered what made Vran's tribe so violent and bloodthirsty, because the people who had settled here with them seemed peaceful enough.

She found the huts of the newly bonded couples and woke them quietly. She commanded them to follow her. She had been afraid that they might ignore her, but the appearance and endorsement of Azal had increased her status considerably. She gathered the couples silently and led them back to the temple. She hadn't told them why they were needed, but only that it had been commanded. When they reached the threshold, the lady of the ocean, Orcas, appeared to Nubia.

"This is a time of change, and you must be the doorway for that change. You must leave here soon and travel over the water. You will be guided and protected. Take heart, for this is the beginning of greatness."

Although Nubia did not understand what was being said to her, she could not stop to question. She bowed in acknowledgment and took the couples into the hall at the center of the temple. "You must stay here tonight," she told them, "and not leave the temple grounds under any circumstances."

They nodded, not daring to ask questions.

Nubia wondered where the old priest was. She had not seen him nor his helper since the ceremony. She wandered around the temple until she found his room. She pulled his entrance cloth to one side and saw him asleep on the bed. She went to wake him. But as she bent over to touch him, she saw the blood that had run from the corner of his mouth onto his headrest. She touched him and his skin was cold. She knelt alongside him and put her hands on his head in blessing. It looked as though he had died in his sleep. There was no sign of the helper and no inner beings had congregated to walk him into death. He had died alone and without help. She lit a candle and silently went into the void, reaching out for a contact who would escort this pathetic soul through the death journey. Afterwards, as she realized that the full weight of responsibility for the temple lay on her shoulders, Nubia began to despair for the future.

Everything was changing too fast, and no one was here to teach or guide her. She was on her own and it frightened her. She began to panic and at first did not hear the tiny voice behind her. She realized she was been addressed and she calmed herself.

You are not alone. I will always be with you. I will teach you and you will be the founder of the greatest and most powerful temple of all time. The learning that will flow through you will go on forever. Be brave, little one, for your enemies have discovered the secret of death and life. They have found the power to shed blood and have tainted the garden. I have prepared a place for you beyond the waves, and I have taken the finest creations of the four friends and placed them there. You, your companions, and your children will be the guardians of this sacred garden. None of the evil influence of the sisters shall taint it. Be brave tonight, little one, and do not let anyone leave the temple. In the morning, you must burn the temple and leave before midday. I will be with you.

She covered the old priest with a cloth and returned to the hall.

The couples were huddled together around the steam well. She stood before them and tried to make herself look as powerful as possible.

"I have just spoken with the Goddess, and she has commanded us not to leave this hall tonight. Nor should we attract attention to where we are. In the morning we will leave this place forever." The couples started to mumble in fear. One raised her hand to speak.

"What of the others in the village? Surely, we should warn them of danger? Can we not bring them here?"

"No," replied Nubia.

"The Goddess has commanded that we and only we should be here tonight. There are powers at work whom we do not understand, and we should not therefore interfere."

One of the men stood up.

"Our families and friends are out there. Can't we help them? It is evil to let them be exposed to this danger. What is the danger anyway? What will happen?"

Nubia shook her head.

"The Goddess told me very clearly that we are not to leave here tonight, and that we are not to warn the others."

Although Nubia was stricken by what was happening, she knew that she should not show her grief to the others. As she thought of her friends, her mother, and her family, and wanted to weep and scream. Instead, she went into each direction and communed with the inner contacts for strength and courage. The couples fell silent as she processed in ritual, not wishing to disturb their new priestess. ·

Suddenly in the distance they all could hear screams and cries. Two of the men rose to leave and, with a voice that came from the other worlds, Nubia commanded them to sit. They sat down and hung their heads in shame. Nubia was in the direction north when she felt something move through her. She turned to the couples and addressed them in the Goddess's voice.

"You are my chosen children. You and you alone can tend the new garden without tainting it. You will be the founders of a new world and I will always be with you. Nubia is my priestess.

"Protect her and honor her. Have courage and strength—for you will need it. Your friends and family will be taken by me. As they die, I will hold them and carry them myself over the threshold of death. Sit now and pray for them."

Nubia fell to her knees as the Goddess left her body. All her energy seemed drained out of her. One of the men gently picked her up and carried her to where the others sat. They tended her, allowing her to rest and recover.

⚶

EVERYONE in the village had been deeply asleep when the tribe of Vran attacked. The men of the tribe of Vran were crazed with anger and hatred. They remembered the stories told to them as children about how the founders of their race, Vran and Bregh, had been cast out of the garden to wander in the wilderness and die. But they had not died. They had survived and went on to establish the most glorious race of the tribe of Vran, beloved of the sisters. The God who is many but one, female and yet not, had treated them kindly and had given them power beyond all others. When the God who is many had finally asked for vengeance, the tribe was more than ready to obey. They had been taught how to use metal and had forged sharp and strong weapons for the day when they would take revenge.

⚶

THE MEN of Vran crept around the huts.

"Kill all!" had been their command.

"Spare none."

The God had spoken to them after many years of silence, and they were now ready to honor that power. They broke into the huts and slaughtered every person they found in the village. After what seemed hours of killing, their leader gathered them and sent out search parties to flush out anyone who could be hiding. They looked all over the village but could find no one. They arrived at the temple compound but were afraid to step over the threshold.

The echo of Orcas sat on the rock beside them and whispered into the leader's ears, "There is no one in the temple."

"There is no one in the temple," shouted the leader.

Orcas' echo whispered again, "We have no need to search this place."

"There is no need to search this place."

"The priest was in a hut with a woman, and he was killed with the rest."

"The priest was in a hut with a woman, and he was killed with the rest," shouted the leader.

The men shouted with relief, for they were superstitious and had no wish to invade the place of Gods. They all nodded in agreement and turned to leave. They gathered themselves together and marched back deep into the forest. Their own settlement was far away. After a couple of hours walking, they decided to pitch camp and take a rest. Dawn was coming up and they needed to rest before continuing their journey.

Nubia felt an inner pull to work in the directions. She commanded the couples to be silent and then went to the altar in the east. She placed her hands on the altar and opened herself to communion with the beings in that direction. While she was deep in meditation, a hand reached out and touched her on the forehead. She looked with her inner vision and saw a man standing before her and smiling.

"I am Taran, Lord of the air. I will be with you in your task. Here is my gift to you."

He leaned over and blew hard into her mouth. Nubia gasped and coughed. She processed to the south. She seemed to reach nothing there. Then she moved to the west. As she approached the west, she saw with her inner vision a sight that amazed her: a young woman who looked just like her. She had never seen any person other than her own mother who looked anything like her.

The woman laughed at her thoughts and then smiled.

"Nubia, child of my own! You and your children will flow out into the world when it is time and will seed greatness. Only beware of those who carry the mark of the sisters for they are truly beings of death and destruction. Use your sight to identify them. Look for the mark of the fish on their heads."

Nubia bowed deeply and then processed to the north. She entered the north and laid her hands on the altar. She closed her eyes and, using her inner sense of touch, reached out for contact.

At first she saw a young man with pain in his eyes. She asked him who he was.

"I am Fynn, lover of Orcas, father of Afari, father of your blood. I search still for my love and will soon come back to your world."

Before she could ask him any more questions, he vanished, and behind him stood the dark Goddess of the springs. Nubia fell to her knees, but the Goddess commanded her to rise.

"Nubia, child of Afari of the line of Orcas. The task you must endure for me is more than any woman should have to endure. I shall give you strength and help. Hold out your arms."

Nubia did as she was commanded. She felt a powerful wave of energy flow through her. It seemed to open her like a door and make her bigger.

"Now you will truly be the mother of all."

Nubia lurched forward as she felt something move into her. Using her inner vision, she saw Azal come out of the direction and step into her, blending with her and joining with her.

"You are now as one being. And yet you remain separate. Together you will build the foundations of the new world. You will increase the line of knowledge and you will give birth to the line of the four directions, the line of the divine."

Nubia tried to reach outside of herself to commune with Azal, but it didn't work. Then Azal talked to Nubia using her mind.

"Child, if you do not wish this to be then I can leave. But if you wish it, we can work together to achieve great things. Talk to me as you would talk to yourself. For as we are now, I am truly part of you. Through my son my blood flows in your veins. My memories and skills are imprinted deep in the pattern of your blood. This allows your body to cope with what is happening. I love you, Nubia, child of my own and of Orcas. I wish to help you."

Although Nubia felt honored that Azal should wish to be with her, she thought that she would find it difficult to get used to having someone within her in this way. The Goddess smiled at her and vanished, leaving Nubia looking at the flame on the altar.

Nubia turned to address the three couples assembled. They were all drowsy and had struggled to keep awake during what had been a long ritual.

"Sleep now, for tomorrow we shall leave on our journey."

They looked at her in horror and alarm.

"What is it? What frightens you? The journey is necessary. But we will be safe."

The people shook their heads. The tallest man stood up.

"It is not the journey we fear. It is you. Your voice is strange."

He faltered and looked down at the floor and wrung his fingers. She urged him to speak further. "It's... it's your voice. It's the voice of two people."

He hung his head in fear of this young girl who stood in front of him, a girl half his size but one who spoke with the voice of a whole army. She smiled at him.

"Don't be afraid," she said. "It is a gift of the Goddess. Now sleep."

❦

NUBIA ROSE JUST BEFORE DAWN, having had little sleep. She felt a sense of urgency around her and woke the others.

"We must pack and leave quickly. Gather your things and meet me by the entrance. Be as quick as possible!"

She left them to gather the belongings they had hurriedly brought last night and ran to the temple stores. She grabbed water holders and honeycombs and dashed down the steps to the spring itself. She stopped abruptly when she saw that the red spring in the forest had snaked its way through the land and was now flowing into and joining with the sacred spring. She bowed reverently and then filled the water holders with the rich mineral water. She struggled back under the weight of the holders, not daring to curse in the presence of holy water.

She staggered through the stilts of the temple to meet them at the gate. When she arrived at the entrance marker stone, she stopped and touched the stone with reverence. One top of the stone was a smaller stone. Its beauty was beyond compare. She picked it up and looked closely at it. It was a crystal with threads of the golden sun shining through it.

"It is beautiful, is it not?"

She looked up to see Orcas smiling at her.

"Yes it is. What is it?"

"It's my gift to you. You may remember me through this stone. It tells of your blood, the clear blood of the ocean and the gold of the sun. Keep it with you at all times."

Azal reached through Nubia to say farewell to her friend.

"May you finally leave this difficult world and be whole with the Goddess."

Orcas looked at the face of Nubia and saw her old friend, Azal.

"Farewell, Azal, child of the four directions. May your line be strong."

Orcas faded and then vanished as the couples arrived carrying their loads.

⁂

"You stupid, cretinous fools! She lives! I can feel her eating away at me and her power has doubled through the night. Return, take your serving women this time, and kill her. And then bring her body to me. I want to ensure that she doesn't come back again—ever!

The priest was rigid as the sisters spoke to their tribal chief through him. The force of their anger was nearly destroying him. They had camped only a short way from the village. If they ran back at a steady pace, they should be there soon. The sisters were determined to wipe out any creature or being that came from the elements. They were determined to make sure that only their creations would survive. They had established two other gardens which were flourishing with their animals and humans. It was only here that the infection of the elements existed. They had wiped out the village and all of the blood of the four friends except for one. Even if she survived she couldn't breed on her own. But they certainly did not want to risk her contaminating the line that they had created. The Vran men and women gathered themselves together and one by one jogged out of the camp clearing.

Nubia and the couples watched as the temple went up in flames.

They then went to the water's edge as they had been commanded. The couples went ahead, and Nubia came behind, sweeping their footprints out of the sand, leaving only hers leading into the ocean. This had been Azal's idea. Nubia did not understand how it could help them. She had decided to ask Azal later when they were out of danger. But then Azal spoke to her.

"They know you are alive, but they do not know about the couples. This will make it look as though you wanted to die in the sea rather than be captured. But now we must hurry. They are getting closer. "

As they walked into the waves, Nubia pushed to the front. She began to panic when the waves rose to her chin, and she struggled to stay on her feet as wave after wave broke over her head. She started to swim, but she was pulled down by her load.

"Do not swim! Walk!" Azal whispered in her mind.

She walked, gulping air and hoping that the others were behind her. The seabed did not slope away, as she had expected, but stayed constant.

They struggled against the waves for what seemed an eternity. Then the sea floor started to rise. When the water was at her waist, she twisted around and saw the fear on the faces of the couples.

"It is safe!" she called. "Do not worry. The Goddess is with us, and she will guide us."

They cheered slightly, but she could not fault their fear. The further they walked, the higher the seabed rose until they were only ankle deep in sea. Now they could move faster. Azal urged them not to slow down, but to push on with all possible speed.

The tribal women were the first to arrive at the village. They stood and watched the remains of the burning temple while the men caught up with them. The leader, who was named after his first ancestor, Vran, looked around the village for clues as to where she might be hiding. One of the women called him to the beach. She pointed down to the footsteps of a small person going into the sea. The woman nodded in admiration.

"She took her own life in the ocean—rather than be captured by us. She must have hidden in the temple when we killed the others."

But Vran was still suspicious. He gazed out to the waves, searching for a body. The waves were high but were breaking quite far out.

Azal cried out for help from her mother the ocean to hide them.

Mother Ocean welcomed her children and surrounded them with her love. She sent out waves that broke like mountains on the shore where the tribe of Vran stood. She also sent a stinging wind that blew sand onto the beach, a wind that drove them back from her babies. The sea creatures which were created by the sisters, man-eaters all, were encouraged by the ocean to hunt for flesh near the shores.

Vran cursed as the wind swept around them and blinded them with stinging sand. They ran into the huts to wait for the storm to pass and the incoming tide to wash Nubia's body back to the shore. Thus they waited for hours, amusing themselves by sifting through the belongings of the butchered villagers. Vran tossed the body of a small girl child out of the hut in which he sat. Her body was beginning to stink, and it made his stomach turn. When the storm eventually subsided, he went back down to water's edge. As the tide came in, he scanned the beach and the waves for a body. Although he could see no body, he did see the long fins of the numerous man-eating fish as they circled just beyond the shoreline. They had probably eaten the body by now.

"We have no body," he snarled. "The Gods will be angry. But I shall not take their punishment. "

He looked around at the assembled men who had gathered to listen to him. One of the warrior women emerged out of the forest and was about to tell him of the river of hot water that flowed through the forest when he approached her and slit her throat.

She looked at him in surprise as the blood flowed from her neck. She slumped to the floor, and he dragged her limp body towards the burning and smoldering temple. He gathered some wood from parts of the temple that had not fully burned and called to the men to collect cloth and wax. He made a small pyre and tossed her body into the flames. When the corpse was burned beyond any possibility of identification, he pulled what remained of the woman from the flames.

"When she has cooled off, we will take her back. It's such a pity that the prisoner decided to run into the flames rather than die by our hands and by this."

He laughed as he grabbed his groin and imitated sex movements. Two other warrior women arrived out of the forest and looked at the burning body. They looked at Vran.

"We found her hiding. She ran into the fire to escape from us."

He looked around at the men, who said nothing, but just smiled.

"We are missing one warrior. You two! Go and look for her."

Vran lay down on the sand to watch the sunset. He would return the body tomorrow when it had fully cooled. The burning flesh smelt good, and he was getting hungry. Pity that she had to be returned whole! He shouted to one of the men to prepare the salt meat which they had brought with them. He needed a good meal after such hard work.

Nubia and the others trudged all day through the ankle-deep water while the sun burned them like fire. They seemed to have walked forever. They rationed the water, fearing that they might be without fresh water for days, and they ate as they walked. They took turns carrying the various loads and only the occasional startled fish broke the monotony of their walk. Their legs ached and their heads throbbed from the sun. Eventually Nubia also felt as though she could continue no longer. But there was nowhere to rest. They finally gave in and sat in the water to rest their feet. The sun was nearly on the horizon and yet she could see no land. She began to fear the possibility that they might die out here.

"Just keep walking. We will get there. Do not fear."

Azal spoke loudly to Nubia, making her jump.

They walked and walked, and although nobody spoke, she could feel the rising panic in all of them as the sun dipped towards the horizon. The seabed neither rose nor fell, keeping a constant level for their journey.

Nubia had discovered—a discovery that nearly stopped her heart—that what they had been walking on was a narrow ledge that ran far out to sea, and that on either side of the ledge the seabed fell far down to its normal depth. The ledge seemed only about four lengths of her foot wide.

When the sun finally sank below the waves, everyone began to panic. The full moon rose slowly, tracing a path of light across the ocean. But it did not seem to provide enough light as they stumbled through the water, terrified of drifting too far to either side They shuffled in single file, sticking close together so that no should fall, stopping every so often to sit down for a while before all rising and staggering off again.

The journey seemed to have endured forever when Nubia realized that she could hear a different sound coming from the sea. It was the sound of waves breaking on a shore.

"We have arrived!" she shouted to the others.

"Just keep going!"

As she was shouting, the seabed rose to meet her, and she walked up on to the dry land. She walked to above where she thought the high tide line would be and collapsed onto the sand. The others followed her.

One by one they fell into exhausted heaps in the soft sand.

While Nubia and the others slept, Azal, relieved that they had all made it safely, gave thanks to the Goddess and to the ocean.

Nubia awoke slowly. Her body ached in unaccustomed places and her feet were swollen. She sat up and looked around. They were on a beach and behind her was forest. She could hear many birds calling to each other, warning of the arrival of strangers.

How did she know that? she thought to herself. She could understand within herself what they were saying. Since she was too tired really to think about it, she just accepted it for the moment. She pulled a piece of cloth from her pack, tore it into strips and bound her feet to protect them and give them a chance to heal. She looked around at the others. While some still slept, others had disappeared. They were obviously exploring. Nubia decided to join them.

She pulled herself up, wincing as she put her full weight onto her sore feet. She walked gingerly into the forest, marveling at the beautiful plants and their blossoms. The birds swooped in and out of the trees, chattering and calling. She talked to them in her mind, allowing them to feel what she felt, reaching out to them, and showing them that she meant no harm. The birds responded by chattering and sending messages through the trees that the panic was over and that the strange new creature was no threat to their territory.

She was laughing with them when she stopped suddenly in her tracks. Before her was the most exotic and beautiful creature she had ever seen. It was a four-legged beast with soft fur, large ears and huge gentle eyes. His face was level with Nubia's, and he cocked his head inquisitively. Animals were new to her. Azal had told her of the existence of creatures created by the sisters— but surely these were too beautiful to be their creation. "You are right, Nubia. These are creatures of the four elements. They are gentle and kind and guard the forest, warning of danger. There are many creatures of the Goddess and the elements, and none of them will harm you. The creations of the sisters eat flesh. That is how you will know them."

While Azal was whispering to Nubia, the creature crept nearer to get a closer look at Nubia. Nubia stood very still, even when the creature started to sniff her body all over.

She slowly reached out her hand to touch him and stroke him. The creature looked up into her eyes. She could feel his curiosity and he could feel the sense of wonder in this tired woman. As he probed deeper into her being he could also feel her pain. He sniffed down at her feet, scenting the blood and weariness. He looked back into her eyes and was startled to see another being in her eyes—two in one— and that confused him. He had never seen two beings in one body before. The other being, Azal, reached out to commune with him. She was also gentle and kind, and there was also something familiar about her, something that he recognized. He decided to take them to meet his dearest friend.

He put the idea into their minds to climb on his back. It took a while for Nubia to be convinced that that is what he wanted. When she finally accepted the idea, she climbed onto his back, and he walked off at a steady pace into the woods. They pushed through the undergrowth, past a spring and a stream where Nubia stopped to drink, and then deeper into the trees.

The trees seemed to get older and bigger, and the forest got quieter and quieter until she found herself whispering to Azal in her mind instead of talking. The trees became majestic—sacred—standing so tall she could not see the tops. From their branches she saw fleeting movements, as of things observing and following them. She tried to catch a glimpse of whatever it was, but they were too fast to follow.

She heard many whispers, mumbles and cautions flitting in and out of the leaves and branches. She called out to them in greeting. Then they would fall silent for a moment before resuming their conversations with more vigor.

Finally, they arrived at a clearing in the trees. The clearing was a perfect circle of trees. In the center of the clear grass was the oldest tree she had ever seen. It was gnarled and twisted. Its branches reached down to the ground, creating a canopy beneath its leaves. The creature she was riding stopped and motioned for her to get down. He turned to look at her and then looked back at the tree. She picked up the thought that he wanted her to approach the tree. She walked slowly towards its branches, feeling the forest watching her, realizing that this tree was very special and that she had been greatly honored by being brought here.

Azal could feel enormous power in the clearing. But she also felt something else, something known to her, but it seemed too far away in the past for her to reach. Nubia could also feel the power and she also felt Azal's sense of recognition. As she reached the tree, she touched the trunk, feeling its life and power. Then she turned back to look at the creature who had brought her here. He was watching her carefully, ensuring that she would do nothing to offend the forest. He pushed deeper, trying to find a place within her where they could come together in communion.

He finally found the convocation within Azal and used that. "This tree before which you stand is the tree at the center of the world, the tree of life, the tree of knowledge. It is the first tree in the world and it was here before any creature or being. It will be here when all the creatures have gone. It is the tree that is the very center of all creation. It houses the king of the forest, the king of the underworld, and the king of the sun that sits in the center of the earth. Pay homage, beings of the four friends."

Nubia placed her forehead against the bark and spoke in her mind to the tree.

"My name is Nubia and I have come across the sea to live in this garden. Will you permit me and my people to settle here and live in harmony with your forest?"

She sat back on her heels, looking at the tree and trying yet again to catch sight of the creatures that moved quickly from branch to branch. She slowly became aware that a shadow had fallen over her and she realized that someone or something was standing behind her. She slowly turned around to see a handsome man with a face that glowed like the sun smiling down on her.

She quickly stood up and became frightened by the response that Azal was having to this man. She could feel Azal's simultaneous fear, panic, and love—and this made her uncertain about how she should respond. The man smiled at her and placed his hand on her shoulder.

"Little one, you carry a great burden for your ancestor."

Nubia was not sure what he meant, but Azal was.

"Belin!" called Azal. "By what power are you here? I have waited throughout time for a chance meeting with you—hoping against hope, that one day in my service to our children I would cross your path. And now that it is so, I do not know what I must do. I cannot use the body of this young woman, for it would be wrong. But if I leave her, I will surely lose you again."

Nubia felt the full force of Azal's pain and sorrow welling up within her, and she started to cry.

"I have traveled across the face of the earth in my endless search for you," replied Belin. "Now that I have found you, let us walk into the cycle together. Let us be part of this garden in the future. Let us walk together into death so that we may be reborn together and carry the seed through the ages for the four friends."

Belin held his hand out to Azal, and she grasped it. She pulled away from Nubia and fell into the arms of her lover.

"My love of love, child of the friends," whispered Belin. "How I have waited in pain and sorrow for you. How I have watched in fear as you lived and died. I tried to be with you in your service to your people, but now that they have reached the garden of knowledge it is time to leave them. Come into me, Azal. Let me make love to you throughout time. Let us be as one thought."

Nubia stayed on the ground where she had fallen once Azal had been pulled out of her. The sudden loneliness of being separated from Azal was something that hit her with a force that she had not been expecting. She had watched as the two lovers reunited and then vanished, leaving her weeping alone in the forest.

After a time, she felt beings drawing closer and closer to her. Through her tears, she could see people not unlike herself in shape but smaller. Their skin was like the bark of trees and their hair was as leaves. They squatted beside her feeling her pain and confusion. They stroked her hair and wove it in strange and complex ways. They brought her dew to drink from the leaf of a tree and nuts to eat from the floor of the forest.

As they talked and chatted around her, she tried to come to terms with what had happened to her in such a short time. Too much had changed. Too many people had been lost and now... now she was in a strange land with strange creatures and no one to guide her. She was responsible for the welfare of the three couples and for founding the garden. What was she to do?

Do nothing, Nubia, friend of the forest, do nothing. Live with us in harmony, eat of the fruits of the forest, drink from the springs, run with the creatures and dance with the faeries of the forest. Give birth to your children beneath this tree and present them to the Gods and Goddesses who reside here and watch over you. Never kill a creature or pick a flower. And never build as humans do, and never use fire, for all that you need is here in this garden called Paradise.

Nubia returned to the beach where the others were waiting. They had been scared to move into the forest and had decided to wait for Nubia to return. She told them of the creatures, but not of the sacred tree.

"Friends, there are many wonderful things here. But deep in the forest there is a danger. You must not go there. We must respect the powers of this land and not trespass into their sacred places."

They nodded their heads in agreement.

"We shall not build here, nor will not use fire to cook. Everything that we need is provided for by the garden."

They looked at each other in surprise. No temple? No fires?

The sisters came together in anger "She still lives. I feel it. But we will find her." One of the sisters rose and started humming. The others joined in until the sound caused shock waves to travel across the surface of the planet. The ocean began to swell, the wind began to blow, and the creatures began to leave their homes.

❦

IT HAD TAKEN Nubia many years to unravel the magical knowledge that had been left as a legacy within her when Azal left her, and now that she had passed it on to the younger ones, there seemed no reason for her to continue. She had birthed and taught the child given to her from the ocean, and she had taught the many children and grandchildren of the couples. She was tired and lonely. She had spent all her life on this island trying to master what Azal had left her—the ways of the forest, the faeries, and the creatures. It now seemed to her that she had scarcely scratched the surface of what there was to know and learn. It would be up to the younger ones now to carry on the work. She looked around her at the children playing and the young mothers chatting as they worked.

She stepped back onto the beach so that she could see over the tops of the trees. The conical hill that lay in the distance had always been a mystery to her. She had climbed halfway up it twice in the past and each time the inner contacts had told her to leave and go no further.

It was special, like the tree, and not to be disturbed. But now she felt it was time to go there. She set off walking into the forest without saying anything to anyone. She pushed deeper and deeper through the trees and the undergrowth and paused every so often to catch her breath. Her body was old now; too many years had passed, and it no longer functioned with the capacity of youth.

She continued her way until she reached the tree in the center of the clearing. She stood and looked at the tree for a while and then bowed her head in reverence. She walked to the center of the clearing and called out to the four directions. Out of the directions walked four beings, the inner contacts she had found during her years of working here. They walked up to her and then walked through her one by one —this being their own form of communion. She communed with them silently for a while, at the deepest level, and then stepped back to address them.

"I have trained many of the young men and women of the Island. You must work with them now for I am too tired. I have given this life for the garden. Now it is time to go. Farewell, friends. Please guide the younger ones as you have guided me."

With those thoughts she left the clearing and climbed up the conical hill. It took her time to reach the top and she had to struggle to breathe, for strong-smelling vapors seeped out of cracks in the earth. It was a strange, noxious smell, and the closer she got to the summit, the stronger it became. When she finally arrived at the summit, she was surprised to find large holes that went down into the center of the hill. Out of these holes came steam and heat. One hole was very large and had soft sloping sides like a dish. Steam and heat poured out of the ground and the soft soil seemed to move and shift slowly.

She held her arms up to the sky and invoked the God of fire, the God of the sun in the center of the earth. Her voice caused a sudden increase in the shifting of the ground, and steam spurted out of the fissures.

Through the steam appeared a tall deity, half man and half hawk. He walked towards her, and she stepped forward to take his hand. They looked at each other for a moment and then she whispered something in his ear. He drew her to him and tore at her clothes until she stood naked before him. He picked her up, turned around in the swirling vapors, and walked back into the heat.

The young boy who had secretly been following Nubia gasped in shock at what he had just seen. He turned and ran back down the rumbling hill to tell the others. As he ran, he tried over and over to repeat the invocations that Nubia had used so that he wouldn't forget them.

♞ 10 ♞

The Next Age

"*The ground heaved and moaned as the Dark Goddess gave herself to the God of the sun. The joining in the underworld of these two powers caused the earth to jump and move as they made love. The ocean joined in by trying to flow over the island. She swallowed some of the forest, but she couldn't quite devour all the island.*

Months later the Dark Goddess gave birth to her children and the children of the God of the sun. They climbed out of the volcano and found a world of wondrous beauty with beaches, forests, hills, and creatures. They looked around the island and decided this is where they would live and raise their children. They went into the forest to search for wood and the trees got older and taller as they went deeper and deeper. Then they emerged into a clearing. In the center of the clearing stood the oldest tree in the world. The eldest of the children looked at the oldest tree and said, "This is the oldest tree in the world, and it would be fitting to use the wood of the oldest tree for the foundation and center post of the first temple that we will build. It will be the temple of the Moon by the ocean."

And so our strong ancestors cut the tree. They carved and shaped it in the most beautiful way, adding crystals of the earth in the four directions of the tree trunk. And that is what stands even now in the center of the old Moon temple, a place lost in time when the new temple was built.

A young woman of striking beauty put her hand up to ask the storyteller a question. The priest raised his eyebrow to signal her to speak.

"Tell us, priest of the Sun temple, great and honorable storyteller, how that started?"

She flashed him a big smile to show off her perfect white teeth. She leant back on her arms and jutted out her small breasts just for good measure.

The priest could not resist. He rolled his eyes back and stroked his long white beard before taking a deep breath.

After the children had all climbed out of the volcano, the last one turned back to give thanks to the fire within the earth for giving him life. The earth responded by asking him to build a temple in that place. For many years the men worked to build this temple—not of wood, but of rock and stone which they obtained by digging deep into the volcano. The inner Gods and Goddesses taught the men about the use of stone and metals, crystals and water. It took many generations and lives to finish.

They then dedicated the temple to the God of the sun in the center of the earth. The God was pleased and gave them the gift of gold from his loins to decorate the top of the temple. When it was dedicated, a young girl stepped forward out of the crowd to speak to the priests.

All the children sighed at this moment—for this was their favorite part of the story.

She spoke loudly and clearly to the assembled crowd of people and priests.

"My name is Azal, which means Shining one. I have traveled through time and through many lives in service to the Gods and Goddesses and I wish to serve in the Temple of the Sun—for that is where I belong."

The priests laughed at this young girl with the serious face and this made her angry. She walked to the center of the square outside the temple and raised her arms to the sun.

"O great and wonderful lover, light of the world, giver of life, face of gold in the darkness, it is I, Azal, your love of loves through time. I have come to you, my love, so that we may work together in power and harmony!"

For a moment nothing happened. The young girl stood with her eyes shut and her arms outstretched. Then the sun seemed to become brighter and brighter until the people had to shade their eyes. A column of light and fire began to form before her and the crowd mumbled in fear.

The column grew bigger and out of it stepped a young handsome man with flowing blond hair and a face that shone like the sun.

"Azal, my love, work with me! Be with me for I am a slave to you in my heart."

He smiled as he took in the situation.

Then he leaned closer to Azal and whispered in her ear.

"You'll have to grow a little yet, Shorty, if you want to really frighten them."

With that he smiled and winked at her and then vanished.

The crowd fell to their knees to honor their new high priestess and the priests looked at each other in worry. The new high priestess, Azal, demanded that the finished temple have a pediment over the entrance.

On it would be carved the face of the God of the Sun, with his wild hair and shining face, so that she might greet him every time she entered his temple. And so was the making of the first Sun temple.

Everyone breathed a collective sigh.

"Nothing like that happens these days," complained the pretty young girl. "Those kinds of things always happen in the ancient past. Why doesn't it happen that way now"? She looked to the priest for an answer.

"Those were the days, child, when the Gods and Goddesses lived in the world with the humans, made love to them and gave them children. Then one day something terrible happened and they withdrew partially from the world, leaving only the temples as doorways through which to reach them. But they do reside in the temples. If you study and work hard enough, you will learn how to work with them and talk to them."

The girl nodded in thanks and sat back down to survey the scene around her. All the other young novices were getting bored, but she never did. Just being near the temple gave her a thrill, but her favorite power was still the ocean. She loved to swim and had abilities and skills in the water that no one else had. She swam like a fish and could commune with the whales, the large guardians of the ocean. No one knew where she got this ability. Perhaps from the same place where she obtained her unusual looks?

Her skin was dark, much darker than the others. Her hair was like wire and her teeth were like pearls. She caught a girl watching her and the girl smiled. She smiled back. Somewhere, deep in the recesses of her mind, that smile seemed familiar.

She got up to introduce herself.

"Hello! My name is Afari. What's yours?"

The girl smiled that familiar smile again.

"My name is Azal."

Afari laughed.

"No wonder you loved that story! So, we have both been named after the ancestors. Well, that's a good start! So what made you want to join the temple?

Azal frowned in thought.

"I don't know really. I have always known that this is where I should be. Maybe I have some of the blood of the high priestess Azal in me. Maybe not. I don't know. But I do feel that I belong here."

The priest called out for the young ones to follow him into the temple courtyard. They followed him in pairs while their parents trailed behind. Once they had settled themselves, the priest blew a conch and everyone fell silent. Out of a hidden doorway emerged an old woman, helped along by two young priests. She walked slowly, pausing every so often to rest before continuing. She sat down on a grand chair provided for her and tapped her stick on the side of the chair. The priest motioned the young ones to go up to her one by one and stand before her. She looked at each novice in turn, probing deep into their minds and hearts. Some she tapped on the shoulder. These were taken to one side. Some she did not, and they sat back down again.

Afari and Azal were the last ones to approach her. As Afari went before the woman, her whole body shook with fear. She looked up as the woman spoke, for up to now she had been silent.

"Do you like the sea, child?"

"Oh yes! I swim in it every day and the dolphins swim with me."

She was about to tell the old lady of her antics when she realized she must be silent and respectful and only answer questions. The old lady surveyed Afari for a moment, looking deeply and thoroughly into her.

"You shall be sent to the Moon temple." She tapped Afari with her stick and Afari stood to one side.

Now it was Azal's turn. She dreaded rejection—particularly since she had now made a friend, a friend she felt she had known for years. She stood before the old lady with her head down.

"Look at me, child!" the old woman commanded.

Azal looked up and drew a sharp breath as she looked into the eyes of the old woman. This was the old woman whom she had dreamt so many times over the years. Every time she felt lonely or afraid, the old woman would appear to her and comfort her. She looked again—just in case she was mistaken. No! This was definitely the same woman.

The old woman looked at the terrified child before her. The child had unusual looks, not altogether beautiful, but strange. Her eyes were as green as the grass and she had dark red hair. But she was too skinny, and it would take some work to strengthen her. She looked deep into the child and sighed with relief. Yes, this was she. Now finally she could die in peace. She had been dreading this day—thinking it would be like all those other novice days during which she had searched fruitlessly for the woman who would be her successor. She looked down on the child again and spoke.

"Azal, child of the ancestors, you will serve in the temple of the Sun!"

The old woman felt the wave of disappointment in the child. She was surprised. What she had just offered was a great honor. Novices usually start in the Moon temple. She probed deeper to find the reason. A vision of Afari and the girl's loneliness swam before her. So! They had found each other already. That was good. She felt Azal's deep sense of isolation.

Although she was an old lady now, she still remembered vividly how the children rejected her because she was different. She remembered the loneliness of those days.

She called Azal and Afari back to her. The priest raised an eyebrow. The old battle-axe usually showed very little interest in the novices. He looked more closely at them but could see nothing that might occasion this kind of unusual interest.

The two girls stood before the old woman with their heads down.

"I wish to try an experiment, and I shall use you two because you are the last in the line and I do not have time to hand-pick people. Afari, you will study in the Moon temple, and you, Azal, will study in the temple of the Sun. But I require you both to meet once a week and tell each other what you have learned in the week that has passed. And each of you must keep a journal. When you are finally ready to be consecrated, you must hand your journals to the presiding priest. They will then be sealed and held for ten years. The journals will be unsealed after ten years by the high priestess of the Sun temple. I will also add something to the journals for the priestess to read when it is opened. The high priestess will then assess if it is worthwhile to let you both be trained together. I have spoken. Let it be recorded."

Without further ceremony, the old woman got up and shuffled away with her attendants on either side, leaving the priest to disperse the crowd.

"All novices on this side have been chosen and will remain here in training for fifteen years. They will not leave the temple compound and will not be able to see visitors. Those of the chosen who wish to leave must do so now. All those who were rejected must come forward for a blessing."

A group of twenty young girls and boys came forward. Some had relief written across their faces because their families had forced them into the selection process—hoping thereby to increase their family's prestige and power if they were chosen. Having a priest or priestess in the family could raise a family to prominence. Many parents had pushed their children forward without the children's consent.

The rejected group knelt before the priest and he raised his arms in blessing.

"Great Goddess of the moon and ocean, lord God of the fire within the earth, the sun at the center of the world, please bless these children who came here with service in their hearts. Their willingness to serve you flows from their depths. May they bear children in your honor and allow the ancestors to walk with us again through their children."

He sprinkled them with consecrated water and then addressed them.

"When you marry, return here with your partner for the ritual mating so that you may bear a sacred child and continue the unbroken line of contact. Now go in peace and with our blessing."

As they filed out, it dawned on Azal that she would not see the city or the people again for fifteen years. She was not sure if she had made the right decision, but it was too late now to change her mind. She turned to Afari and smiled. Her new friend sidled over and they hugged each other.

"See! We will still be together. It's perfect. In the Moon temple you will be with the sea every day. Perfect!"

Afari looked at her. She was confused. Azal laughed.

"Don't you know anything? The Moon temple is its newer name. It was originally called the Sea Temple. I don't know why they changed the name, but it works with the sea and the moon. It's perfect for you. I'm glad I didn't get sent there. Water frightens me."

Azal's face clouded over. Afari put her arm around her friend. "Why does it frighten you?"

"I don't know. It's not really fear. No. It's more like sadness. The sea makes me very sad and I don't know why. But the Sun temple is perfect for me. All I've really wanted to do since I was very small is work in the Sun temple. Now we will see each other every week. Did you see the priest's face when she said we must meet once a week? He certainly didn't like that! Oh Afari, it's going to be wonderful. I have a friend at last!"

The priest called for everyone to line up. Most of the novices went into the Moon temple line. Some novices who had served in the Moon temple were now qualified to do service in the Sun temple. Azal lined up with them. The priest frowned as he looked at her. What was he going to do with her? He was used to novices who had been taught the basics in the Moon temple. He was not used to dealing with totally fresh novices and he was most unhappy at the prospect of having to teach this rather awkward-looking child.

Azal looked around for the last time. She would not see anything outside the temple compound again for a very long time. She looked over the low wall to the city below and beyond it to the sea. She always felt a sense of awe as she looked at the old and magnificent city with its winding streets and canals that wound around the base of the hill. She looked at the sea and the port where ships bobbed in the water and she wondered what it must have looked like before humans came here and started building. She tried to look around the corner to catch a glimpse of the sacred stairway that stretched from the sea to the summit of the hill—the hill which had been built into a pyramid. At the summit of the pyramid stood a secret chamber in the shape of a cube. One day, she thought, I will be allowed to go in there and I will emerge as a full priestess, and my headdress will glow like the sun. She looked up at the chamber surmounted on the pyramid—the holy of holies at the peak of the temple. The temple's golden tiles glittered in the sun, and she wondered what it would be like now to live in this magnificent temple.

She looked back at her mother and brother who were waiting to say good-bye. She waved to them since they were no longer allowed to approach her. A lump formed in her throat. Her brother was standing tall and strong, determined to be strong for his mother's sake, but Azal could tell that he wanted to cry. She could feel his pain deep within her.

After her father had been killed on an exploration expedition, her brother had accepted the hard work and responsibilities involved in protecting and providing.

Azal had known before her father had left their home on that occasion that he would not return. But she was not convinced that he was dead. She imagined that she could sometimes see and feel him—living in a remote land that was cold and forbidding. She thought she could see him playing with children that were his and she had sent out messages of love and hope to him so that, in whatever place he might be trapped, he might enjoy a measure of peace within himself. It was easier for her mother, however, to think of him as dead. Today he would be proud of her, and her brother reflected to her the pride that he would have felt.

She waved to them for one last time before turning to leave and pass through the novice gateway, a one-way entrance into the sacred temple of the Sun.

Once inside the temple she became very excited, but tried to act like the other older and more experienced novices. They largely ignored their surroundings and didn't comment or even look at the amazing pictorial scripts on the walls. She tried to take in the pictures on the walls without seeming too obvious, but eventually her curiosity got the better of her. She began to gape unashamedly at the intricate and delicate pictures that told the story of the beginning of the world.

The priest noted her interest and came to stand beside her. Azal gazed at the sequence of paintings in front of her that showed a group of people walking on water with their leader, a woman, radiating a circle of light around her.

"Who is that? What are they doing?"

She turned to the priest. The others hovered in the background, pretending not to listen.

"That is Nubia, our Matriarch, the founder of our world here. Thousands of years ago she chose the best humans she could find and brought them across the water to colonize the garden, thereby giving birth to our race."

"Why don't they show the boats in which they came?"

Azal didn't know if she was overstepping the mark by probing for a hidden secret. But she did know that these pictures told a different story from what she had heard as a child.

The priest looked at Azal before replying.

"They did not sail. They walked on the water. Our Matriarch could perform many miracles, and that was her first."

He turned to go, leaving Azal to study the pictures. At the center of the story was a beautiful tree with branches that spread out over the whole scene. She gently touched the picture of the tree and an overwhelming sadness tore at her heart, a sadness so intense that she stepped back and put her hand to her mouth as though it had been burned.

Behind her, with a sound so soft that she did not hear it, a metal spy hole cover dropped back in place. The old woman who had been watching intently now smiled to herself. She had seen what she had hoped for. "At last!" she murmured to herself. "Now it will come. The tide will turn. But not before many seasons have passed."

⚘

AZAL LAY on her bed and gazed at the stars painted on her ceiling, reciting their names and power properties. She scrolled through the powers of the directions, the names of the elements, the dates when the seasons changed, the invocations, the prayers, and the rituals until she thought that her head was going to burst. She had been here now for three years and all she had done was to memorize words and numbers.

Tomorrow she would start her class in pictographs She looked forward to this, but the temple training was not what she had expected. She had dreamt of powerful rituals, the secrets of the ocean, the power of the volcano, how to use the elements, how to control the weather, how to control birth and death. These were all the secrets that she had hoped to attain. But so far, all she had learned were names, dates and numbers.

She sucked in her breath and held it, counting how long she could hold it before blowing out.

Boredom had pushed her to an all-time low. Even the men here were not worth chasing. She mentally went through each man in the priesthood, pondering the profiles she had assigned them. Too fat, too thin, too stupid, too ignorant, too arrogant, too slimy, too sterile or just plain ugly.

She gave thanks to the Matriarch for arranging for her to see Afari. The old nanny goat must have known we wanted to see each other, Azal thought. She was so funny.

Each week Azal and Afari met on the walkway that linked the two temples. They would sit in the middle and exchange gossip, jokes, tricks and insults before rattling off the facts that they had learned. The Moon temple training seemed more interesting to Azal, for they were now learning how to talk to the crops and plants to make them grow better and yield better harvests. All she had done was to learn numerical balance and harmony and how it could be used to extract energy from water. The sparking power was stored in batteries made of copper and clay, and then used in the inner sanctum. That did not interest her in the slightest, but it seemed to grab Afari. Afari would grasp Azal by the shoulders and her dark eyes would pierce Azal's brain looking for more details and facts. Afari in turn told Azal of the technique used in plant communication and Azal decided to try it out in the temple garden the next time she had a chance.

The priest seemed to work Azal twice as hard as the others and Azal resented it. She was sure he was angry with her because he had to teach her from the beginning. Although she had to study everything in the sun temple novice course, the priest also had to teach her the very basic knowledge she would have acquired in the moon temple.

What confused her, however, was that what he was teaching her in the evenings was not what Afari was learning. Afari seemed to be doing a lot of practical things while she was just learning facts. She could not complain or comment. Because there was no way out, she just put her head down and worked. Although it seemed to her that they were each in the wrong temple, she certainly did not regret having access to the story walls in the temple corridors. They fascinated her and she spent any spare time she had looking back over the creation and exodus stories. Each time something new shone out to her and she stored it in her heart.

After two further years of mind-numbing boredom, Azal finally progressed enough in her studies to leave the first stage of the novitiate and enter into the next level of the temple training. Afari too had progressed and had now been given a patch of temple garden to tend. She had undergone all the training that had to do with plants, the elements, the oceans and the springs, and now she was progressing to animals and birds. She talked at length to Azal during their weekly meetings about the techniques she had learned that enabled her to talk to animals. Afari had been chosen to do a higher training than some of the others and she was now about to embark on a whole new study of animals and humans. She would learn how the body works and how breeding lines can be changed, while her fellow students moved on to the sun temple to complete the studies that Azal had just finished. Azal ached to do such work. It fascinated her. She too had been chosen for a higher level of training; instead of learning how to make robes and attend priests and priestesses, she was to train in the art of ritual pattern making.

She had also been chosen to learn how to manipulate the elements and work with them. Here was finally something that had grabbed her interest, and she had decided to excel in every possible way. She knew that this was the first stage towards the priestesshood at the highest level. Azal and Afari lay for a while in the light of the setting sun and dreamed of the future.

"Azal, I cannot remember what my mother's face looks like. It has only been five years since I last saw her, but I can't picture her."

Azal rolled on to her side to look into the eyes of her friend. She saw the pain and sorrow etched in Afari's face and was at a loss as to how to help her.

She moved forward and embraced Afari as she started to cry. The girl sobbed as if her heart would break at the loss of her family, while Azal just held her tight. The sun slowly melted into the vast ocean as Azal stroked her hair and calmed her down. Finally Afari sat her up and wiped her face.

"Afari," said Azal, "I have a feeling that this is your real training. Your whole life will be one of separation and loss, but out of that loss will come something new and powerful. I can feel it. You will travel to new lands as you search for what you are looking for, but out of that newness will come children—a whole civilization descended from your children."

Afari looked at Azal in shock. She realized that Azal had just used the sight. Then she collapsed in a fit of infectious giggles that mingled with her tears.

"Children... me! That would mean having... sex!"

They both rolled around with laughter at the thought of such forbidden fruit.

The old priest was listening and watching from a balcony overhead. His face grew dark and angry. She had the sight. She could see into the future without training. God's fire! Why did he not see it before? She was going to be far more dangerous than he had anticipated.

He had watched her for two years now and had heaved a sigh of relief at the lack of enthusiasm she had shown for her studies. Most novices gobble up anything you throw at them, but she had been different. He had questioned the wisdom of the Matriarch many times, but now he was beginning to see something. He had put much greater pressure on Azal in her studies—much greater than on the others—because he had resented the interest that the Matriarch had shown in her. But for the last few months he had relaxed his pressure and had allowed her into the higher level, thinking that she was of no consequence and that she would fail. He knew very well that failure at that level meant death. But now, after what had been seen tonight, even though it was only a small hint of Azal's sight, he knew he was going to have to tread carefully.

Fifteen years passed. It seemed like forever to Azal, who had worked hard at her studies as the subjects came and went. The more she applied herself, the stronger and more powerful she became. The first level of initiation had awoken her powers in a way that no one was expecting—least of all Azal—and these last few years she had bounded from power to power and was now ready for the final test. The old priest was on the verge of hysteria. He had become obsessed with destroying Azal ever since the day when she and Afari lay crying and giggling, the day on which Azal had revealed her natural sight. The Matriarch must have suspected that something had shifted, because before she died, she had assigned the old priest to the training of only new novices. Azal's training had been allocated to an experienced priestess of low but steady power. And so the priest no longer had any opportunities to be near her—until now.

Azal stood veiled and anointed before the huge doors of the secret sanctuary at the top of the volcanic temple hill. The temple was shaped like a step pyramid with a square box structure on the top. Steps ran from the water's edge up the pyramid to the sanctuary and Azal had just completed the ritual walk from bottom to top, meditating on the steps in her life story as she climbed.

She reached the doors but could not find a handle or a lock. She pushed, but they did not open. She knocked and nothing happened. She became nervous and wondered if this had all been a mistake. Perhaps she was not ready, maybe the Gods had rejected her. Maybe the Goddess did not want her as a priestess. She stilled herself and reached within for the answer. *Place your hands on the door and feel.* The message rose into her mind from deep within her. She placed her hands gently on the door and moved them around. She found a pattern into which her hands fitted perfectly and as she settled into the pattern, the doors slid open.

The crowd below roared with approval as she stepped within. The doors slammed shut behind her, leaving her in total darkness. The crowd below sat down to wait. They had brought food and drink to ease the wait, which might last for hours. If she did not emerge within three hours, she would have failed and they would all know that she was dead. Either they walk out of that door alive—or the powers that they meet kill them. That is how the highest priestesses are selected. No woman had emerged out of the chamber for nearly fifty years. The matriarch had been the last. When she had died ten years before, the old priest had assumed her power, as it is written in the book of the law. Until a woman emerges out of these doors, the eldest priest holds the power of the temple and he will pass it on to the next priest in line upon his death, and so on.

Only women undergo the test for only women have access to the highest Gods and Goddesses. The old priest was not interested in such power, even if it existed, and he was not sure that it did. He was only interested in controlling the temple and therefore the city. He loved the honor and respect that people gave him. His greed and lust for worldly power had not gone unnoticed in the city. How fervently the people longed for this beautiful young priestess to succeed! When the matriarch had died, leaving the temple and city in the hands of the priesthood, the people had felt the change and shift in the power. They wanted a woman back in control and this woman might well be the one.

Azal stood quietly in the dark for a moment, trying to orientate herself. She reached out from within, feeling each direction and its qualities.

She realized that she was facing west and that the doors were behind her even though she felt for them and they were no longer there. All she could feel behind her was a cold stone wall. She was in a cubic stone room with no doorway or exit. She had to find a way out and she had to do it by communing with the Gods.

She sat down and tuned herself inwardly. She saw before her a fire and as she looked through the fire she could see faces on the other side.

She stood up and walked through the fire towards the faces without thinking about it. She found herself in a large hall that seemed to go on forever. In the center was a column of fire, the very fire that she had just stepped out of. What seemed like thousands of people were circling around the fire in meditation. Out of this crowd stepped a man and a woman.

"Greetings, Azal, child of the four directions, we have waited a long time for you to return to us." Azal was confused. She recognized the place, but she couldn't remember where or when she had seen it before.

Many of the faces looked familiar, but again, she couldn't place them.

"Where am I? I don't remember you. I'm sorry... I don't understand .... "

"Be still, Azal. You have returned to the convocation of those who serve the worlds and the divine power. You are our sister. You have been here many times before, but because you are now deeply entrenched in a human life, your higher memory is not yet accessible. We will help you."

The priestess reached out her hand, and with her nail cut a long gash in Azal's forehead. The blood trickled down her face and into her mouth. She felt a tension building up in her forehead. The pressure grew and grew until it suddenly exploded with a loud crack. Azal felt something open deep within her and memories came bubbling up to her. They came fast and at random, making no sense whatsoever.

She saw a sailing ship in a storm and saw herself screaming and weeping. She saw herself holding a child. She saw a group of humans tearing each other apart. She tried to block the memories but she couldn't. The priest put his hand to her head and the touch stilled the flood of memories.

"They will come and go. Do not become attached to them. They are no longer you, but they are simply waiting to be released and cleansed. Lives are simply vehicles that allow you to function. They are of no importance in themselves. This release will allow whatever knowledge you have gained before to surface slowly. Accept the memories that surface—but do not cling to them or make much of them. You have a lot of work to do, Azal of the four friends, and much to learn. We will be with you and we will help you"

Azal became confused. Was she not supposed to be communing with the Gods?

The priestess laughed.

"The men who told you this know nothing apart from what they have read. Each time a priestess enters the sanctuary, she learns that there are many beings with whom she has to work and commune. And yes, you will commune with the powers of divinity—but only when it is necessary."

They faded through the fire leaving Azal behind. She cried out to them to return, as there were still so many things she did not understand. She sat in the darkness for a while until she realized that she still did not know how to get out of the sanctuary.

Once more she went within herself, using her inner vision as she had been taught, until she saw that she was walking on the plains of death. If I am going to die in here, she thought, I want to die properly. She walked across the plain of death until she heard someone call her name. She looked around but couldn't see anyone. She heard the call again and began walking in the direction of the voice. She walked and walked, away from the river of death, until she came to a huge abyss. A whimpering lion was stretched out on the other side of the abyss. She could see that he was licking an injury to his paw, and she instinctively wanted to help him. She remembered from the creation pictures that animals had once been the friends of humans before the fall from grace, and she wondered if he would remember this and would allow her to help him. As she formed the thought in her mind, the lion looked up in pain and cried out in his mind to her.

Azal looked around desperately for a way to cross the abyss, but there was no way across. It was too wide to jump, and its length seemed to go on forever. She began to despair when something within her whispered for her to just walk out over the abyss. The voice told her that she would not fall. She shook her head in denial.

No! That is not possible. The lion whimpered even more and his pain drifted in and out of her consciousness, urging her forward. She looked down into the abyss. The bottom was too far away for her to see. Well, she thought to herself, I have to die anyway. I have failed in life and in the sanctuary. If I live and that voice is right, I will help the lion. If I fall and die, then so be it.

With that, she stepped out off the cliff edge, her throat tight and her heart pounding. As her second foot left the ground something came up from below her to support her foot. She opened her tightly shut eyes to find herself standing on the hand of what she could only describe as a giant. He smiled at her as he stood in the abyss holding her in his giant hand. As she was too shocked to speak, he spoke to her.

"The lion is my friend. My hands are too big to help him, but yours are tiny and nimble. You have goodness and compassion in your heart and you are the child of the four friends. I will help you."

He placed her carefully on the other side. She managed to work her mouth to say thank you as he slid away. She turned to the lion and bent down carefully to look at his paw. It was very red and swollen from a thorn that had lodged in it. She very gently pulled on the thorn.

The thorn slid out and a stream of yellow pus drained out after it. She dabbed at the wound with her skirt and then tore a piece off her robe to bind it.

She felt the intensity of the lion's pain and started to cry. Her tears fell like a waterfall. They fell and fell, forming a river of sweetness and sorrow that washed over the lion's paw, cleansing the wound. She tried to apologize to the lion for crying so much as they sat in a shallow pool of tears that was slowly building up into a lake. But as she looked at his paw through her tears, she saw the wound fade and vanish. She looked up in astonishment. The lion smiled.

"Your tears have healed my wound. You carried my sadness and pain so that I may recover; I am eternally grateful for your selfless service. I will be your friend. Climb onto my back and we will journey together. "

She was about to climb on his back when something disturbed her. It was something that her body had heard as she sat on the floor of the sanctuary. She began to feel strange, and realized that she was in two places at once—both in the sanctuary and on the plains of death with the lion.

She heard the noise again: a scraping noise, as though a heavy old door was being pushed opened. She became more aware of her presence back in the sanctuary and she was surprised to see that the lion was still with her and had crossed into the sanctuary with her. Out of the darkness came a soft glow. In the dim light she saw the face of the old priest, twisted in hatred.

"You will not get out of the sanctuary. I have come to make sure of that. In the morning, when they open the doors as the sun rises, they will find your body and assume that you failed. You will not take the temple away from me—you who are nothing!"

His eyes glittered in the light of the fire stones he held in a basket of metal. Azal knew that it was forbidden to use the glowing stones in this way, and now the stones reflected the light of madness in his eyes. Azal wanted to scream but nothing came out of her throat. She could see nothing that she could use as a weapon and she was about to surrender to the inevitable when she felt the lion press against her.

The priest lashed out at her with a knife, slashing her arm. She cried out, jumping back and holding her injured limb. She lifted her bloody hand before her face so that she could see it and then, driven by instinct, she tasted her blood, smearing it across her mouth. Something within her shifted and changed. She felt a rush of power building up in her, engulfing her. Azal stood tall and strong, her hair afire with power as it cascaded around her.

The lion roared and its roar seemed to come through her and out of her mouth. The priest's face changed into a picture of horror. The girl that stood before him changed. She seemed to get bigger and bigger. Her hair had become flames and her whole being shone like an exploding star. But it wasn't until he saw the blood around her mouth that he realized what was happening.

The dark Goddess was moving through her! So it was true; these women could bring in the divine presence. He was about to cry out to her for forgiveness when she pounced on him. She caught his throat in her mouth and tore at it. She savaged him with animal power and stopped only when she was sure that he was dead.

She collapsed back on the floor as the Goddess of Death withdrew from her, leaving the lion licking her face. She lay in confusion for a while, and finally sat up to face what she had done. The lion, who was now fully present before her, spoke within her mind.

"Do not be revolted by what has passed. It was the justice of the Goddess and you had no choice but to be her vessel. She demands the blood of those who kill in hate, anger or lust. By their own thoughts and lusts shall they die. I will stay in this world with you as the Goddess has commanded me. Now you must leave this place."

Azal looked around, trying to avert her gaze from the pulped mess of blood and bone that had once been the old priest. She could still see no way out. She felt around the directions again and turned to the east, where she knew the door should be. She went to the wall and put her hands on the cool stone. She felt for the element of earth within the stone and was shocked when she didn't find it. Then she realized that the stone was not really there, even though she could feel it. She felt deeper for the fabric of the door. She felt it through the false stone and communed with the door. It needed light to open! She looked around for the glowing stones. No, that is not it. She cried out in despair. She had no other light!

What light did they want?

The lion leaned against her, purring. He looked at her. As she looked back into his eyes, she saw the strength of the inner flame within him and how beautiful his soul was. She looked at him for a few long seconds before she got the message.

The inner fire!

She calmed herself and went deep within. She reached inward for the flame within, the flame at the center of the void, and drew it out. Her inner fire spread out over her body until she glowed with the light of divinity, the divine expressing itself within the human. As she glowed, the door clicked and swung open. The light of the sun burned her eyes and her body struggled to hold itself.

"Come, my beloved Azal, ride on my back. I will carry you over the threshold."

She sat on the lion's back and felt unable to move or even think. The wound on her arm throbbed badly and the gash on her forehead still trickled blood that dripped down her face and into her eyes. But I've made it! she thought to herself. I've made it!

Afari waited for what seemed an eternity on the viewing balcony. She wished she could join the people down below as they partied and sang.

As the three-hour deadline drew near, everyone became quiet in anticipation. Now the crowd was silent, praying for the life of their last hope.

No other priestess had made the training. If this one failed, they would be at the mercy of the priests forever.

Afari had just about given up hope and had resigned herself to Azal's death when the sanctuary doors slid open. The crowd whispered and gazed, waiting for the priestess to emerge so that they could greet her.

Afari breathed a sigh of relief for her friend and was about to start the greeting shouts when what she saw stopped the call dead in her throat.

Slowly, out of the sanctuary, emerged a lion. Upon the lion sat the priestess. She was covered in blood. On her forehead was a huge bloody gash and there was blood around her mouth. Her arms were slashed and her robe was torn. Her hair had turned white and there were streaks of blood on it. But her whole body glowed with an unearthly light.

The crowd sank to their knees. What had gone in had been a young priestess. What was emerging was surely a Goddess. The crowd lay facedown on the ground—not daring to look upon the sight that had emerged. Afari bowed deeply and offered prayers to the Goddess to protect her friend in the days and years to come. She stood back up to look at Azal and cried out.

The lion had vanished and Azal was lying on the ground as though dead. The crowd looked up. They called out offerings and prayers to the unconscious priestess, and the priests stood by and watched in grim silence.

Afari started to run up the staircase. She did not care that it was forbidden! Her friend lay dying and no one was lifting a hand to help her.

She dashed up the stairs, ignoring the outraged shouts of the priests and dodging past the guards as they raced to prevent her.

She reached Azal, who was unconscious but still breathing. Afari wiped the blood from Azal's face with her robe and ran her finger over the gash in her forehead. You have truly been touched by the Goddess, she thought. She called gently to Azal but Azal did not react. Afari sat back on her heels, wondering what to do next. The guards and priests arrived, but Afari merely motioned them to stop and be silent.

She sat aside her dying friend and reached out with her inner vision. She saw the lion again with Azal slumped over his back. The lion sniffed her. When he was sure that she loved Azal, he said,

"Azal, child of the four directions, will live. I will always guard her and you will always love her. Take her to a place of rest and be vigilant. Many unseen forces want to destroy her and now she is still vulnerable from the initiation. Be with her and protect her!"

Afari rose to face the priests and told them of what she had just seen and heard. Many of the priests began to shout and protest. How could this mere slip of a girl be allowed to guard their new Matriarch?

They called for the elder priest. The young runner returned to say that he could not be found. A young priest then stepped forward and volunteered to keep vigil over the Matriarch. This would help to subdue the chaos in the priesthood. It might also enable the priests to keep an eye on Afari.

The oldest priest among them nodded his approval in the absence of the elder. He looked anxiously around for him again. How very odd that he did not attend the coming out. Where could he be? He sent off various people to search for him and find him.

Then he turned and scowled back at the slumped figure on the ground. He was aware that certain factions in the priesthood, including the elder, did not wish to have a Matriarch. Perhaps he had gone off in disgust?

With any luck the girl might die and then everything could return to normal. It made some sense to let Afari care for Azal since she had received little healing training and so would not be able to care for someone who had undergone the trials that this young priestess had endured. He felt a stab of guilt as he looked at Azal, for he too had seen the vision of the lion.

"Madness!" he muttered to himself as he turned to leave.

He looked back at the sanctuary doors which once again were tightly shut. They had slammed shut behind the lion as he and Azal had emerged—yet another sign that she was the true selection of the Gods. Even so, he rankled at the thought of having to accept orders and bow before a mere girl. All other Matriarchs had been much older at the choosing. Maybe the elder had calculated that she would die if she went in too early.

The young priest laid Azal gently on her bed and brushed her hair from her face. He sat and gazed at Azal in adoration as Afari made her comfortable and cleaned the blood from her tired body. She had not once spoken. Her silence was frightening. Only once had she opened her eyes, but her gaze had been empty and glazed. Afari sang to her as the priest took his position as guard at the door.

"Why do you guard the door, handsome priest? From whom are we to be protected?"

Afari was half joking, but could feel fear and tension in the young man.

"The priesthood would like to see Azal dead. By choosing her they have lost their power. They have never before had full control of the temples. Now this brief taste of power has unseated their reason. They would have preferred it if she had died from the strain of the choosing. And there is no other woman in the training who has the sight. Thus, there is no one to take the Matriarch's place. They certainly want to assume power again. We must protect her at all costs."

"And what is your attitude, young priest? You could kill her. Are you not, after all, one of them?"

The priest surveyed Afari for a minute. He knew she was totally devoted to Azal.

"Not all priests think in the same way. I worshipped her as she rode the lion. I have seen that scene many times in my dreams—a woman riding upon the back of a lion. I knew as soon as I saw her that she was a gift from the Gods. I will defend and serve her with my life."

Afari looked at him and wanted to believe him. She needed help from a friend at this time. She decided to trust him.

"What's your name?"

Afari knew the power in a birth name and was curious to hear what name he had been given.

"My name is Kyndrum. I am a priest of the sun temple and a servant to the Matriarch."

Afari was about to ask him more questions when Azal started to moan. They both drew near to her bedside as she moaned and talked.

Afari stroked her hair, trying to calm her, but her agitation only increased.

She started to talk, at first in a language that they couldn't understand, and then in their own language.

"I didn't mean.... He tried to.... The blood was everywhere.... I cannot see. Belin, please help me. I love you .... "

She raved and moaned until Afari was forced to give her a draught of the seed sap of the sleep plant. She finally settled into a deep sleep and Kyndrum went off to find out how the priesthood were reacting.

He entered the great hall of conversing to find the priests and priestesses locked in deep discussion. They fell silent as he walked into the room and turned to look at him. One of the elder priestesses of the Moon temple stood and invited him to approach.

"How is the Matriarch? Is she well?"

Although the priestess seemed to have genuine concern about Azal, he could feel the collective hatred of the priests as he walked through the door.

"She is well. She is resting."

He held his face and mind in a blank so that nothing could be drawn from him. They asked him to be seated at the table.

"We were just discussing the validity of the Matriarch's position. We entered the sanctuary chamber this very hour and found what was left of the elder. He had been torn to pieces. She was the only other person there. This shedding of blood might very well invalidate her claim to power. Murder is punishable by death. There can be no exceptions."

The young priest struggled very hard not to allow his feelings to surface. If he made one wrong move, Azal would die. He had to think fast.

He could more or less guess what had happened. He was sure that some of the priests had come to the same conclusion as him, but they would not speak out. This he was sure of. He had to fight her case here, now, and quickly.

He stood up and inwardly pleaded with the Dark Goddess to be with him. He slowly looked around at the assembled faces, pausing to look deeply into the eyes of each one of the priests.

"The elder," he began, "entered the initiation chamber against all our laws—through a secret passageway known only to the priesthood. This entrance should only be used if the initiate had died. He therefore broke the first law. He then tried to kill the initiate as she communed with the Dark Goddess of the Underworld..." A roar of protests arose from the assembled priests, but he continued.

.. thereby breaking the second law. She killed in self-defense, and because the Goddess was flowing through her, he died with the full force of the Goddess's anger. How dare you question the choice of the Gods? How dare you accuse the Matriarch? If she had been guilty, she would never have been able to open the doors. The inner doors can only be opened by those who are blessed and chosen. You know that! And yet you—all of you—stand in judgment against her when you are not worthy to lick the dirt beneath her feet."

"I curse you, servants of greed and power, in the name of the Great Goddess and her manifestation of destruction. I curse you in the name of the God of the sun who will burn and sear the flesh from all your generations. I curse you by the roaring wind that will blow around you, unseating your power. I curse you by the ocean that will swallow up your foulness. I curse you by the power of the fire mountain, that you will be consumed forever—trapped in the swirling heat, unable to release and be reborn. I curse you and your lines that you will reap everything that you have sown. You will not escape the full force of the power that you have been playing with."

The assembled group sat in complete silence, each person weighing up the individual consequences. Curses were no light matter and his was a particularly dangerous one. Now that he had fallen silent, he realized that he had set a new chain of events in motion. But at least it seemed as though he had saved Azal from a death sentence.

※

AZAL SWIRLED and turned in her dark secret world. Faces appeared and disappeared. Visions came and went. She saw herself giving birth with her friends around her. She saw herself making love to one who had no name to her, but had a face that she had yearned for all her life. She saw fire and desolation and she saw destruction. She saw the fire temple explode and the priests killed in the explosion. She saw many people fleeing. And then she saw the temples being rebuilt by women. She saw a lion licking her wounds and the Goddess reaching out and touching her.

Each vision drifted and faded before she could grasp the meaning of what she was seeing.

Afari held Azal's hand as she fidgeted and twitched. Azal would occasionally call out in some strange language. Afari was just beginning to wonder whether Azal would survive when one of the very old priest-esses from the Moon temple slipped quietly through the door

"How goes she who was chosen?"

Afari did not answer, but merely shrugged her shoulders helplessly. She knew that she was out of her depth and she did not really know what to do to help her friend. The old woman sat down and looked carefully at Azal. Then she closed her eyes and looked at Azal with her inner vision.

"It is as I thought. The touch of the Goddess has gone deep, very deep. It has awoken her at the deepest level and now her personality in this life and her eternal soul are in confusion. She must join the two together and maintain full awareness with understanding. That is the only way."

Afari looked at the old woman in confusion. She did not know what she was talking about, but at least she felt that she could be trusted.

"How can you see? The priests say that none of the women have the sight."

The old woman smiled, showing her few remaining teeth, of which she was very proud.

"We all knew this day would come. Yes, I have the sight. I saw this day and I knew that I was not to be the Matriarch. But I also saw that I would be the one to save the life of the chosen one. She is a gift of the four directions to our world. She will destroy in order to create. She will be the door through which the Goddess can pass. She will be an adversary to the divinity that is many while yet being one—that secret hive of power that the priests of the sun temple work with. They are false gods and will be destroyed. This is a time of change and the doorway always appears at such times. Now we must make sure that the doorway does not die—as the priests hope and pray that she will.

"At this very moment, a gathering has broken up and a group of priests are preparing to work a ritual to tempt Azal into death. There are priestesses of the moon who are gathering to counter the rituals of the sun, for they are devoted to the new Matriarch. Now, quickly, for I have to rouse her before the ritual is completed. Go get me some water, some earth, and bring a fresh flame."

Afari paused only for a second before bolting out of the door to collect what was needed. She passed Kyndrum in the hallway and quickly told him what the old woman had said. He nodded and then ran to the room where he found the old woman stroking Azal's hair. She looked up at him and smiled. The deeper she looked into him, the more she smiled. The young priest wondered if the old woman was slightly mad. She couldn't seem to stop grinning. He smiled at her cautiously before settling himself protectively next to Azal's head on the other side of the sleep platform. The old woman did not speak to him but merely nodded and smiled occasionally to herself as she busied herself with rearranging the room.

Afari returned in a breathless state. She put down all the things that she had collected and the old woman set about preparing for the ritual. She drew a circle and put the soil in the north, the water in the west, the small bowl of fire in the south. Then from beneath her robes she drew out a small jeweled dagger which she placed in the east. She commanded the priest to place Azal in the center and for him to stand in the south. She commanded Afari to stand in the east. The old woman sat on the floor in the north and all was silent. After a few minutes she got up and started to process around the directions by first moving towards the east.

The old priestess reached within herself and found her inner fire. Out of that fire she pulled a flame and placed it at the threshold of the void in the east. She called upon the creatures and beings of the air, the Goddess of balance, and the God of justice. She called on all the ancestors of the element of air to come out in union to assist their beloved child of the four directions. She turned and processed to the south, calling on the God of fire, of the sun. She called to the element of fire and to the Goddess of fire within the earth to assist her. She went to the west and then to the north, calling on all the powers, deities, directions, and elements to help them in this dangerous task. She then turned to the woman who was laid out on the floor, and placed her hands on her head. She created a doorway into a tunnel where Azal could speak with the deities and powers, where she could find herself.

Azal drifted in and out of a darkness that was warm and protective. A voice in the distance called her name, but she resisted responding, wishing only to drift and to rest. The voice grew more and more demanding until she could no longer ignore it. She began to move towards the voice, which became familiar as she drew nearer. She felt an urgency in the voice and became aware of something pursuing her. She tried to fight her way out of the darkness, calling for the lion and for her lover through time, Belin. All she could find was darkness. She began to despair, crying out to the Goddess to help her. As the cry left her lips, she tumbled through the darkness, through the void, and beyond.

The old priestess hunched over Azal as she warred for her soul. Afari and Kyndrum could only watch helplessly as Azal twitched and moaned in her battle to survive. The two observers began to pray to the Goddess for assistance in the work that was happening.

As Afari prayed, she felt something building in her vision. She turned her vision inward and saw the dark Goddess of regeneration standing before her. She bowed deeply in fear and respect, touching the feet of the Goddess in reverence. She asked the Goddess if she would help Azal.

The Goddess replied: "On one condition: I want you to leave this place to travel over water. I will be with you always. Sail to a new land and give birth to my people whom I call beloved. Will you do this for me?"

Afari nodded, and then, realizing that a vow must be made with breath, she said "yes" slowly and carefully.

The old priestess cried out and collapsed over the body of Azal. The two friends rushed forward and lifted her to the side. Afari checked her. She was dead. She looked back to Azal who was beginning to stir and gave thanks to the Goddess for the life of her friend. At the same time, she mourned the loss of the old woman who had given her life for the Matriarch. The young priest attended to Azal while Afari tended to the body and soul of the old woman.

They would take her later to the Moon temple for the death rites and they would bury her with great honor. She had made this tremendous sacrifice for Azal. Afari stroked the hair of the old woman, allowing the gray strands to trickle through her fingers. She was only just beginning to realize the total selflessness of this great priestess. Her real sacrifice was that she had hidden her sight and allowed herself all her life to be thought of as stupid—so that one day, when she was old, she would be able to give her life for the Matriarch and save the future of the temples.

The sun priests assembled as quickly as they could and began the ritual that would lead Azal into death. While she was unconscious they would seek her out in the inner worlds and lead her to the threshold of death and beyond. They were very excited when they found a veiled priestess walking with them in the death vision. They led her to the threshold and told her that the power of the Matriarch lay beyond the threshold and that she must cross it if she wished to assume her power. Much to the relief of the assembled priests, she crossed the threshold. But before she stepped out into the void, she turned back to address them.

"Priests of the sun! You have been cursed by the son of the sun. Your false Gods will not and cannot help you in your treachery. You will suffer the full force of your transgressions in time and your stories will be wiped from the memories of the races to come. But for now, I delight in knowing that you have failed because of your corruption. The Dark Goddess will not be spurned by the likes of you."

She pulled off her veil to reveal her face. The priests shouted in frustration and anger when they realized that they had been fooled. Before them stood the old priestess of the Moon who laughed deep and loud as she stepped into the void.

Azal called a gathering of the convocation, which brought together the priests and priestesses of the Sun temple and the Moon temple. There was little love between the two temples and Azal was determined to change that. She scanned the assembled crowd and smiled when she saw Kyndrum. She felt as if she had known him all his life. He had appeared out of nowhere and was accepted for training in the Sun temple.

Azal had an idea that would break the power of the priests of the Sun. She raised her hand for silence, and then recited the prayer of gathering. After that, she spoke.

"Gathered priests and priestesses. I have become aware that there is much imbalance in the way the power is used. The balance must be maintained if we wish to keep harmony. I propose that certain priests of the Moon be transferred to the Sun, and certain priests of the Sun be transferred to the Moon. I say only 'priests' because it has come to my understanding that the imbalance is caused only by the male mediators."

Angry shouts drowned her words and many cast dark looks at Kyndrum.

"We will not allow it, Matriarch! Our training does not provide for such a switch and we will not do it!"

The highest-ranking Sun priest stood in defiance, daring Azal to answer.

As Azal rose from the throne of power, she felt the power of the lion and of the dark Goddess flow through her. Her eyes grew large and dark and she seemed to grow in height. The senior priest felt less brave as he looked at her, and he took a step back, but did not sit down.

"You will not allow it? YOU... will not allow it?" She transfixed him in her stare, holding him like a trapped animal.

"You dare to talk to me in that way? Do you know who I am and what you have done?"

"You are Matriarch, our leader," stammered the priest.

His eyes darted around, searching for allies. No one met his gaze.

"No, you are wrong. I am not your leader. I am the doorway of the Goddess. You have just told the Goddess that you will not do her will. If you will not do her will, you do not deserve to be a priest—for a priest is a servant of the Goddess. Come closer."

The man inched closer to Azal while her stare held him in her grasp.

"I touch you with the touch of the Goddess. Let whatever flows through you be appropriate to your needs."

She touched the man on his forehead. For a minute nothing happened. Then suddenly he let out a terrible cry and fell to the ground. A Sun priest ran forward to assist him, but found him dead. He looked up at Azal with fear and loathing. She caught his thoughts and smiled at him.

"This is not caused by my power or will—but that of the Goddess. Do not stand in judgment of her lest you be judged yourself."

The man colored and shrunk back into the crowd

"I will draw up a list of the transfers next week."

With that she got up and signaled an end to the meeting. She swept slowly out of the courtyard, being careful to keep the image of power around her, for she knew that it was the only thing that would keep her alive.

As she arrived in her chambers she was greeted by Afari, who had already heard what had happened. Azal had requested that Afari be her personal attendant, as she needed someone she could trust in these troubled times.

"Afari, I know that the Sun priests are doing something terrible. I can feel it but I don't know what it is. I have to find out and stop it. I thought that if we transferred some of the priests to new positions, it might help. But now I'm not so sure."

She was interrupted by a knock on the door.

"Enter!"

Azal's word was clear and precise. She was not aware of the change in her voice since the choosing, but those around her were.

A priestess of the Moon came through the door and bowed in deep reverence to Azal. Azal bowed deeply back saying,

"Priestess of the Moon, do not bow so low to me. You are older than me and bear greater responsibility. You carry a heavy burden. You are my sister. We should then greet as sisters."

She put her arms around the priestess and hugged her. She then motioned her to sit and waited for her to speak.

"Matriarch, we are concerned about having priests of the Sun in our temple. We have been working with the three sisters hidden deep in the center of the earth. Our wave of humanity is slowly coming to an end and a new wave is ready to be born. We have been working with the sisters on the bloodlines, the threads of knowledge and the deity connections. We are concerned that if the priests of the Sun find out they will interfere, for they have their own plans for the future which are not so pleasant. They do not as yet have access to the Sea Temple of change so at the moment there is little they can do about the future. But if they enter our temple, they may learn our ways and find access to the forbidden places. What should we do?"

Azal thought for a while.

"Is there any way of keeping them from the major rituals or from the workings? For the influence of the Moon on these men will be very important."

The priestess nodded.

"I agree that they need the influence and I think there is only one way to achieve it. But it is closed to us. Only the Matriarch holds the key."

Azal's curiosity was aroused and she leaned forward.

"There is an access gate to the old temple which lies beneath the new. It is the same in the Sun temple. We could work down in the old temple. It is well hidden deep underneath a terrible labyrinth and many people have died trying to get through it. We could conduct all the important work in there if we could organize plausible cover for those who are missing. The same labyrinth also gives access to the Sun temple. You may wish to go there yourself, Matriarch."

Azal nodded at the priestess's hint.

"I don't know of any key to the labyrinth. I was left many things by the last Matriarch but that was not among them."

The priestess shook her head.

"No, great Matriarch, it is not a physical key. It is a guardian who will guide you. The guardian will be someone whom you helped on your vision journey, someone who has vowed to help you. They will show you the way. I will go with you and memorize the path. It must never, never be written down."

"What is your name, priestess of the Moon—you who would risk so much?"

The woman blushed.

"My name is Isca and I risk everything for my mother, the Goddess."

Once she was alone, Azal finally picked up the journal that she had written with Afari when they were students. She had avoided it for a long time, knowing that once she read the words of the old Matriarch, her life would change forever. She fingered the pages, noting her childish script and the neat hand of Afari. Then she came to the pages written by the Matriarch and noted that the old woman addressed her as Azal, Matriarch of the new world. Azal put the book down, not wishing to read any further yet. She would know when the time was right.

Four days later, at the turn of the dark moon, Azal, Afari and Isca, the priestess of the Moon, set out to walk the labyrinth. They climbed down the steps that led from the sanctuary to the sea. On the second from last step, the priestess stopped. She pushed against the stone step. It slowly gave way and slid to one side, exposing a small entrance. Afari held up the lantern of fireflies to see the entrance more clearly.

"Will we fit through it?" she exclaimed.

She looked around, amused at the other two women.

"Good thing we didn't have to bear children and get fat."

She grinned at the others and stepped through, holding the lantern backwards for the others.

When they were all inside, the priestess pushed the stair back to conceal the entrance. Azal stood up and took out her tinderbox. The walls were lined with torches ready to be lit. She lit the torch near the entrance and left the rest.

"We will only make as much light as we absolutely need." The others nodded.

She closed her eyes and reached out to the lion in her mind. He appeared beside her in her vision and brushed against her leg. She told him what they had planned and he agreed to guard and guide them. They set off, wandering through the many tunnels, occasionally coming across the remains of some unfortunate priest who had tried to walk the labyrinth. There were many legends about fabulous wealth and riches being hidden in the old temple—enough to tempt a greedy priest to his death. It seemed that they found entering the great labyrinth of the Mother an easier option than joining the overseas trading voyages that sailed once every two years.

They walked and turned for what seemed forever, nudged this way and that by the lion. Finally they reached a heavy wooden door carved with the symbols of the moon. They pushed, but nothing happened. The lion told them to beware. There were traps built into the door designed to kill any unworthy person from stepping through into the sanctuary.

Azal surveyed the door for a minute. It was covered in many symbols, but one in particular caught her eye. It was a symbol she had seen in her dreams since early childhood. She had never seen it before in the outside world and the sight of it gave her a momentary shock.

She reached out to touch it and the lion smiled.

"You are truly worthy, my Matriarch."

She maneuvered the carved symbol until she had turned it on its side. A large click resounded around the hall and the doors slowly and nosily creaked open. The others cringed from the loud noise.

"Do you think that this noise can be heard above?" Afari asked.

"No," replied Azal.

"We are deep below the temple. As we walked around and around, the floor slowly led us downwards. We must be a great distance below the surface of the earth."

The doors finished their slow movement and the three women stood together peering into the dark. Azal held the torch high but could see nothing. They moved forward cautiously, stirring small clouds of dust as they went. Azal swept the floor with her foot and held the torch down so that she could see the floor. It seemed to have been engraved with many labyrinth patterns with snakes intertwined around them. She saw some old half-used torches around the walls and went to light them. As she did so, she realized that the other two had become silent. She looked back at them. They were standing with their mouths open and bodies shaking. She turned to look at what they had seen, and she drew a sharp breath.

At one end of the hall was a statue of a deity that reached nearly to the vast height of the roof. The deity was a black woman with a lion's head. Her eyes glittered red from precious stones and her legs were splattered with red blood. She sat upon a throne of stars and a crescent Moon was beneath her feet. To her left was what looked like the trunk of a very old and gnarled tree, carved and decorated with crystals. It stood alongside by her arm like a staff of power. Between her feet was a door and a bowl for fire. Azal went straight to the bowl and saw that it still had fuel in it. She lit the fire and fell to her knees at the feet of this ancient dark Goddess.

"O great Goddess of the Moon and the Underworld, I am the Matriarch from the surface world. We wish to use your temple to rebalance wrongs that are being done in the current temple."

She turned to the others,

"I will go into vision and try to commune with this Goddess and ask her permission to work here."

"Azal of the four directions, do you not know who I am? Have your successive lives caused the memory of our friendship to fade so quickly?"

Azal stood up in terror, looking around her. The others had fallen to their knees, not daring to look up.

"Look at me, all of you! Azal, I am the Goddess who reaches out to you. I am she who walks with blood from the ocean. I am she who brings days of destruction and nights of renewal. I am she who is with you at birth and at death.

Fear me not, for I am truly your mother. Many who worked in this temple became corrupt and so I fell silent. Now you must come here and work under my protection. But you must work exactly as I guide you. The work of the sisters is not work of the Divine power. You must take my name to every reach of the wind, to every mountain and to every plain, for I am truly forgotten in the world."

The three women bowed in reverence to the manifestation of the female divinity, realizing how inadequate up to now their work had been. The doors between the legs of the Goddess swung open and they slowly crept in. They found an empty room with a well in the center.

"Look into the well, my children! Look into the well!"

The Goddess spoke in their minds. The three women peered into the well and gasped with awe and joy at what they saw. The well seemed to fall away through the center of the earth and out on the other side. It was a well of stars. They saw all the stars in their beauty and, as some fell to earth, the three women saw the souls of people fall with the stars to be reborn.

❊

AZAL DID NOT AS YET TRUST Kyndrum fully. He was keeping her informed of the politics of the Sun temple and telling her about the uncomfortable time that the priests of the Moon were having in their new home. She watched him intently, trying to grasp at something about him that eluded her scrutiny. Why did she feel that she had known him from long ago?

She retained recollections from the most important events and personalities of her past lives as a consequence of the choosing. She knew he was not Belin. But she had known him before—of that she was certain.

She decided to do some inner work on the problem. She did not like being ignorant of what was ahead.

Her thoughts turned to Belin. She knew he was in this life with her, on the planet somewhere, but she had not found him. Her heart ached for someone to touch her, someone to reach out to in the deep of the night, but no one would be acceptable but him. She had ordered that a pediment bearing the likeness of his face, as she remembered it, be made and placed above the entrance to the Sun temple. The work was nearly ready and she inwardly braced herself for the conflict with the Sun priests that would inevitably come.

As her thoughts drifted to the Sun temple, she remembered that the labyrinth went under the Sun temple. It was a hot afternoon. Because everyone was sleeping, no one would miss her for at least four hours. She decided to walk the labyrinth to the old Sun temple and explore it.

She cloaked herself in plain robes and moved like a whisper down the passageways of the Matriarch's palace that lay between the two temples. She moved quietly and quickly through the pathways that led to the stairway of the sanctuary and finally slipped beneath the second great stair. As the stair slid back to conceal her, she struck her tinderbox. She reached within for guidance from the lion, and found that he was already waiting for her. Together they descended the sloping passageways that led to the temples of past times.

They arrived first at the temple of the Moon. Azal stopped and lit the light in front of the great dark Goddess. She remembered somewhere deep in her past that she had dedicated herself to the work of the Goddess throughout all lives. She restated those vows, swearing that her soul would be of service in the work of the dark Goddess throughout time and beyond. To seal the bond, she cut a lock of her hair and placed it at the feet of the Goddess. The lion waited patiently until she was ready to move on. They pushed deeper and deeper into the living land until finally, after what seemed an age, they reached the doors of the Sun temple. Azal looked up and saw the face of Belin smiling down on her.

She took in a short breath at his handsome face and realized that the pediment she had ordered for the surface Sun temple was almost the same. This face had been cut from quartz with gold running through. Azal marveled at how beautiful this representation of Belin's face must have been when the light of the Sun hit it. She stood for a while and drank in every detail of his face. Her body ached for him and the lion rubbed his head against her to comfort her. Her hand fell down to ruffle the lion's mane as she tried to pull herself away from her past.

The door to the temple opened with a push. She smiled at the lack of an inner device. The Sun temple, run chiefly by men, was renowned for its exteriorization of power. It amused her to think that even in the ancient times when this temple was in full use, that outer expression of power was dominant there. This, she thought, is what the downfall of the Sun temple will be. She hoped that it would not destroy everything else with it. Maybe, she thought, if the priests and priestesses of the Moon temple work hard enough, they can limit the damage. First they had to find out what had been happening, and what the priests of the Sun temple had been doing.

She entered the temple cautiously. She lit a torch on the wall and it was immediately evident that the temple had been used recently and that it was being used regularly. She noted the lack of deities—except for a large gold disk in the south of the temple. A perpetual flame burned in the center of the hall and to the east there was a square tent covered in gold.

Azal's curiosity got the better of her. She pulled the curtain over to one side and slid into the tent. A table stood in the center of the tent and on it was a miniature model of a golden city. It was a strange city with curved lines and domed roofs and every building was gold. Only the temple in the center of the city had the straight column lines that she was accustomed to.

She traced her finger over the curves and arches, marveling at their shape. How on earth could they stay up? Surely they would fall down. What were they going to do? Rebuild the city? Azal thought not. No, she thought to herself, this has something to do with the future. But what?

She looked around the rest of the temple, which was orderly, finding nothing that would give her clues about what they were attempting. She decided that she must come back alone when she knew that the key priests were missing. She looked around the temple for hiding places and other exits. She could not just walk through the great doors during a secret ritual. The lion nudged her into a corner behind some columns near the main door. She looked around but could see nothing. He nudged her harder until she fell against the wall. She complained to him, crying out, and then suddenly she fell silent. Her arm had disappeared into nothing. She had fallen against a wall covered in embroidered banners with a hidden doorway behind the fabric.

She pulled the hanging to one side and entered a small passageway that rose steeply away from the temple. She had to climb on her hands and knees to ascend the steep secret way. It emerged, not by the sanctuary steps, but in an antechamber off a meeting room intended for senior priests and priestesses of the Sun temple. She had emerged in the heart of the Sun temple.

She brushed herself off and quickly looked around to see if she had been observed.

Both room and hallway seemed empty. She entered the hallway and had walked only a few steps before she encountered one of the most senior priests of the Sun.

"Greetings, priest of the Sun."

Azal smiled blandly at the priest who fumbled for words that would hide his anger. How dare she enter the Sun temple without telling anyone? And for what reason? Azal read his thoughts clearly on his face and smiled even wider.

"Surely, priest, you do not expect me to wait for an invitation to enter my own house? Come, come! How can I minister to my priests and priestesses if I only visit them formally to perform rituals and judgments? No, priest, I wish to share my power openly and informally with all of my children."

Azal spoke in a patronizing and sugary way purposely to aggravate the man. Calling him simply "priest" instead of his titles reduced him to the lowest status in the temples. He was turning blue with rage.

"Surely you are not angry with me, priest? Forgive me. When the Goddess speaks through me, she knows not of petty temple etiquette."

Azal gave the priest a curt bow and walked down the corridor before he could speak. He swore under his breath that he would destroy the Matriarch, the Moon temple and everything in it. The time had come to rid the world of such pestilence and those old ways that were long overdue for burial. The Sun temple must reign supreme and only then would real power return to the world.

⊙⋇⊙

AZAL PONDERED OVER the craftsman's message that the pediment was ready. If it was mounted now, the priests of the Sun would assume that she took the design from the pediment of the old temple and that would reveal that she knew about the old temple and had access to it. That must not happen, she thought to herself. They must not realize that she was watching them. She gave orders that the pediment be stored in a secret place somewhere until the correct auspicious star patterns were in place. She threatened death to any craftsman who broke silence, and her deadly stare melted away any thoughts of disobedience from their minds.

Kyndrum spoke softly to Azal, daring to reach out and touch her hair as she idled at the side of the private court pool watching the fish. She caught his hand and smiled.

"Kyndrum, I am aware of your devotion to me, but I feel a waiting within me. I cannot move away from it nor do I wish to hurt you."

He withdrew his hand and reddened at her rejection.

"Do not feel rejected, friend! You are very precious to me, and I wish you near me, but I cannot take a lover. It is forbidden to me."

"By whom?" Kyndrum sat up straight to challenge this statement. "The Matriarch can take whom she chooses. Who dares to forbid the Matriarch?"

Azal looked at him. His pouting lip and his anger seemed so familiar and yet so far away in her memory.

"The Goddess," she replied.

The mood broke as Afari walked into the chamber, carrying fabric to make worker clothes for Azal, to conceal her as she traveled to watch the priests. She had covered this fabric with her cloak lest the young priest's curiosity broke their cover.

Kyndrum got up to leave. He paused at the door to look back at Azal. He was now convinced that she loved him and that she suffered because of the Goddess's prohibition. He was going to find a way to defy the Goddess and take what was rightly his. Then he remembered the reason why he had come to the chamber.

"The senior priests of the Sun have arranged a deception for tomorrow at noon. They have organized a ritual that the Moon priests must attend, together with most of the Sun priests and priestesses. They will pretend that they are working in the hidden inner sanctum, but only some novices will be in there to make the appropriate noises. I do not know where they are going or what they are doing, but I thought you would like to know."

Azal got up and placed her hands on his shoulders.

"Thank you, my close and precious friend."

She planted a light kiss on his cheek before turning away. He left the room elated and determined that he was going to find out as much as possible for her.

Azal and Afari looked at each other after he had left.

"He is getting dangerous, Azal. Be careful." Azal nodded.

"I remember him from somewhere, sometime, but I cannot quite reach where. You are right. He is becoming increasingly dangerous. He must not find out what we are doing, and I must find a way to get rid of him."

As the words left her lips, an idea flooded into her mind.

"I know! I will send him on a mission. I will send him to distant lands to build an outpost."

Afari's eyes lit up. "Wonderful! With any luck he won't come back."

Azal giggled at Afari's words and added, "Don't be so cruel. He's only a boy."

She smiled though, proud of the idea and relieved that she could finally release herself from him. He made her uncomfortable. Something within her knew him and liked him, maybe even loved him, and that scared her. She was bonded with Belin throughout time, wherever he may be. She could not be unfaithful to him by bonding with this handsome young man who adored her. He would have to go.

Kyndrum was summoned to the main hall the following morning. All the priests and priestesses were present, including the senior Sun priests, who looked extremely uncomfortable. They were holding back great power. Azal could feel it around them. They were obviously holding it for the noon ritual. What on earth could they be doing with such power? she thought to herself.

She surveyed all the waiting faces after the morning prayers. It was obvious that she had something to say. She rose from her throne and put up her hand for total silence.

"Gathered priests and priestesses of the Sun and Moon. We have been here on this island in isolation for all time stretching back through history and beyond. We know only a little of the outside world beyond the ocean and, through our trading, we have come to learn of a new wave of humanity flourishing in its infancy beyond our shores. The last wave was destructive and twisted. It is our responsibility to ensure that this new wave does not follow the path of those to the west of us, the people of the sunset ocean, but rather that they follow our path. We must be the midwives of the new races—those that are here and those that are to come.

To do that, some of us must build and teach in the new world. Some of us must guide and mediate. Those who are chosen will be held throughout time as heroes in legend. The parties will go out at two-yearly intervals for six years. After that we will wait for the next generation so that we do not leech our own shores of our finest.

"The first party will leave soon, very soon, to take advantage of the spring currents in the ocean. Everyone is charged with assisting the party by gathering sacred objects, food, and other things.

"The first party will consist of priests and priestesses of the Sun Temple. The next will be of the Moon. I choose three novice priestesses, one herbalist, two novice priests and... "

Azal scanned the crowd as if making up her mind,

"... the leader and senior priest will be..."

As she looked around, the senior priests cringed away from the choosing. They were in the middle of a series of terribly powerful rituals which would fall apart if even one of them had to leave. "The senior will be Kyndrum."

The seniors heaved a sigh of relief and surprise. He was but a boy. How could he be a senior? At least, thought the priests, they would be rid of him and his spying ways.

Kyndrum was shocked and confused. He was proud and pleased to have been the chosen one and yet it meant leaving his beloved Azal. He looked at her in pride and anguish. She smiled at him and summoned him closer. He stood by her as she dismissed the others, ordering that the ship be prepared immediately.

"Do not speak now, my friend. I have chosen you because you are the one that I trust and I know that you have it within you to be a great leader of the new world. My love and blessings will go with you and you will return triumphant to me one day when you have established a temple and city. Now go and choose your novices. Choose wisely! Look for the spark of strength in their eyes and tell them to prepare. You sail at the waning of the Moon."

Azal left the hall, swiftly circled by her attendants and ordering that she not be disturbed for the rest of the day. Kyndrum heard the order and smiled.

"She is going to weep for me today. She does love me! I have to prove to her and the world that I am worthy of a Matriarch. Of course, that is why she sent me away. I have to return as a leader and Patriarch."

He muttered to himself all the way back to his rooms, determined that he would succeed beyond her wildest dreams.

As soon as Azal reached her chamber, she tore off her clothes and Afari helped her to dress in the worker clothes. Afari too changed her robes and together they slipped through the temple hallways to the back entrance that was used only by the servants and workers. They arrived at the sanctuary stair just in time to see the last of the morning traders lift their heavy packs and walk away from the square at the stair foot. The two women waited until it was clear and then quickly pushed the moving step to one side. They descended into the hidden passage, closing the stair back in place behind them.

Azal moved quickly and Afari had to run to keep up. She was aware that it had taken them longer than she had anticipated to arrive and she did not want to miss what the Sun priests planned to do. She darted in and out of the maze of tunnels, her mind moving swiftly through the memorized key. They arrived breathless at the door to the temple. She realized that they could not just walk in and so she started to look around for another way. They tumbled around in the semi-darkness, until she found a small rock fall where part of the exterior wall had collapsed. She motioned silently for Afari to follow her as she slid herself through this narrow crack in the wall.

They emerged behind two enormous pillars that stood at the lower end of the temple. They could see the ritual being prepared without being detected. They were hidden enough to be invisible to the senior priest as he entered the inner worlds. Nor would they be identified by the beings that worked with the priests.

Azal and Afari settled down on the floor to watch and listen to the magic being woven by the priests of the Sun. Azal noticed that there were no priestesses and was thankful that they had not felt it necessary to include women. That was probably their mistake. Women are much more powerful in ritual than men, and to have a woman working with them would have made the ritual more difficult to unravel.

The priests had aligned themselves to the directions and the senior priest nodded to two younger ones to remove a large stone plate in the center of the floor. They turned the wheel that maneuvered the heavy plate to one side, revealing the fire of the volcano below. Azal became very curious. What were they doing? The priests all went into inner vision, signaling that the power was going to be higher than Azal had previously thought. The less action or ceremony that happened in the outer form of a ritual, the more powerful the final results would be. She sat quietly and slipped into vision herself, first touching the scar on her forehead in recognition of the Goddess. The lion appeared quietly by her side, watching and waiting. She looked around the temple with her inner vision. She was surprised to see that it had been reinvigorated and aligned.

The priests were each reaching down to draw up strands of fire from deep within the earth, and connecting them together, like weaving a large cloth. They all merged above the volcanic fire, forming a sphere within which developed a series of helix patterns. They worked tirelessly, pulling and weaving until they seemed to be unable to withstand more. At that point, the senior priest called out for the guardian he had created during their last ritual. A large, almost shapeless being stepped out from the wall behind the priest and stood by the flames. The guardian was charged with holding the sphere to protect it from any intrusion. The large creature reached out and took the sphere into its hands, holding it out over the volcanic flame. It stayed there motionless as the priests slowly withdrew from the inner worlds back into the outer world. They quickly broke up the circle and doused the flames, leaving only the volcanic fire still exposed in the center of the hall.

As the last priest left the temple Azal breathed a sigh of relief. When they were sure everyone had gone, they silently crept out to look around them. Azal was intrigued by the sphere and what they might try to do with such energy. She moved as close as she dared without alerting the guardian, trying to feel her way around the sphere, and sensing its use. Nothing. Nobody had spoken during the ritual. No one had indicated what they were going to do. She cursed under her breath, realizing that she would have to go through it all again. Then she stopped suddenly in her tracks. Priests often talked of their work with pride after the ritual. She remembered the back stair and the passage that led to the upper Sun temple, hidden by the wall hanging. She motioned to Afari, looking around for her. She strained to see into the shadows, but Afari's black skin and dark eyes had vanished in the darkness. Afari, giggling, emerged out of the shadows, showing how she could appear and disappear.

Azal motioned for them to go up into the upper Sun temple. Afari caught her arm.

"If we are caught dressed like this and no one recognizes us, we could be slain where we stand." Azal nodded, but still they had to go.

"The lion will guide us."

Afari was not aware of the presence of the lion, but knew that the guardian Azal had was powerful and would not allow the Matriarch to get into any danger.

They crept up and up until they came to the side chamber of the

Sun temple. They could hear the priests talking in their meeting room. They were arguing over the danger of the power that they had worked with. They talked about the golden city and how they could give it an outlet in the outside world. The `one who is many yet one` would be able to work through the city, absorbing the power of the people, and the priests would control the people. They argued about who should be senior, how they would justify the exodus to the Matriarch, and how many years would it take to train the local people in the land where they would settle. Humanity in the outside world was weak and still primitive. They would be as demigods to the people and the one who is many, the sisters, would give them endless power.

Then they started to talk of the sphere. Azal inched closer so that she would not miss anything. They talked about how the power strands of fire from the Sun within the earth were beyond anything they had previously known. They argued about the different ways of applying that power to alter humans, to light the dark, to kill in large numbers, and to shape the face of the planet. The Senior Priest stood up. He had been silent up to now, but had decided this was the time to pull these silly children together.

"You must understand that the Matriarch will not let us go and will not support our dream of the golden city. She is opposed to the 'one who is many.' She fears that power, thinking it evil." They all sniggered at the Matriarch's superstition.

"It is vital to the future history of this planet that the golden city is built in at least one place. The temples here have become homes for milksops and eunuchs, run by a silly female child who has nothing of real power but her sexual frustration. The city is stagnant and the people degenerate. There is nothing for us here now and nothing for history. I propose that we use the inner fire power to destroy the island and leave to seed anew."

The others fell silent while Azal's face burned with humiliation and hatred. Afari fingered her moon dagger, weighing up how many she could kill before they felled her. Hot tears of rage splashed down her face as she struggled to be silent. The priests looked at one another and nodded. "We agree, Priest of the Sun. You are right. We will do as you say. Just tell us where and when."

The senior Priest of the Sun smiled and nodded.

"A ship sails in a few days to take Kyndrum away. We will wait until he has gone and then plan for the dark of the moon. When the moon is at her darkest, we will raise the power and destroy the island while the Moon priests and priestesses are at their weakest. The Matriarch will be able to do nothing and the people in the city will not even feel anything. It will be so swift."

Afari and Azal looked at each other. They had found his weakness. He did not know about the dark moon power! The darkest phase of the moon is the secret pole of power, the balance to the full moon. At the dark of the moon, women can tap into a power that would horrify any man in battle. They both smiled to each other. He couldn't have picked a better time for them to defend themselves. Azal motioned for Afari to follow her and they crept quietly away down the humble tunnel used only by the lowest servants.

When they arrived at the Matriarch's chambers, Azal summoned Kyndrum. When he arrived, he could see that she was agitated.

"Listen well and do not argue with me. You will sail tomorrow if the ship is stocked and ready. Have the men work through the night. You will also take with you some priests and priestesses of the Moon. They will be dropped at two locations on the way. I will commune tonight to draw you maps of where they should go. You will keep contact with them through the convocation and you will be responsible for them. Do you understand?"

The man nodded mutely, wondering what was going on. He had heard of seeding projects happening many times in the past. Indeed some had been most successful. What he could not understand was the urgency. Azal felt this rise in him and knew that she must justify her actions to quell any suspicion from the Sun priests.

"I had a vision from the Goddess about her children spreading across the world. I wish to take advantage of the ship and send more people out. The ship can comfortably hold you all. If we delay much longer, the sea streams will be unusable."

The young priest nodded, proud that he would be leader of such an important expedition and such a group of people. Azal smiled inwardly when she realized that she had led his train of thought in the right direction.

"One last thing: do not speak of this to anyone but the chosen travelers. I do not wish the Sun temple to hear of this."

He smiled at the intrigue.

"I will serve you well, my Matriarch."

Azal gave her blessings for a safe journey and vowed to bless the ship in the early morning at first light.

Afari was posted outside to guard the door while Azal communed to obtain the maps. She lit a gentle flame and sat down before it. She touched the sacred mark on her forehead in a gesture of reverence to the Goddess before going in vision to the water's edge. She called across the sea to the first ancestor of the ocean, Orcas. She called and called until she was aware of movement in the ocean. A beautiful young woman rose out of the sea with dolphins swimming and cavorting around her. She stood on the water's edge and greeted Azal. Azal told her of the plans and Orcas listened. When Azal had finished, Orcas spoke with a voice of the waves.

You must send others out, even after the fire is released. Work in the fire temple. They will teach you how to avoid the death of your people. The first ship must sail east and north across the great ocean, following the path that I will guide your hand to draw. The first set of Moon servants must land there. Then they must follow the coast south until they reach the pillars of power, the opening to the hidden sea. They must pass through the pillars and sail east past the many islands until they reach land. When they arrive there, they must travel east and north until they find lakes with flames near the mountains. There your young son must build his temple of fire. It will be named after him. It will be known as the land of Parsa.

You must also send out the child of my own blood, Afari. She must sail east until they reach the pillars and then turn south. First she must set down two priests and priestesses of the Sun and two of the Moon.

Then she must travel further south, to the hot lands, until she reaches the mouth of a river. She must travel up this river until she can travel no more. That is where she will build the land of the chosen people of the Goddess. Later you must send out more, just as many went in times past. Your people must scatter as seeds upon the face of the earth.

Azal sat for a while after the vision, trying to absorb what Orcas had told her. She had drawn the maps but was still shaken by the revelation that Kyndrum was her son of times past. She knew now why the many conflicting feelings she had were well founded. She held within her, as Matriarch, the memory of everything that had happened before. She now remembered her son, the son of Belin. She had been granted the honor of being with him again, only to send him away from her. She knew now that his journey was not of her making, but that she had been steered by fate. It was important that he leave and found a new colony of the Sun—a line that would be uncorrupted and balanced, a line that would bring forth the Golden City in a balanced and harmonious way.

She walked out of her chamber and onto the walkway leading to the Sun temple. She came to the wall of history. She traced her fingers across the pictures that told the story of the past. She smiled at the many hours she had spent here while she was training. It seemed so long ago.

She looked at the story of the garden and the tree of life—the tree that had been so badly treated and cut down to feed man's vanity; the tree that now stood at the hand of the Goddess in the old temple. She looked at the story of the people and the animals walking out of the water, how the ocean had given life to the garden. She smiled at the simplicity and ignorance of the story she once held to be so true.

She then moved on to more recent events, looking at the exodus of the stone builders. She looked at the ancestors who built the temples from large living beings of the earth, the giant stones, and how their temples were filled with the power of the divine within substance. She looked at one of the exoduses made more recently, when her grandmother was a child, when five fleets of ships left over five years. One went as far as they could go to the roof of the world, a land of mountains, snow, demons and power. Others stopped at the hot land of the five rivers just beyond the mountain range that would now serve as a horizon for her son. A team of the best builders traveled the usual route through the pillars to the land in the east and found two large rivers that ran from the mountains in the north to another sea in the south. They had settled there at the mouth of the river and built towering sanctuaries.

She then stopped at one of the last exodus trips. It had gone in two directions. One had been through the pillars of strength to the strip of land that lay along the south of the enclosed sea. The river that flowed into the sea spread at last into many directions, giving rich strength to the land there. It was a beautiful land, full of forests and flowers. The priests had trained the people well and had erected an image of the guardian of the Goddess, the lion. It had been recently finished and guarded the inner sanctuary of the Goddess of the Underworld. The small sanctuary under the ground had worked as powerfully as the pyramid sanctuary on this island, but the local humans in the new land were incapable of understanding the flow and skill of building such divine structures. So seed bearers taught the knowledge of divine power in substance to these people and taught them how to bring the deity into the image so that they could talk direct to the God or Goddess. They introduced the people to the dark Goddess and erected images of her, the black woman with the lion's head. This distant land had been sending young priests of the local blood back to the island for formal training. It had been one of the most prosperous of all the recent exoduses.

The direction of the last exodus had been across the narrow sea towards the setting Sun. There they had found lush green lands with a river of hot water. The architects had set about teaching the local tribes, who seemed to share some common history with their own people. Their ancestors had preserved similar names and similar stories. The priests and priestesses of the mountain temples in the far lands only communicated now by inner means. They had sent some young people for training but the journey was too difficult and long.

Azal wondered what the future would hold for the young ones who would set off tomorrow, and if she would ever see them again.

A zal considered the gathering of priests and priestesses assembled in her quarters. The sun had still not risen yet but she was aware that she had little time to convey what she needed to say to these young people before they left the island forever.

"You are to journey across the seas to the new land to the east. The island here is in great danger and you must act as seed bearers for the knowledge of the temples. There have been many such voyages in the past, but I feel that this will be one of the most important. You must understand your history and the mystical history of this world if you are to build anew, for your foundations must be strong. Be seated."

They sat on the floor, casting confused glances at one another.

"The priests of the sun are working with a power which they believe to be divine. They are mistaken and will possibly cause the destruction of our island. You are descendants of a migration your-selves. Our people are not originally of this land, for back in the dark-ness of the distant past we came from the land that you are about to return to. You have the blood of the four elements within you, and our ancestors migrated first to the west and then to this island to preserve the power and blood of the four elements. The rest of the world was dying, and a previous race of people became extinct. They had been created by the 'one who is many yet one.' The one who is many then created another race that has flourished in the outside world, but they are not of our blood. They are not linked through all the worlds as we are and cannot reach divine power, the land, the faeries and the flowers because their whole being has been focused on obedience to the false god.

"The one who is many is not a divine being but is of the first wave of creation. They are known as the 'sisters.' The Gods gave them too much knowledge and power and they abused it by setting themselves up as creators. You must train your inner sight so that you can distinguish those humans created by the sisters from those humans created by the elements. Some of the priests and humans from the sisters use the symbol of the fish. You will also recognize your fellow humans and animals because no creation of the elements will take blood. Only the creations of the sisters eat each other, for they cannot sustain themselves naturally within the flow of the elements.

"Go out into the world. Work on the land. Contact the deities of that land. Work with the beings of the forests and seas. Always use the image of the lion to distinguish yourselves from the others, and work with the inner contact that flows through that image. Teach the humans some things, but preserve the higher knowledge only for those who can cope with it. Breed children and train them. Let the power of the elements not be lost with this island but allow the power to cascade down the generations."

Azal dismissed the group, telling them to go quickly to the waiting ship and not to stop or be distracted by anything. She touched Kyndrum on the arm, indicating that he should wait. She looked into his face and smiled.

"My son, my love for you will follow wherever you go and I will always be linked to you throughout time. Call on me through the convocation should you need help and guard yourself and your charges against the sisters; their power is vast now. Here are your maps. Take the pediment that is wrapped and waiting for you on the ship and erect it over the entrance to the first temple you build. It is the face of the son of the sun, my lover throughout time, and your Father. Go now and may the Goddess walk with you every day of your life."

The young priest wanted to say so much but was pushed out of the door by Afari, who was waiting to usher him to the ship. Azal fought hard to maintain balance as she watched her son of past times leave her. She knew she must not forge emotional ties to him in this life, but that she must allow bonds to build anew.

The ship pulled away silently as the sun rose over the ocean. Azal watched from her viewing ledge, whispering words of power on the wind, protecting them from the perils that lay ahead. She turned her thoughts to getting Afari out on the next ship. She gave orders to an attendant priestess to summon the master of the ships to her chambers. She also had to think quickly about how to deal with the impending disaster which loomed on the horizon.

Azal entered the convocation that night and searched for Belin, but was unable to find him. In her search, she approached a priest of the sun, a tall handsome man robed in white and gold.

"Forgive me, my lord, for this intrusion, but I seek Belin, the son of the sun. I urgently need to commune with him now."

The priest looked at Azal and smiled.

"Ah, the shining one of the four directions! I can see you have a troubled heart, but Belin cannot be found here. He is preparing for life. He will be seeded from the loins of his son. Can I help you? I am also of the line of Belin and I, as his brother, am devoted to you."

After saying this, he bowed, before grinning at her. Azal wondered if she could trust him. He was, after all, a sun priest, and that was the priesthood against which she now fought.

The priest looked deeper into her and saw how she doubted his loyalty.

"Child, I am not of your time. The priests of the sun in your time are misguided and corrupt. I am of the sun throughout time, but at the moment I have life in the distant future. I can and will help you to right the wrong that priests of my line have done. Tell me the story. "

Azal told him of the plan to destroy the island and reseed in a new land. He nodded and then fell silent when she had finished. He stood in silence and stillness. After a short while he breathed out and looked down at Azal.

"It has been spoken that what is to happen must happen, but the knowledge and power of the moon and sun in their truth must not be lost.

"The priests who scheme and plan will set in motion a tide of fate and time that will ultimately wipe from the face of the earth all the creations, human and otherwise, of the sisters, or the 'one who is many but one.' That wave of balance must flow at its own time and pace. But to preserve the knowledge and lines of the elements, you must withdraw the temples of the sun and moon into the underworld. The temples will be withdrawn from the outer world, from time and from space. They will pass into a state of timelessness and the priests and priestesses will work from that place to ensure that the truth of the world will unfold silently, like a flower.

"You will not pass to this place, but you will be called to join the outer world in birth and death at times of great change. This you must agree to."

He watched her take in all that had been said to her and saw the sadness within her. She nodded, agreeing to such a fate, but her heart felt heavy.

"How will I take the temples into the underworld? Is it not a skill that was forgotten? Does it not need the body of someone to pass through?"

She cast her mind back to a previous life, to when the sisters used her frail body to pass through on their withdrawing. She did not want to be involved in such a terrible thing and she began to fear that she would become as corrupt as the sisters. The priest followed her thoughts with interest.

"No, you will not become corrupt. They degenerated because they created beings unnaturally. They tasted the forbidden fruit. You are and always will be a servant of the Goddess and not of your own greed. I have put within you the knowledge of the mystery of withdrawing. You will have to do it soon and you will have to do it without fear or regret. Now go, Azal, and be rested." He paused before he turned away and looked back at Azal as she stood dejected.

He raised an eyebrow and tried not to smile.

"When it is all over and you are in a new life, I will give you cooking lessons. I have always prided myself on being a good cook and you don't eat properly, girl."

Azal looked up in astonishment at the priest, but he had vanished into the flame.

The following morning Azal made her way through the new sun temple into the old temple. It was empty but charged with power. She wanted to know the future of the beautiful city she had seen before she died so that the images might be forever imprinted on her soul. She knew that the city was important, but she could not fathom how.

She found the model city hidden behind veils and she sat down beside it, stroking the models with her fingers. She closed her eyes and tried to sense what had been passed into the models by the priests, but she could not find anything. She then passed into vision and looked at the model city. She saw many lines of power leading off through time into the future. She held one line and followed it.

She passed through many circles and waves of times, turning around and around the directions as she passed through the ages. She felt a change in the power and stopped her travels to see what had caused such a change. She found herself in a strange room with many inner symbols marking the doors and walls. As she looked around, she realized that she had somehow stepped forward into the distant future and that whatever was happening was critical to the Golden City.

To the east a man sat in a magnificent chair with carved faces covering every corner. He had gray hair, bushy gray eyebrows, and laughing eyes that were invoking the angelic guardians of the Golden City. Opposite him was a woman who was an inner contact, a priestess of the future Moon temple. She was a tall, powerful looking woman, with the symbols of the lion on her forehead.

To the south was the tall handsome priest who had offered cooking lessons to Azal, and to the north was an empty space. The man in the chair motioned for her to stand in the north. She took up her place and watched as the man wove power in strange and complex ways with the movement of his words and his hands. The weaving created a vortex that was upheld by the three other directions, allowing a thread of divine power to emerge. The thread was directed to an image in his mind.

The image built before them into the Golden City, and the thread of power wove its way through existing chaotic patterns, changing them as it passed. The patterns became increasingly harmonious, pulling the city into balance.

Azal watched in fascination, but could not understand what they were doing or why. When the man in the chair had finished his work, he turned to Azal. He was aware of her confusion.

"The city has various manifestations in my world and time, but the power source that feeds them is unbalanced and causes terrible conflict and death. The purpose of the work that we do is to undermine the corrupt power and replace it with a power source that has harmony. The best and most harmonious energy is true divine power. My name is Knight and I thank you for assisting in this work."

Azal looked around the room in curiosity. She had realized it was far in the future and she was glad to see that the thread of the elements still ran through some people in what she felt to be a terrible and corrupt world.

"Will you work with us again, priestess of the north?"

The woman addressed her with great dignity.

Azal answered, "My name is Azal of the four directions. I will work with you as often as I can; but now I must go."

The woman studied Azal for a moment before speaking again.

"My name is Fortune. Call me through the convocation and I will be willing always to assist you in your work. I know of your struggle with the island and when the time comes for removal, I will allow you to draw on me for power and support."

Azal's eyes widened. How could the future know of such things?

Fortune laughed kindly.

"We are all of the timeless convocation and we all share the struggles of one another. That is why you are here. We needed someone of pure blood of the four directions, someone whose blood is not tainted as we all are, by the Elohim, the power whom you call 'the Sisters.' We will all be with you as you withdraw, and we will always support the seeds of the island we know today as Atlantis. We have worked through many lives to support the work you and others have done. In the future, others will support and uphold the work that we do now to cleanse the land."

Azal bowed deeply in reverence to these dedicated souls. She looked at each of them and felt a profound link to the man with laughing eyes. She could see the thread of the sun temple on his forehead but she knew it was more than that. She did not pursue her instinct, deciding instead to let it be. The pain of losing her son had taught her not to try and renew old connections with people from beyond the present life. She turned and walked through the wall of the north and appeared once again in the old sun temple. She looked briefly around the temple before getting up and quietly leaving.

๛

SAYING good-bye to Afari was harder than she had expected. Now she had to sail out at night under cover of the fading moonlight. Azal wept openly for her friend, knowing that she would not see her again in this life.

"Don't forget, Afari, have plenty of sex .... The Goddess said you have to have babies." Afari giggled through her tears at such a thought.

Azal then turned to the frightened Isca.

"I am sorry that I could give you no warning of your journey. Your bravery and devotion to the Goddess must not be lost in what is to happen here. I thank you for all that you have done in your service to the Matriarch. The Goddess will protect and guide you, and may you take your knowledge and goodness to the corners of the earth, Isca of the Goddess."

She turned back to Afari and they hugged again until the master of ships coughed politely to signal the time to leave.

Azal watched the tiny frame of her dearest friend vanish into the darkness. She seemed to have so many memories of losing people. The pain of losing her mother, Belin, all the people who had been linked to her through time: it was always the same, pain and loss. Could she bear to be in this cycle for much longer?

A voice whispered across the face of the earth:

"Be still child and rest. You will feel pain and sorrow, for your charge is to

bring endings into the world. You are a servant of the Dark Goddess, and as such you bring about endings that are necessary. Regeneration cannot happen without first breaking down and clearing away. I will always be with you and you must carry this burden in my name."

Azal sat in the main temple hall and looked across the heads of the priests and priestesses who had gathered for the passing of prayer. After the gathering, as Azal was preparing to leave, a sun priest raised his hand as a sign that he was requesting permission to speak. Azal settled herself back into the chair and nodded.

"It has to come to our attention," he said, "that the young priestess and handmaid to the Matriarch have left the island in a ship with a small band of novices. Is this correct? And if it is, why was she allowed to leave without discussion?" The other sun priests nodded and looked to Azal for her reply.

She looked around the room, increasingly able now that the withdrawing was closer, to identify corrupt priests. She fixed in her mind each person that had to be watched.

"Indeed, I gave orders for the young priestess and a small group of novices from the Temple of the Moon and of the Sun to circle the island in a ship and then to explore the gulf that lies to the west of the island. I was told in a vision of the convocation that such an expedition would fill our treasury with precious metals of the sun. Do the priests of the Sun have objections to the search for more gold to decorate your temple with? If so, your objections are rejected. I will order what I please and when I please—and you will not question my actions again."

She leaned closer to the face of the offending priest and hissed at him, "Do not anger me, priest, or I will look in more detail at how you and your colleagues spend your time."

The man reddened and backed off. It had not occurred to him that she might know that they were up to something. He did not want to risk the project which was so close to completion. He bowed ceremoniously to Azal and left.

Azal waited until the senior priests and priestesses had left the hall and then held her arm up to prevent the younger ones from leaving. She looked at each and every face, searching for any mark of corruption or weakness. When she was satisfied, she asked the young ones to come closer and sit around her feet. She warned them that certain unspecified powerful things would be happening in the next few days and that they should prepare themselves by going into the convocation every day and finding a mentor who would guide them. They all nodded seriously, looking at each other in surprise as they realized that they had been told something by the Mother that was not being communicated to the seniors. They knew that they must work silently and in a disciplined way as, one by one, she touched them on the forehead in blessing.

She chose a Priest of the Sun and a Priestess of the Moon and asked them to remain behind. She dismissed the rest and asked the couple to accompany her to her chambers. As they walked down the passageway that led to her apartments, she had a strong feeling that she must not talk there anymore. It was no longer safe. She cursed herself for being so stupid as to threaten a priest. They knew now that she knew something, and they would work hard to find out exactly what she knew. She took a gamble and decided to lead the couple to the old Moon Temple, where she sensed she could talk freely and where she could introduce them to the full power of the Dark Goddess.

Azal stepped to one side to allow them to enter the temple first. She lit the torches and smiled as they gasped at the image of the Goddess with the tree staff. She took them to the foot of the Goddess and told them to commune with her. She stood back to allow them space, and stood watching, wondering if she had made the right choices. She pulled on a lock of white hair that still held the red stain of blood, a stain that would be with her forever.

The young priestess fell back in fear when the Goddess addressed them directly.

"Do you know why you are here?"

The young couple shook their heads. Azal stepped forward.

"Great Mother, I thought it would be better for them to learn of their fates from your lips. In that way it will neither be cast aside nor forgotten."

"The Priests of the Sun are about to destroy the island and all who reside

there. Azal of the four directions will take the temples into the inner worlds before the destruction so that they will work out of time and will be my window on the worlds forever. You two have been chosen to be Matriarch and Patriarch of the inner temples, to lead and teach both those of the inner worlds and the outer worlds. You will act as inner contacts for the priests and priestesses who work through time, and you will guide the outer world in its quest for balance and harmony. Do you agree to such a fate—for it is a fate that must be chosen and not forced on anyone? If you choose this path, I will support you and provide you with the power you will need. Do you choose this path?"

The young girl did not hesitate. She stood up before the Goddess and pulled out her blade of the moon.

"I cut my hair in your service. All that has gone before this moment is wiped from my memory and my hair. I am yours in service forever and I worship you, my Mother, with every word that spills from my lips."

The young girl cut her hair as close to the scalp as she could and vowed after that moment never to cut it again. The black bundles of hair fell at her feet and her dark brown eyes glowed in love for her Goddess. She took off her robe and stood naked and her smooth muscular body glowed with a sheen of oil as she held her arms up to honor the Goddess. Her clear young voice echoed around the temple.

"Why, when nothing is veiled before the Goddess, should it be veiled before her servants?"

Azal watched the young priest struggling to control his body in the presence of such naked beauty.

"Because, beautiful child, if it is not veiled, the priests cannot do their work."

Azal paused for a minute and thought about what she had said.

She smiled and added, "Maybe that's not such a bad thing!"

The young priestess laughed and the priest reddened in embarrassment.

Azal knew that the Goddess would speak again and knelt at her feet.

"My children, you two must not leave this temple now. You must stay here until it is time to withdraw. You must bond with each other until you are as one. Make love. Learn the secrets of opening the worlds through love. Learn how the

beings of creation move through the worlds on the breath of a lover. You will be guarded here and Azal will provide all that you need. You are chosen and I will carry you in my right hand in honor of your devotion. Priest, stand!"

The young man stood at the feet of the Goddess.

"Do you accept this fate?"

He nodded mutely and then, realizing he must use his voice, he uttered a *yes* that echoed back to greet him.

He felt a hand upon his genitals and a power flow through him.

Another hand touched his forehead, another his feet, another his heart, another his throat.

"These are mine and will only ever be used in honor of me. Never ever misuse them nor forget to whom they are dedicated. Even in inner life, the pattern of the human body is mine. When you make love to the priestess, you make love to me. Remember that. Whenever you make love to me, you recreate the universe and allow life to pass into the surface world. I am the door through which all substance passes and you are the door hinge. Honor me, Priest of the Goddess."

The young man bowed deeply in reverence at the feet of his Goddess. The young priestess placed a hand on his shoulder and she too whispered the words of eternal power and love to her Goddess.

Azal stood back in the darkness. She wept for her lost love, for the aching body that had never been touched in this life. She wept for her mother, and for her friend, Afari. She wept at the horror of the blood on her hands and wept for Belin. Her gray, white, and red hair trickled through her fingers as she sat with tears streaming down her face. So much had happened that she could not control. Where would she go from here? What pains must her soul go through now in service to the Goddess? Would she have the strength to carry the burden that she knew must come to her? Azal felt a light touch on her shoulder, so light that it was like the touch of a shadow. She turned but saw no one in the dark. She turned her vision inward and saw the handsome tall priest from the convocation, the cook.

"I'm not quite ready for the cookery lessons yet," she said in her inner voice, trying to sound light and uncaring.

He said nothing, but held her in his arms. She felt his own personality fade away and another take its place. As the personality got stronger, she began to recognize it. The power of Belin flowed through the priest, comforting her and smoothing the pain in her heart. He pulled away, and Azal reached out, not ready to let go.

"Blessings, Azal! If I had been a receiver of your love, I would have surely died from happiness."

The priest vanished into the darkness, leaving Azal empty and exhausted, yet with a new reserve of strength to endure the last days of preparation. She got up to leave and called to the young couple.

"I will arrange for food, water and bedding to be brought for you. I wish you blessings and ask that you look kindly on me when I return to this world under your watchful eyes."

The priest and priestess bowed for the last time to their Matriarch and watched her as she vanished into the darkness. Azal gave orders for a young priestess to attend the couple in the Moon temple. She swore her to secrecy, holding her with an oath of silence to the Goddess, which, if broken, would result in death.

Azal watched the waning moon rise and fought the fear that gripped her body. The time was near and still she did not know what must be done. She knew, however, that the older temples of the Sun and Moon would be taken to the inner realms, for they held harmony and balance.

She sat in the moonlight and began to clear her thoughts. She must allow the knowledge to surface. There were only a few days left. Something in the darkness distracted her. She looked down from her balcony to the water's edge. She smiled as she saw faint outlines of breathless, fat priests heaving heavy loads onto a ship. They scuttle about, gathering their treasures, she thought, and yet they do not realize that what they leave is the most precious.

The senior sun priests had gathered in the old Temple of the Sun while the others loaded the ship. They moved around the directions in ritual, drawing up the power of the sun in the center of the earth. They pulled on the power to release it into the world so that they could harness and control it. Although the release of such star power would most certainly destroy the island, it would nevertheless allow the power to flow out, allowing the priests to control it from a distance. It would be funneled through lines of inner power to be channeled across the land. It would provide such explosive power that they would be able to do anything. When a fraction of this power is released in a storm, it is an energy that jumps and burns, lighting the sky for all to see. The priests could hardly contain themselves at the idea of having total control over such a power that could destroy, create or move mountains.

The time for releasing the power drew close. The priests made arrangements for loading all precious sacred writings, objects and symbols into the ships ready for their escape. They would release the final power through two seniors who had agreed to die on condition that the others would guide them through death straight back into the lineage of the Sun Priests. The remainder would be at a safe distance, waiting for the moment on their ships, ready to leave that part of the world forever.

Azal sat cross-legged on the floor in front of her small private altar.

The candles shed their light across the room, dancing in the light breeze that flowed through her chambers. She looked around the room that she had come to call home, fixing each detail in her memory. The plain white walls prepared for murals, the simple wooden bed, the soft rugs with their beautiful colors, the floor tiles depicting dolphins and ships. She looked at the rounded stone, black and shining from being touched over many years, sitting on her altar. Her Goddess. The Goddess as stone, sacred substance, the earth itself. She touched it reverently and closed her eyes, preparing herself for death.

Azal walked calmly through the streets and slipped under the huge sanctuary step and into the labyrinth unnoticed. As she wove her way through the maze, she hummed and sang. She sang of the birds and the fishes, the trees and the wind, the sun and the joy of touching another in love. She sang about all these wonders of life as she wove her way around the labyrinth that drew her to her death. When she emerged in the Moon Temple she was greeted by the couple who had prepared the room for ritual. They had erected altars in the four directions, with the altar in the north at the feet of the Goddess. In the center was the bowl of fire.

Azal prayed for the strength to do this ritual properly and without mistakes. Her head whirled with questions and fears. What if it went wrong? What if she did not manage to take the temples into the inner worlds? Then everything within them would be lost and it would be her fault. She nervously tugged at her white hair, biting her lip like a young child. She felt a hand touch her shoulder lightly and knew that others were there to support her. She called to the couple to stand on either side of the altar in the north as she stood by the central flame. She closed her eyes and called on the convocation to join her in this working. She processed around the directions, stopping at each altar to commune with the beings that approached the threshold of the altar, the threshold of the worlds.

When she went to the east, she was greeted by the Knight from the future, the man with the laughing eyes. She remembered her work with him and the others and remembered the promise that they would help her when the time came. He smiled at her and held up his arm in greeting. As she bowed to him, he moved closer to the threshold so that he stood between the two worlds. She moved on to the altar in the south and looked through the flame. She smiled when she saw the face of the "cook." He stepped forward and greeted her with a deep bow. She bowed back and moved to on the west.

The tall woman from the future completed the trio that she had worked with before. She was already at the western threshold, waiting impatiently. She tapped her foot, indicating to Azal that she should hurry. Azal moved on to the north and was greeted by the three sisters of the mountains who now resided deep within the earth. They held their arms up in friendship and each vowed to help Azal throughout time to fight the havoc that those other sisters had visited upon this planet. Azal was ready.

She briefly communed with the Goddess before taking her place by the central flame in the south, looking through the central flame to the north. She felt many beings and powers assembling to help with this task.

She still felt that she was incapable of doing this, but she knew she could not reverse it now. She closed her eyes and saw an inner picture in her mind of the two temples, with the remaining priests and priest-esses in them. The new Temple of the Moon still had a few priests and priestesses within who were going about their duties, oblivious to what was happening around them.

They too would be taken into the inner realms to serve as inner contacts for the outside world. Azal worked and worked to build up a solid picture of the old and new temples and the people who served in them. She felt her own self fade away until all she could see and comprehend were the temples she had built in her mind. She started to process around the directions, humming a very deep note. The sound resonated around the temple and changed the power that flowed through the hall. She moved faster and faster around the directions, drawing them into herself, bringing the world around her into herself.

The two remaining priests of the sun who were working in the old Sun Temple were oblivious of what was happening in the old Moon Temple. They sat on either side of the volcanic fire that lit the temple and joined their minds with the priests on the ships. They worked to release the buildup of power that had been accumulating over many weeks of work by the senior priests. As they undid the strands that held the power, they moved ever closer to the explosion and release that would destroy the island. They worked without pause, strand by strand, until there were only two threads of power holding back the explosion. They looked at each other across the flames in recognition of each other's work, and smiled.

Azal stopped in the center by the flame. By stopping suddenly, she caused all of the remaining fragments of the temples to whip around her as a whirlwind. The lines of power, so painstakingly constructed by the sun priests, wrapped around her, tearing themselves from the path that had been laid for them. She absorbed the inner power of the volcano, the lines of power, the temple shapes, the life forms and the inner symbols into the whirlwind and stood very still in the center of the circle. The contacts in the four directions stepped over the threshold and stretched their arms out to reach each other, creating a circle of power that condensed everything into one space.

Knight looked into the staring eyes of Azal as she tried to hold focus on the power. He, in friendship, wished that he could bear some of the agony that was now tearing at her body. As she looked out through the pain she saw Knight smiling at her, and in his smile she saw something familiar. Azal recognized that he was a part of her distant past, but her discipline would not allow her to be distracted by his face. She blanked out all outer images and focused more deeply, collecting form within her.

The young priest and priestess were within the center and walked slowly towards Azal. The circle of contacts also moved closer to her. The ground around them began to shake as power built to an unmanageable level. The inner contacts and the couple moved right up to Azal and then, with a loud humming that came from the lips of the Dark Goddess, they stepped into Azal, vanishing into her body. The inner temples, built over thousands of years in the minds of the priestesses, also slid into Azal, leaving no trace of their substance behind.

Azal pitched forward into the flame, setting her clothes and hair on fire. She stood for a moment, stunned by the intensity of the pain. The flames licked around her body, cleansing and purifying her for a new life. The pain reached her scalp and became exquisite as she fought to keep herself steady for the last part of the ritual. She moved slowly while the fire destroyed her skin and made it difficult for her to move.

She inched her way to the north, to the feet of the Goddess. Holding onto the feet of the Dark Mother, she pushed herself into the sanctuary between her legs. She stood on the edge of the well and looked down. She no longer felt any pain—only an inability to move or think or be. She hurled herself down the well. As she fell through the inner realms towards the stars, she released the temple, the people and the contacts into the underworld. As she fell she was aware of the three contacts from the future withdrawing from her. As Knight pulled away from her, she finally recognized him: Parsa, her beloved son.

She emerged in the stars and allowed herself to flow into the void, caring nothing about lives, fate or existence. She wished only to become the void, to be as one with divine consciousness. A hand stopped her and pulled at her as she faded into the void. It pulled her by the hair and she found herself surrounded by a group of beings with many eyes and many wings of fire. She felt them reach out to her and she knew that she could not simply merge, that she had vowed service and that she was still bound by that vow.

They took her to the edge of the abyss. Behind her was a mountain down which people seemed to be falling. At the edge of the abyss was a magnificent angel who was made up of many smaller beings of fire and wind. The angel stretched out his many wings to prevent people from falling into the abyss until they were ready. Azal stood at the edge and the angel touched her on the forehead. She looked out over the abyss and saw many lives that could or would be hers. She knew that she had to choose one among the many that she saw—all of them lives to which she had agreed to, in order to serve. But one in particular caught her awareness. She saw many children, horses and Belin. That was enough to draw her. The angel let her go and she fell. She fell into a whirlwind that stripped her of her thoughts and feelings. She whispered the name of the Goddess in devotion as she fell into darkness.

※

THE SUN PRIESTS waited on the deck of their ship to witness the explosion of the island. As the island disintegrated, molten rock spewed up to the sky lighting the dark moonless night, and the priests smiled. The inner power released during the explosion was channeled across the land down a network of power, constructed through inner arts by the sun priests, or so they thought. They hoped to send their power across the ocean to sites where the priests would build new temples, using the power to control and build a new society free of Matriarchs and priestesses. The 'one who is many' would assist them in the use of fire-power and they would be the new creators, the new gods and so the world would bow in acknowledgment of their achievements.

Two of the priests went below deck to the small sanctuary that had been assembled for the journey. They sat down and went in inner vision to the plain of death, to honor their side of the bargain and guide the sacrificed priests through death as agreed. They looked and looked but could not find the two sun priests who had died in the explosion. Again and again they looked, and by daybreak they realized something had gone wrong. They consulted the senior priest, who became confused. They could not have survived the explosion and they were not advanced enough to have merged with the void. He shook his head in confusion but came to the conclusion that they could do nothing more, and that they should start the long arduous journey to the land that lay through the pillars of strength.

KNIGHT, having recovered from the strain of the ritual, drew strength and grounded himself with a small nip of whisky. The working through times and worlds had taken a bigger toll on his strength than he wished to admit to himself. But as he sat on his chair, the chair of the many faces, he knew that the ritual had changed the world in which he lived and had started a chain of power that would rebalance the Golden City.

He looked out of his window at the cars that passed his house and knew that each city in the world depended on the balance of power within the Golden City, the city of God upon which all cities are founded. Wherever many people come together and build a communal space that includes power and commerce, so there shall be the influence of the original city. In a world that was so degenerate and in its last stages of decay, he knew he was one of the few people left in the world who held the blood and knowledge of the elements. He also knew that the strength of the city depended on him and him alone. Many others wished or thought that they too carried that burden, but the bloodline was near its end and the Knight struggled to carry his burden.

He thought of Azal and smiled. He thought of her terrible death and the many lives that now lay before her and all the richness that would be contained in them. He thought of the many times their paths had crossed and would cross. He opened the old Bible he had been reading before the ritual and found the text he had marked.

He started to read: "And God planted a garden eastward in Eden; there they put the man whom they had formed .... "

As the whisky began to take effect, he drifted into sleep and dreamt of lions.

EPILOGUE

The rain lashed and tore at the windows, tearing the wood of the frames into splinters and shards. Debbie inched closer to the window, checking on the layers of masking tape she had stuck in crosses across the glass to stop it shattering into dangerous spears. She tried to re-tune the television in an effort to get some useful information about the coming hurricane. Nothing. Only fuzzy pictures and the occasional snatched word. She looked harder trying to see something that would make sense.

A map with a weatherman faded in and out as he talked and the screen scrolled up emergency numbers for people to ring. She looked behind him at the satellite picture that tracked the storm. She tried to make out the outline of the land path that had been marked out. When she realized what it was that she was looking at, she groaned inwardly. It was heading straight for the Keys.

She tried to use the phone but it was already dead. She began to regret having such a gung-ho attitude to staying behind.

"I will be fine!" she had said.

"Good Lord! If everyone had run from all the storms that have hit here in the past, there would be no one living here by now."

She had lived on this island for over twenty years and considered herself a fully blown conch. Although she had been born here, her mother left with her within months of her birth for New Orleans and had refused to return. She never gave an explanation and could not even bear to hear the name "Key West" uttered around her. Debbie had waited until her mother's death to return to the island. It had been her whole life's ambition to live and die on this fragile outcrop laid low in the ocean. It didn't feel like America, this little island. It felt more like the real Caribbean.

She had always had problems with being teased as a child. Not only was she black, she was very dark, and all the other kids in her neighborhood took turns teasing her. But on Key West, it was different. It was her home, her land. She could feel it in her bones. This was the place where her bones wanted to rest when she died. She didn't have any rational explanation for it. There was little work here other than pampering tourists, and everything had to be imported. There was no landscape other than row after row of T-shirt shops.

Her house stood opposite an old Methodist church on a crossroads. The house had survived the last hit nearly seventy years ago but she wasn't so sure it was going to survive this one. She stalked around the house, checking windows and doors for the fiftieth time. She checked her water and food supply which she had dragged upstairs to avoid the flooding that would inevitably happen. She had just re-floored the whole house and so, of course, it was going to flood. That's how the world worked, didn't it?

She was about to check her first aid supply when the electricity went. Shit. It was dark now and it was still daytime and the hurricane was miles out southeast. By the time it got here it would be total darkness.

She waited for her eyes to adjust to the dim light and then systematically rounded up every torch and oil lamp that she had placed around the house. It would be best to have them all together, she thought to herself. She tried everything to keep herself busy so that she would not be aware of the noises outside that were slowly getting louder and louder.

The house started to groan under the weight of the wind bearing down on its old bones, and Debbie started to panic. What if the house just fell apart? What if it blew away? Would she die? Would anyone find her? She realized that she had been stupid to try and brave it out. Although she had always wanted to be looked upon as a tough woman, this was probably taking it a bit too far. What was she to do?

The emergency services had evacuated everyone two days ago and told her that if she did not leave, she would be on her own. She knew that other conches had tried to brave it out too, but she did not know where they were, or if she could reach them. A shelter had been erected inside the elementary school, but as she looked through the tape and out of the window, she knew she wouldn't make it. It was too far and too many streets away. The wind would just pick her up like a doll and tear her to pieces. She carried on gazing out of the window and looked at the concrete church opposite. She had an idea. If it was unlocked, which was unlikely, she could shelter in there. It was solid enough—more so than the house she was in. The Methodists wouldn't mind, would they?

Debbie mobilized herself. She packed a torch, matches, a candle, some food, water and a knife into a small backpack. She wrapped a length of rope around her body and shoved her small first-aid kit into her pocket. She scanned the room for anything else that she might need. She filled her pockets with painkillers, candies, small bottles of water and a cigarette lighter. She paused for a moment. She had never really been religious. She was raised as a Catholic but stopped going to church on the day she left school. With no nuns to cane her hands for non-attendance, there was no real incentive anymore.

But now, as she was about to brave the winds and rain that might kill her, she stilled herself with a prayer. She remembered the chapel dedicated to St. Mary, Star of the Sea, with its blazing candles and its rosary path outlined in the grass—a place where all kinds of people lit candles to Mary in offering, asking her to protect them from the sea. She saw the chapel in her head and started to recite the rosary. She went to the front door and placed her hands on the doorknob: "Hail Mary, full of grace. The Lord is with thee .... "

She battled to open the door. As she unlocked it, the door flew at her with an horrific force, hitting her on the shoulder as it spun past her...

"Blessed art thou amongst women...." She screamed out at the storm as the pain tore through her body, and her arm went dead. Shit. Shit. Shit.

She cursed under her breath as she tried to move her right arm. She pushed forward into the storm, finding it hard to breathe as the wind slapped her full on in the face. Her backpack hung down on her right side, just where her shoulder had been damaged, banging against her injury, causing waves of pain to knife their way into her brain. "...and blessed is the fruit of thy womb, Jesus...."

Her head bowed out of childhood habit as her mind got to the word "Jesus." Because of the driving wind and rain, she couldn't see across the street and so she stumbled in the direction of the church, fighting to stay on her feet, fighting to stay alive long enough to reach out and open the church door. "Holy Mary, Mother of God, pray for us sinners..."

She reached the church door on the corner of the street. She rattled the door. It was locked. She cried out in anger and frustration, banging her left fist on the door and sobbing loudly to the wind. No one heard her. No one was there.

She remembered that there was a side entrance to the Sunday School. Maybe someone had left it unlocked. She must try, for she knew she could not make it back to the house. The wind screamed around her, lifting her off her feet and pushing hard against her body until her rib cage felt as though it was going to collapse under the pressure. Her right shoulder hung uselessly and the backpack strap had slid down her right arm, pinning it to her side. Inch by inch she pulled herself along the outer wall of the church, grasping the concrete with her fingernails. The pack weighed her down enough to prevent her thin frame from being lifted by the wind and tossed into a tree." ...now, and at the hour of our death. Amen."

She reached the small garden wall that surrounded the tiny piece of garden at the front of the Sunday School entrance. She thanked God for getting her so far. Her eyes swam with rain and she screwed up her face, trying to see the door through the lashing rain that seemed to intensify with every second that passed. She stumbled and fell over the small wall and bush that separated the outer wall of the church and the outer wall of the schoolhouse. She fell heavily on her right side and her mind swam in a tide of pain as her shoulder took the full weight of the fall.

She tried to get herself back on her feet, but could not use her right arm to lever herself up. She fell back and cried out for help, even though she knew no one could hear her. She knew that if she didn't get up, she would surely die here at the threshold of the church. Maybe it's because I'm a Catholic and this is a Methodist church, she thought as she used humor in an effort to hold herself together. She managed to roll herself onto her stomach and lever herself up onto her knees. She stood up, falling heavily against the school door that opened under her weight and she fell into the hallway. A cold damp musty smell assaulted her as she tumbled into the hallway of the disused school. She cried with relief.

She gave thanks to the Virgin Mary for getting her so far. Debbie threw her backpack to one side as she pushed the door with her good shoulder and forced it closed against the wind. She fell back exhausted against the door, relieved that she had made it into the building. Her eyes scanned the school in the semi-darkness. Before her was an open cafe area and a staircase that led up to the kitchens above. She had been here once, many years ago, for a festival—she couldn't remember what or with whom but she did remember the wonderful food that had been served. When all other memories ceased, Debbie always remembered food.

The building seemed silent and calm—in mysterious contrast to the havoc that was being wreaked outside. She got onto her feet and staggered to the tables and chairs that had been left out. She dropped her backpack onto the table, screaming out in pain as her shoulder moved under the weight of the bag. She fumbled for her first-aid kit and emptied it onto the table. Band-aids. "Fat lot of good they're going to be," she muttered, cursing out aloud.

She found the small homeopathic kit and silently gave thanks that she had had the brains to pack it. She downed a dose of a high potency remedy to help her muscles and then looked around for something to bind her shoulder. Nothing. Her hands fingered the rope still tied around her body and she had an idea. She loosened out a length of rope, cut it and let the rest fall to the ground. Then she tied the rope lightly around her bent arm, pinning it to her side, using a dusty table-cloth to pad her arm and shoulder against the rope. Once her arm was securely tied down without the circulation being cutting off, she stopped to breathe through the pain.

She felt light-headed. She sat down on the floor and looked at the wall that separated the church from the school. It had a beautiful stained-glass window that looked into the church. At that moment, someone walked past the window. From the outline it looked like a big woman, but it had moved too fast for her to tell. Debbie cried out, thankful to find a living soul in the middle of this hell. No answer. She called again, louder, putting all her fear and urgency into her voice. Again nothing. She got onto her feet and went to the door that led into the church. She pushed it open just in time to see someone disappear into a small side room that led off from the altar. She stumbled through the church, aware that the ever-stronger winds were banging on the window, demanding to be let in. When she reached the room, it was empty.

She looked around the room with its desk, piano, wall banners and crosses. No one here and nowhere to hide. She leant against the wall and fought back the scream that was in her throat. She was not mad! She had seen what she had seen! She desperately wanted someone to be with her, to share this terrible fear. Maybe she just wanted it too much and her mind was playing tricks. She was in such pain. She turned to go back into the church and as she looked through the door-way, she saw an old black woman seated in the pews, all dressed up for a Sunday service. Debbie knew that she was seeing someone or some-thing that was not of this world. The hair on the back of her neck stood up and every cell in her body screamed at her to run. The old woman smiled at her and then vanished.

Debbie did not know what to do. She had to come out of the room but she was too scared to go into the church where she had seen the woman. After cowering in the room for a while, her bladder forced her out. She bolted through the church and slammed the door shut as she got herself back into the Sunday School. She found the bathroom and prayed as she sat with the door locked.

When she felt brave enough to emerge, she got herself busy and began to organize herself into survival mode. That was the only way to shut out what she had seen—or what she thought she had seen. She looked around and found a small area under the stair that had no windows. This would probably be the best place to hide from the fury of the hurricane in its full force. Judging by the sounds outside, it was very near now. She kept her pack close and the torch on dim. The darkness had fully descended.

Her only source of light, the dim glow of her torch, did nothing to quench her fear that the old woman was about to jump out and eat her. She chewed on more remedies for her pain and tried not to hear the windows in the church blowing in, nor the creaking of the roof or the groaning of the three towers that stood guard around the outside of the building.

The remedies started to take effect and Debbie found herself drowsing and drifting. The noise around her was horrific, but her brain seemed somehow to be filtering it out. She slipped into an exhausted sleep, twitching from the pain and the noise. Despite the storm, her mind was pulled deeper and deeper into sleep. She dreamed of the sea and of her mother. She dreamed of her college days and her proud graduation from Harvard, the greatest gift she had given her mother and her community.

She fell deeper and deeper into sleep, unaware of the water that was starting to lap around her body.

She dreamed of volcanoes and explosions and she found herself standing out in the sea with the old woman she had seen in the church.

"Look at the storm, girl. Look how it cleans them islands. See how it lets things settle back into the place where they belong. Look at the children playing."

Debbie looked harder and saw little girls, their wiry black hair teased into braids and curls. They stood around the island, holding their hands out. String was wrapped around their fingers. They seemed to be playing cat's cradle across the island, teasing lines of power back and forth between each other.

"They are your sisters, child. Don't you know them?"

Debbie shook her head.

"Go play with them, girl. You are back home now."

Debbie approached one of the little girls, who smiled and held out her hands for Debbie to take some of the thread. She teased her hand under the web pattern and took some of it up.

Her whole being shook under the weight of the threads and she looked up in amazement at the small children carrying the threads with no apparent strain. They giggled, smiling at her, and then gave her a spare thread to weave that seemed to come from deep within the ocean. As she wove it into the pattern, she had a deep urge to hold onto the thread and follow it down to the ocean floor. The old woman smiled and then scratched the end of her nose with a large red painted fingernail.

"Go then! Follow it!" She laughed a very unusual and deep laugh as she saw Debbie's hesitation. Debbie held on to the thread and slid down. She traveled at great speed, flowing down through the ocean to the floor and then down through caverns and tunnels until she emerged in what looked like the remains of a city. She followed the threads down deeper as they twisted and wove through tunnels and passageways. She emerged in a place that looked like a scene from her favorite movie, *Raiders of the Lost Ark*.

She found herself in a temple building shrouded in darkness. She could feel the stillness and presence that she had once felt in church when she was a small child. She tried to look around her, but could see so little. A small light in the distance approached her. As it drew near, she could see that it was an oil lamp held by a beautiful woman with long red hair and brilliant green eyes. Debbie did not know if she should run or stay. The woman smiled and told her she was safe. She touched Debbie on the forehead and then on the heart.

"It is with great honor that we greet you, child of Afari. What brings you here?"

Debbie could not think of what to say but her mind conjured pictures of the children weaving and the woman nodded.

"I see that the storm has finally come. Do not fear it, for it heralds the beginning of a new era, the resurfacing of the mysteries of the elements and the death of the power that the sisters hold over humanity. Your presence on the island allowed the mysteries to flow once more and we are grateful for your return. The storm will do damage, but the island will recover. It will not sink as many foretold. It is the last fragment of the garden and it will rise again through the blood of the children of the elements and will once again be a place of sacred learning and worship. Leave now and make your peace with the Star of the Sea."

The woman and the temple vanished and Debbie found herself on the public beach. There was no storm but she could hear singing drifting towards her. She saw many people, some naked, some partially clothed in European dress. They all had chains around their ankles and shuffled along in procession down to the water's edge. They held aloft a litter holding the body of a small child, decorated with herbs and grasses. Debbie realized she was looking at a procession of slaves and her heart lurched in ancestral pain and sorrow. They could not see her as they held up their fire torches and looked around. The white men and women who were escorting them fell back to allow them privacy.

They took the litter to the water's edge and held the child up to the ocean.

"Behold, mother of blood, queen of the ocean, star of the sea, giver of life and death, woman of fire and breath of true life. Take this child back into your belly and whisper songs of love to her as you guide her through death. Call on the Ancestors to greet her so she may tell them of our suffering and captivity, so they may in turn warn our brothers and sisters, our uncles and cousins, our mothers and grandparents."

They laid the child solemnly in the water and doused the fires by dipping the torches into the seawater. They then knelt and laid their foreheads down to touch the mother earth, searching for solace at her breast.

As their heads were down, Debbie fought a cry in her throat as she saw a Goddess rise out of the sea. A black woman, naked, with long hair decorated with flames of fire, with blood running between her legs, rose out of the sea to take the child. She reached out to touch each slave one by one, resting a flame on their heads in love.

"This is my fire which I give to you, my beloved children. May it give you strength in this time of darkness and may it mark you through time as my chosen. As the power of the sisters falls away so you will strengthen and give

balance back to the world. Forget me not, children, in your long exile. May you scatter in freedom to the four directions, taking your legacy with you."

The Goddess then started to whip her hair around her head, chanting and screaming as it swirled faster and faster. Suddenly her hair whipped out and twisted around the child, pulling it into her and absorbing the tiny soul within her.

She then turned to Debbie.

"I heard your prayer to me, daughter of Afari, and I give you a choice. Come with me into the ocean, or stay and tend my shrine. Which shall it be?"

Debbie didn't need to choose. She knew it was not yet time for her to die and that she still had much to do. She chose to stay and tend the shrine. As soon as that decision was firm in her mind, she was transported back to the old wise woman and the weaving children.

"So, you choose to stay, eh?" The old woman eyed her up and down. "Then make sure that you are of use. Never leave the island and never let the shrine go unattended. Do you promise?"

Debbie nodded. The old woman chuckled and then reached out to Debbie and sliced through her forehead with a long red fingernail. She cut deep into the flesh and Debbie licked the warm salty blood as it trickled down her face.

◈✸◈

SHE LAY for a long time in the water under the stairs and did not fully come around until she heard shouts echoing through the church. She tried to call out, but her throat would not make any noise above a whisper. She reached out with her good arm and felt for the flashlight. She banged it repeatedly on the wall until she heard the footsteps coming closer.

"Bloody hell! Quick! Over here!"

The man leant over her, shining a torch into her face. He swore quietly under his breath as he summed up her injuries. He saw the deep gash in her forehead and the obviously dislocated shoulder. He checked her over for breaks and then put a mask over her face.

"Breathe deeply. It will help the pain."

She breathed deeply, thankful at last for some relief from the never-ending sea of agony that she had swum in and out of.

"You're not American?" She tried to speak through the mask.

"No, love. We're an English rescue team. We were working in the area. They asked us to drop by here to check it out. Lucky I heard you calling out, eh?"

She tried to smile but her forehead hurt.

"Engleeshh."

She tried to speak as the painkilling gas befuddled her brain. She hadn't called out, she tried to tell him. Maybe someone else was trapped. As she was lifted on the stretcher her head fell to one side and she caught a glimpse of the old woman peering through the church door.

⚜

WHEN DEBBIE HAD RECOVERED, she walked with her new roommate, Sara, to the chapel of St. Mary Star of the Sea on the way to her new apartment. She knelt down at the altar and was saddened to see that people had not relit the candles. Although they felt betrayed that the hurricane had hit, she knew that it was necessary for the island.

She lit all the candles and they both knelt on the ground before the statue. "Hail Mary, full of grace, the Lord is with thee. Blessed art thou amongst women, and blessed is the fruit of thy womb, Jesus. Holy Mary, Mother of God, pray for us sinners, now and at the hour of our death. Amen."

Behind Debbie stood a woman with long red hair and brilliant green eyes. Her hand rested on Debbie's shoulder as she recited the prayer with the young woman, the prayer to the Mother of all Creation, the Mother of the Ocean and the Goddess of Blood.

ABOUT THE AUTHOR

Josephine Stewart, now known as Josephine McCarthy, is a well-known occultist and author living in the UK. Her most recent non-fiction books include the Magical Knowledge Series and Quareia Magical Training Course. For more information, visit her website at www.quareia.com

ALSO BY JOSEPHINE MCCARTHY

It is often the actions of ordinary people who do extraordinary things that determine the fate of a land and a nation.

Stretching from Pre-Roman Britain, through the 19th century Golden Dawn Magical Group to the present day, *The Last Scabbard* tells of the magical mysteries of ancient Britain/Albion, told through the story of the magical sword Caliburn, the Stone of Destiny, and the Last Scabbard—the final Guardian of the sword.

A tale filled with magic, occult rituals, love and the confrontation of death and reincarnation—*The Last Scabbard* peels back the shroud of the distant past to expose our potential future.

Read *The Last Scabbard* today!

https://books2read.com/scabbard

www.ingramcontent.com/pod-product-compliance
Lightning Source LLC
Chambersburg PA
CBHW031058020726
47495CB00007B/1947